THESE
VENGEFUL
HEARTS

KATHERINE LAURIN

THESE
VENGEFUL
HEARTS

inkyard
PRESS

Inkyard Press
22 Adelaide St. West, 40th Floor
Toronto, Ontario M5H 4E3, Canada
www.InkyardPress.com

Printed in U.S.A.

To Justin, Henry, and Asher.
I'm so grateful for the light and joy each of you bring to my life.

CHAPTER 1

OF THE WAYS I'd want to start a Monday, finding a car covered in blood was not one of them. The murmurs began just after first period, and fragments of muted conversation led me out to the Heller High parking lot. I was curious to see the spectacle drawing so much attention.

The crush of students flowing out of the school buoyed me along in a tide of bodies. Between gaps in the crowd, I caught glimpses of the word smeared across the car's windshield in bloodred relief.

LIAR

Gray clouds hung low, casting the macabre tableau in watery light. The chill that slithered up my spine had nothing to do with the brisk October morning. I skirted a group of girls in front of me, recognizing familiar faces from my Geometry class, and found myself staring down at the thick crimson streaks. The letters looked nearly dry, and I couldn't fight the morbid impulse to touch them. A distinct tackiness remained. Was it corn syrup or actual blood? I didn't care to investigate further.

There was no proof that the infamous secret organization made up of Heller High's elite even existed, but this exhibition had all the makings of a Red Court takedown. Whispers from the ring of students surrounding the car reached me and I stepped backward, edging away from notice until I was part of the throng gathered to witness the scene. It didn't seem like anyone was paying attention to plain old jeans-and-a-tee-every-day Ember Williams. Good.

Other words, some so ugly I couldn't look at them for more than a moment, marred the rest of the car's windowed surfaces. My eyes skipped to a girl huddled beside a tree next to the parking lot. Tears mixed with mascara ran in inky rivulets down her cheeks. Two of her friends rallied around her, whispering softly.

No amount of consolation was going to wash away the stain from this one. More than a few heads from the crowd were turned in her direction. I didn't know her name, but I had a feeling she'd be remembered as *that girl*, the one whose car was vandalized with blood. She'd been marked by the words we'd all seen: *liar, cheater, tramp.*

Why did the Red Court target her? Who wanted this girl humiliated—to be brought so low in front of the whole school? Or had she been reckless enough to throw in with them and ask for a favor she couldn't repay? No. The vulnerability in her expression was too raw to fake. This girl was a pawn in the Red Court's game. The pull to learn more about the group known for dealing out ruin and favors in equal measure went beyond cursory interest. I *needed* to know more.

My stomach gave an uncomfortable tug, as if my body was eager to put distance between me and the girl now that I'd seen the damage. A sob shuddered through her, and I tore my gaze away, shifting my feet and noticing a stickiness beneath my sneakers. A thick coat of red clung to the bottom of my shoes, marking me, too. *Ugh.* I must have stepped in a pool of the blood. I told myself it was fake blood because I couldn't stomach the alternative. I'd have to go change into my running shoes before next period.

"Everyone back inside," a teacher called from the main doors. His tone left no room for argument.

The mass of students quickly dissolved, moving back into the school. The whispers rose to chatter as theories were passed around like mono on prom night. I trailed behind a couple holding hands as they maneuvered through the crowd.

"This is the worst one so far," the girl said.

Her boyfriend scoffed. "Worse than the video of Brett Shultz's keg stand? No way. He got kicked off the football team for that. Brett had Division I schools scouting him, too."

A rogue Facebook account had cropped up just after the school year began with some incriminating footage of the varsity running back at a party in a stunning display of upper body strength and chugging technique. The video had made it all the way to Principal McGovern, who reluctantly had him removed from the team, along with the school's shot at a state title.

"Do you really think she cheated on her boyfriend?" someone behind me asked.

"Does it matter?" his friend responded.

I shook my head in silent reply. It didn't matter. That was the power of the Red Court; gossip and innuendo were all it took for a star student to fall from grace after accusations of academic cheating.

As I passed a small cluster of teachers just inside the doors, I stepped nearer to catch the edges of their hushed exchange.

"—needs to do something."

"The district's policy on bullying—"

"I know the policy, but this is beyond 'bullying.' It's the third time since the school year began."

This may have been the third public display of destruction in the last six weeks, but it was hardly the third time the Red Court had struck. Their takedowns were legendary and highly visible to ensure maximum exposure, but they also excelled in the small things no one would notice unless they were looking for anomalies. My eyes were wide open.

For as long as anyone could remember, there have been rumors that the mysterious Red Court was pulling the strings behind the scenes at Heller High School. Its ranks were shrouded in mystery, but its influence was undeniable. Rigged student council elections, changed grades, and ruined reputations were all in their repertoire.

Half of the school treated them like the boogeyman, the near mythical thing that was out to get you. It was easier to deny their existence than to acknowledge the specter of their presence. Takedowns like the one outside were as likely to be attributed to the Red Court as they were to be pinned on anonymous wannabes posing as the Red Court to allay suspicion. It seemed like the other half of the over two thousand students at Heller made a sport of trying to guess which members of the prom court were legitimate and which ones owed their wins to the Red Court.

But I knew the truth.

The Red Court was real, and I needed in.

I pushed my way through the crowded halls to get to my locker. All around me a chorus of voices carried the news of the Red Court's latest victim, the story spreading faster than I could move.

My phone buzzed in my pocket. It was probably my best friend. I ducked into an alcove to check my texts.

Gideon: Did you hear?

Me: I saw, actually

Gideon: And?

Me: It was probably them. Who else would mess around with that much blood?

Gideon: Ew. Was it real blood?

I thought of my shoes again and shuddered.

Me: Who cares? The car looked like the prom scene from Carrie. They got their point across.

Gideon: I saw Mrs. Martin leading the girl into her office.

If something like that ever happened to me, I'd want to be put in the hands of the nicest—and most capable—guidance counselor, too.

Me: Yeah, I saw her outside.

Gideon: It's too bad. She looked wrecked.

We were reaching the point in the conversation at which I was supposed to condemn the monsters who did this. I wasn't ready to go there with Gideon. Revealing the true depth of my disgust at everything the Red Court stood for was not something I could do over text. Truthfully, my feelings about the Red Court were this gnarled mass inside of me, too big to start talking about at all.

Me: I gotta run. Lit is calling.

Gideon: Ok, see you after.

Before I'd made it halfway across the school, the warning bell rang. I gave up the attempt to change my shoes and turned to book it upstairs so I could suffer through American Lit with a room full of disenchanted sophomores. Oh, joy. On an ordinary day, class was a chore to get through. On a day like today, with my mind busy dissecting the latest Red Court takedown, it seemed like my school would live up to its nickname after all. Welcome to Hell High.

"Ember?" Mr. Carson called my name like a question.

Crap. I must have missed something. I couldn't seem to concentrate on Mr. Carson's analysis of *Leaves of Grass*, which was a shame. Whitman had some serious nineteenth-century game going on. "I Sing the Body Electric" gave me chills the first time I read it.

"Yes, Mr. Carson?"

He sighed impatiently. Or perhaps disappointedly. "Do you have any thoughts on the final section?"

I glanced at my notes from the night before to read the scribbles aloud, but a mocking voice cut in.

"Whitman's talking about the physicality of the body and how it is part of the soul or is the soul. Like it's just as important as the soul, which at the time was elevated above a person's body in significance."

I threw a baleful look toward Chase Merriman—insufferable know-it-all—and was given a smug half smile in return. He just loved to one-up me. Mr. Carson turned his gaze to me for more input, but my premeditated discussion points wouldn't add anything to the dialogue. I gave my Lit teacher as unaffected a shrug as I could manage even though a sharp retort branded with Chase's name tried to claw its way out of my throat. I pushed it down, not deigning to give Chase the satisfaction of knowing he got under my skin.

Mr. Carson continued droning on, asking for our "thoughts" and "feelings" about the poem. Poor guy didn't seem to understand his audience. Disengaged was our default setting. It really took some doing to rouse us. Though Whitman's work was taboo back in the day, most of the students here had probably seen something more risqué in their Instagram feeds over breakfast this morning.

The bell rang and Mr. Carson's shoulders slumped. Another day of not making a difference. I almost felt bad for him, but this was his chosen career path. He had to know what he was getting into when he signed up to teach freaking poetry at a public school.

"Could you hang back a minute, Ember?" Mr. Carson's words caught me six inches from the door and freedom.

I smiled tightly. The next period was my off-hour, but Gideon would be waiting. Every moment I wasted in the classroom diminished the chances of running out for my caffeine fix, which were already slim since I had to trek back across the school to change my sneakers first. I would not spend a moment longer than necessary in these shoes.

"What's up, Carson?" He was one of those teachers who thought using "Mr." in his title meant he was uncool, so I dropped it whenever I needed extra brownie points. Not that my brownie point bank account was in that much need.

"It's unlike you to space out during an epic poetry discussion. Everything ok?"

Mr. Carson was probably my favorite teacher, and we had a strong rapport, but I couldn't tell if his use of *epic* was sincere. I hoped for his sake he was being cheeky.

"Just having one of those days, you know?" *Vague, Ember, be vague.* "I'm sure I'll be back to contributing the only meaningful insight tomorrow," I added with a rueful smile, which he returned.

"Sounds like a plan. So you know, I'm always here if you need an ear." He shut his copy of *Leaves of Grass* with a snap, effectively ending our conversation.

"Thanks!" I bolted out the door as fast as I could without seeming rude.

Running down the steps two at a time, I nearly crashed into Gideon as he waited at the foot of the stairs near the school's main entry.

"What's the rush, Em?" His words came out in a whoosh as he caught me.

"I need to stop by my locker before we get coffee. Let's go!"

"Seriously? There isn't time for a detour if we're going to make it back before the hour is up. Let's just hit the library instead."

He was right of course, but I was in desperate need of a large Americano. I wanted to argue, but once Gideon made a decision, there was no way he'd change his mind. If only there was someone as bullheaded as him on the debate team with me.

Gideon broke down what he'd heard about the takedown this morning as we walked through the halls. I was too busy sulking to add to the commentary. I spun the combination on my locker, wondering how in the world I could explain the bloody shoes to my mom. The door swung open, and I tossed my bag to the ground. I was already toeing off my sneakers when a flash of red caught my eye.

The Queen of Hearts sat alone on the top shelf of my locker. The coy smile on her face said she knew something I didn't. If the rumors were to be believed, she did. A Queen of Hearts was the eponymous calling card of the Red Court's leader, and its presence could mean only one thing: my invitation had finally come.

CHAPTER 2

I THREW A furtive look around, my ruined shoes forgotten. The passing period between second and third hour was almost over. Only a few stragglers and slackers lingered in the halls. Gideon was parked against a column, the door to my locker blocking his view of what was inside. I rubbed my hands together, willing feeling back into my suddenly numb fingers, and gingerly plucked the card from its place.

My hands shook so badly it took three tries before I could make any sense of the message written on the back.

> *YOU'RE IN*
> *BE READY @ 2:30*
> *THEATER ROOM*
>
> *THE RED COURT*

The words were scrawled in a haphazard block font. I wondered at the hand that wrote them. Was it the Queen of Hearts herself who issued the invites?

"What's that?" Gideon asked as he peered over my shoulder.

I jumped in surprise and slid the card into my pocket. "I'll tell you when we get to the library." Gideon eyed me while I changed my shoes, content for now with the promise of an explanation.

As far as Gideon knew, my interest in the Red Court was the same dark interest every Hell High student felt. With the first step in my plan complete, I was ready to tell my best friend the only secret I'd ever kept from him.

Gideon led the way to the library at the heart of the school. Most people could count close friends on one hand; I could count mine on one finger. It was a hard fact to admit sometimes, but at least I had him. He got me from the very first day of middle school when we were the only two kids not laughing at fart jokes during lunch. Being Ember Williams, model student, was exhausting. It was nice to be around someone else and not worry about what they were thinking of me. Because Gideon would tell me exactly what he was thinking. All the time.

"I have something to tell you." We'd settled on a couple of armchairs in the center of the library. The familiar old-paper smell wrapped around me like a cozy sweater and I soaked in the atrium's abundance of natural light.

"Don't tell me you're breaking up with me. I couldn't stand it. Who knows what I'd do?" Gideon's gray eyes blazed with mischief. Smart-ass.

"How can I break up with you when you only have eyes for everyone's favorite barista, Damien?"

"He does make the best lattes," he said with a dramatic sigh. Gideon brushed a jet-black lock of hair, courtesy of his Korean heritage, from his face. I was envious of the way it seemed to obey his every styling command. Sometimes it was slicked back or combed to the side, but today he wore it tousled, which he managed to make look effortless and cool. My hair had a permanent ponytail crease. Le sigh.

"Really, though. Don't flip out at me." I pulled the card from my back pocket and slid it across the table.

He paused to read it and then picked it up and examined both sides. "What the hell is this? Because I know it's not what I think it is."

"Keep your voice down. It's my invitation." This was not the kind of news you broadcasted in a library with the acoustics of an amphitheater. The Red Court hadn't survived for years because they invited girls who didn't value discretion.

"Your invitation?! This isn't a dinner party, Ember. This is the actual Red Court. I wasn't even sure they were real. I always figured it was just a bunch of kids using the rumors to cover up their pranks." His eyes scanned my face, seemingly checking my features to make sure I wasn't a well-devised impostor who kept things from her best friend. "I didn't know you wanted in!"

The last part sounded like an accusation. It probably was; I didn't normally keep secrets from Gideon. The rest of the school typically existed outside our sphere of notice, but we were all each other had. This part of me, the one who knew the Red Court was real and needed to join, was secreted away from my best friend. It was born in the darkness of my anger, and that's where I'd left it. It felt too big to talk about or even

acknowledge to myself in the presence of others. It was easier
for me to let it own a small corner of my life. But if my plan
was finally working, it couldn't remain that way anymore.

"I'm sorry. It's complicated."

He shifted back in his seat to a slouch, like an experienced
interrogator waiting for me to break. "What's going on? No
bull."

I took a deep breath. It was time to pull the Band-Aid off
the truth. One, two, three. "I'm not joining because I want
to."

"Oh, I see. They abducted you and forced you to swear an
oath to the Red Court. Cool, cool, cool."

"Are you done?" I was feeling defensive and exasperated.
This already wasn't going well.

Gideon paused to let a gaggle of chattering girls pass. I recognized Gigi, Mrs. Martin's daughter and the newest member of the debate team, in the group. She gave me a small
wave and I waved back, fighting to smile against the strain
of the conversation.

"I don't know. I feel like I'm learning a lot about you right
now. Why don't we continue this sharing session with you
telling me exactly why you're getting involved with a clan-
destine group dead set on the destruction of others?"

Even with our conversation at an aggressive hiss, it was
enough to make me reconsider our location. "Follow me."

I rose from my chair and moved to the back of the library,
where a few lonely chairs sat without a table. No one ever
came back here unless they wanted to balance their work on
their knees, which was no student ever. I sat and gestured for
Gideon to join me. He threw himself down into the over-

stuffed chair with such dramatic flair that I wanted to applaud the performance. His expression was set to fiercely irritated.

"I've known the Red Court was real for almost two years, ever since April told me that they were the ones who caused her accident. They're the reason she may never walk again."

"So, you're doing this for what? Like revenge or something?"

"Or something. I'm not becoming one of them. Not really. I'm joining so I can destroy the Red Court."

I pulled out my battered journal, the one I'd been using since the beginning of the year, and flipped to the first page. "Here. This should help."

Gideon took it, staring at me with a dark, questioning look. I didn't let him look at my journal. Ever.

He mouthed the words I'd written to myself, ones I knew by heart.

1. Join the Red Court.
2. Find out the Queen of Hearts's identity.
3. Take down the Queen.
4. Dismantle the court.

"How long have you been planning this?"

"A while," I whispered. "In every journal I've kept since April's accident, that's what's been on the first page. I'm going to find the Queen of Hearts and cut the head off the snake."

Gideon's expression turned thoughtful, with a level of intensity reserved for the things he truly cared about. It was something I saw only in flashes when he was talking about photography or his family. And me.

"How do you plan to accomplish this?" he asked.

"By doing to her what she does to everyone else."

We all had secrets, things we'd rather not shine a spotlight on, but that's exactly what the Red Court did. They found the one thing with the power to wreck your life and paraded it out in front of everyone. Just like the car outside, they made shows of the destruction they wrought, and that's why someone had to stop them. Someone prepared to see it to the end. Whatever end that was.

Gideon chewed on his thoughts before speaking. "Be careful, Ember. We've all heard the stories, and you saw yourself what happened outside this morning. Remember Tessa, my lab partner from last year? She moved to live with her grandma in Phoenix after the Red Court revealed she cheated her way through Algebra—"

"Really? I didn't hear that."

"No one can confirm it was them, of course. But she was *expelled*, Ember." Gideon paused and his face softened with a rare expression of remorse. "I'm sorry for what they did to April, but they mean serious business. What if the same thing happens to you? Don't think you can swim with sharks and not get bitten."

I gave him my best vicious smile. "What if I'm one of the sharks?"

He scoffed. "Sharks eat their siblings in the womb, you know."

"Too much Shark Week for you." I hauled my messenger bag onto my lap to unpack my geometry homework. It would look weird if we didn't have something in front of us. Probably best not to attract any attention right now.

"I'm sure you think a plan and your stubborn streak will

be enough, but have you thought about what you'll need to do? Could you write slurs on someone's car in blood?"

I swallowed down my revulsion. There would be things I didn't want to do, but I couldn't borrow any trouble. One step at a time. "For someone with a pronounced vain streak, you're surprising me with how much you care about others."

"Em, you know I don't care about most of the people here. I care about you and what being a part of the—" He caught himself. "What all of this will do to you in the long run. What happens when they ask you to do something like what happened to Tessa? You don't have a grandma in Phoenix to run to when things take a nosedive. *I* need you to be ok."

Leave it to Gideon to mask his concern in selfishness. What was that in his eyes? Worry? Anger? Frustration? Probably all three. And all three unnecessary. Joining the Red Court was phase one of my plan. I clenched my fists tight to stop them from shaking as I said, "I can take it."

At two thirty on the dot, a student aid came into my final class of the day and handed my French teacher a note. My palms were itching so badly that conjugating verbs was impossible. Before every track meet and debate tournament, nerves tickled my palms with an invisible feather. It took my entire freshman year to learn to control the impulse to rub them along the tops of my thighs.

The messenger scampered out of the classroom with a concerned look on her face as Madame Anderson summoned me to her desk. Who knew what the girl had done to be in the Red Court's pocket, but the look in her eyes was a warning I didn't need.

Rather than going to the attendance office as written on my pass, I made my way toward the theater room. Stress weighted my steps as I walked, so I pulled out my journal to expel some of my worry.

October 1
How can I feel so lost when things are going exactly to plan?

As I descended the steep staircase that led to the theater room and the rest of the performing arts classrooms, I reflected on the steps I had taken to get to this moment. My careful planning, cultivated over years of hard work, had paid off. From my straight As and teacher's pet status to my position as a leader on the debate team and underclassman on the varsity track team, I was undeniably well positioned to be an asset to the Red Court. April had helped me cultivate the traits the Red Court were rumored to be looking for. They only recruited girls who were the most influential members of the student body, girls who'd shown they could handle leadership among their peers and the ability to win the trust of their teachers. You couldn't just gather a bunch of nobodies to break up the star football player and cheer captain.

Red Court jobs took finesse and the best of the best at Heller High to execute them. Regardless of how I felt about them personally, I couldn't deny the allure of their organization to my inquisitive mind. How were prom queens elected and failing grades made passing ones? What was the strange Machiavellian mix of brutal efficiency and cunning that made it work? A sick feeling settled in my stomach at the wave of grudging admiration that hit me.

Since starting at Heller, every move I made was part of a choreographed dance, bringing me ever closer to the Queen of Hearts and retribution for what the Red Court did to April. This was the moment I'd worked for—the culmination of my sweat and tears and all the blood staining the Red Court crimson. I kept my attention focused on that thought to edge out any doubt that might have been lingering in the back of my mind. Getting involved with the group that hurt my sister and countless others was as dangerous as Gideon said, but this was the way. This was the only way. This plan may have started with my sister, but it'd become more than that. My need to take them down was an obsession.

The theater room was wide and open, flanked by thick red curtains on either side that also lined the back wall. It was large enough to hold some of the school's smaller performances in, but not so large that I would miss my…whoever I was meeting. I glanced around and saw only an arts student crashed out and snoring softly on a weathered couch in the far corner. I'd seen her around, but she was two grades ahead of me; we didn't exactly travel in the same circles. Poking around the room, I checked behind the curtains and in the costume closet so I could discreetly pull the playing card from my pocket to check the time and location again, even though I knew I had it right.

"September Marie Williams."

My full name startled me like a thunderclap, and I shot out from the costume closet to see who it was. I couldn't hide my shock when the girl from the couch sat up and looked expectantly at me.

"September Marie Williams," she repeated. "Daughter of

Steven and Jo Williams. Resident of 1328 Belleview Street. 4.0 GPA. Track prodigy. Youngest captain of the debate team in Hell High history, yet you're only able to convince your friend Gideon to get coffee with you once a week."

The girl rambled these facts off as disinterestedly as if they were a particularly boring weather forecast. From the sound of it, I was sunny with a high of seventy-five. Her face was familiar and pretty in an unruly way; she had a lot of her paintings and drawings displayed in the halls for art shows, that much I knew. Her curly blond hair was long and floated around her face in corkscrew tendrils. Black fitted pants and a long dark tunic sweater hugged generous curves. The whole look was very art house, which I could only guess was the desired effect.

I finished examining her and answered coolly, "You could have found most of that online."

"True, but you don't have Facebook or an Instagram account or any other kind of online existence. You—" she emphasized the word with a point of her finger "—are a ghost."

I smiled. All true. I deleted my accounts over a year ago. It was a risk to be one of the only ones at school without a place to upload snaps and videos of my life, but there was a level of vulnerability in it I couldn't afford. "You know all about me. Who are you?"

"I'm Haley. I'm the one who invited you here."

This girl was part of the Red Court. I hadn't realized until I saw her that I had a preconceived notion about the kind of people who made up the secret group. At first blush, she was everything I wasn't—artistic and laid-back. What would the

Red Court do with a painter? How could someone so left-brained run such calculated operations?

"How do I know that this isn't some prank?" I asked and scolded myself for not questioning the invite before this moment. Could someone have found out about my plan?

"You don't, not really. Guess you'll just have to trust me. Well, this, too."

She tossed me a folder, which thwacked against my chest when I grabbed it. Inside were my transcripts, detailed notes on my freshman year, what I'd been up to the first few months of my sophomore year, and copies of graded tests I hadn't even received back from my teachers yet. No one person could have collected this information, but the Red Court had resources.

I looked back up at Haley with new eyes; she was the real deal.

CHAPTER 3

I CLEARED MY throat and gathered my scattered thoughts back together. "What now?"

Her face shifted to a professional smile—a magnanimous Don Corleone with an offer I couldn't refuse. "Now we talk. If you don't like what you hear, you walk. No harm, no foul." To my surprise, she raised her hands in a supplicating gesture.

"You would just let me leave? But I've seen you. I know who you are and what you do."

"Of course. We wouldn't hold you against your will. Joining has always been a choice. Even after you agree, you can change your mind whenever you want. As for seeing me, you've seen your dossier. You know what we're capable of. I doubt you'll be talking." Her eyes twinkled like she knew the punch line to a joke I missed.

She waited a beat before continuing. "Here's how it works.

We're a team. Everything we do, we do together. There are other teams of two, but we don't know them and they don't know us. We get assigned jobs from one central contact—"

"The Queen of Hearts," I interjected. The Queen of Hearts. The ultimate prize. I hoped my excitement at saying her name was masked by the anxiety rolling off me.

"Yes, she accepts all the requests and hands out assignments. Sometimes they are our own projects, sometimes we run support for other teams."

"What kinds of jobs do we do?"

"Everything. The Queen of Hearts makes all the decisions. She knows us and our strengths, but my personal specialty is election rigging."

I felt a jolt of excitement at the idea of rigging a student body election. All those hours spent designing posters, campaigning, and making promises could mean nothing in the end. What would it be like to be the one in control?

"So, tell me what you know about us and I'll let you know what's real." She took a seat on the slouchy couch and tucked her long legs under her.

I pulled a chair over and sat in front of her like we were conducting a bizarre job interview. "Requests don't cost any money, and any student can make a request of the Red Court in exchange for favors later on."

"True. We don't need money. We work on favors. We can call in our markers at any time, as often as we want. Those favors can be supplies for an assignment, which can cost money, but we only ask when the Favored can easily acquire what we need."

Favored? Interesting term. Ironic. "If you don't pay up, you're ruined."

Haley cut me a sharp look. "*Ruined* is a strong term. Kids know the rules. There's a cost, and they agree to pay."

"Ok," I said, thinking of the girl from the parking lot. Ruined was exactly the way I'd describe her reputation. Only, she didn't make a deal with the Devils of Hell High; she was just their victim.

"What else?"

"All communication is done by locker." I held up my playing card to demonstrate my point. "But if you want to make a request or would like to join, you slip a note into locker 1067." A nervous laugh bubbled out of my mouth. This was the part that had made me the most anxious, dropping my name through the slot. I could only go off theories and rumors I'd heard and April's educated guesses. No one spoke openly about requests they've made. "But no one has ever seen anyone opening that locker before," I continued.

"And you never will."

I waited to see if Haley would share any other details, but she remained tight-lipped.

"You must have access to every locker, though, right?"

"Yes, we have skeleton keys that get us into every locker in the school."

"Handy," I replied. "What about the Whisper Wire? Is that real or myth?"

In addition to the unassigned locker acting as the mailbox for requests, there were rumors that students slipped notes through its slot for the Red Court to use as leverage.

"Real. We get anonymous tips and secrets constantly. A lot

of it is nonsense or things we already know, but we keep track of what we hear. You never know what might be useful later."

I nodded. Sifting through fact and fiction when it came to the Red Court was hard. No one ever talked about it, but it was always there, roiling just under the surface.

"That's kind of it for what I know. Can I ask some questions?"

Haley made a sweeping gesture, indicating I could proceed.

I didn't ask the questions burning to get out. Those would only raise suspicions. Instead, I asked, "What's with the name?"

She pointed at the school logo and mascot painted on the wall behind me, a red knight. "We rule the school. Royalty holds court."

"And the playing cards?"

Haley produced some playing cards, fanning them out in her hand. "Inside joke. It started with the Queen of Hearts. Who else would lead a red court? All our jobs were coded to follow suit. You'll learn them, but a Straight is something to do with fixing grades, a Queen of Clubs is a breakup assignment, a Joker is for a takedown. When you get playing cards in your locker, it's the beginning of something. Since you're the newbie, I handle all the cards and communication. If you stick with this next year, it will be you."

It seemed so easy—this tampering with people's lives and handing students grades they hadn't earned. Somehow, it seemed to devalue what others had worked so hard to achieve. Not that any favor came for free; the payment was the equalizer. In the end, either you put in the time to earn what you wanted, or you paid for it. And payment was never cheap.

The Joker caught my eye, reminding me of the weight of

a single card. That Joker may have already ruined a life, like another card hurt April.

I asked the first question that came to mind, needing a moment to recover my composure. "What's your favorite color?"

Haley's smirk was amused, like she could tell how unsettled I was but decided to play along. "Black, like my cold heart and the pit I'll throw you in if you betray us."

My vision went fuzzy around the edges. Did she know that was my plan?

She rolled her eyes. "That was a joke. But, from what I heard, the last girl to betray us had to change her name and move to Canada after she was caught selling her mom's Xanax at school. That was over a decade ago."

I gave a short cough to clear the dread clotting my throat. I didn't particularly want to relive any more of the Red Court's greatest hits. The Red Court had to know that my sister's injury was their doing, but as far as anyone else knew, my family had bought the story that it was just a terrible accident. Could Haley suspect that I was one of the only ones who knew anything more than the public story?

"Why me?"

"You're only a sophomore, but I picked you because you've managed to make a name for yourself. You're a good student, you're an athlete, and you're on the debate team. That tells me you're a hard worker, you're competitive, and you're driven. That's all I needed to decide you have potential."

"*You* picked me?" This girl wouldn't have stumbled across me in the course of a day, heck, a week even. How had she pegged me as a good prospect without ever so much as speaking to me?

Haley gave me a knowing smile. "We have our ways of selecting ambitious underclassmen, and you hold influence in some areas we needed filled. After some observation, we could tell you might be the kind of person that would…enjoy the work we do."

"What's that supposed to mean?" It seemed my defensive streak wanted to come out to play today.

"Don't act innocent now. There are certain personality markers that we look for, and you had them all."

For someone deliberately trying to join a secret, potentially evil, mafia-like group, I didn't realize I was broadcasting such a ruthless vibe.

I gave my brain a mental shake, hoping it would come up with a different response like a Magic 8 Ball. "I heard the Red Court was a no-boys-allowed kind of club. Is that true?"

If this rumor was accurate, it would narrow down the pool of potential members by half.

"It is." Haley regarded me with a cool gaze.

It was probably time to wrap up this Q and A session before any seeds of doubt sprouted into genuine suspicion.

"Is there anything else I should know?"

"One of the best parts is that you'd be under the protection of the Red Court. We'll never move against you." She paused as if letting that sink in. What she didn't know was that I wasn't the one who'd need protection.

"So, what do you think?"

"There was never a moment I was going to say no." This was the most honest statement I'd made all day. I was in this for as long as it took to take the Red Court down.

"Good." A chime sounded from Haley's bag, and she pulled out a phone to silence it. "We better get moving."

"Moving where?"

"We, September Marie Williams, have a job to do."

CHAPTER 4

MY STOMACH TIGHTENED with doubt. Could I do this? I knew I agreed to join, but saying you'll plan to ruin someone's life and then carrying it out were not the same thing.

Haley strode out of the theater room without looking back at me. Apparently, blindly following was expected. Noted.

"Think of this as your initiation. You pass, and you're in. You fail, and we'll part ways and never speak of this again." She whirled back toward me, a tornado of blond curls. "And I do mean that literally. We'll *never* speak of this again. Not that you'll be talking to anyone else about this even if you do get in." Haley held her index finger up to her lips, face impassive. It was the expression of someone who'd destroy me without a second thought.

I bobbed my head at the implied threat. Art student or not, she had a streak of iron at her core.

She kept walking, purpose in her steps, and marched up the stairs. Heller's main halls were built off a quadrangle with the library situated in the middle and the performing arts department in the basement. Haley shot out into the quadrangle and toward the gym on the opposite side of the school.

"You have a small but important role to play in another team's assignment. You're going to be a damsel."

"In distress?" I asked, struggling to keep up with Haley's long stride. She had to be several inches over my five foot two and that was without the killer heeled boots she was rocking.

"A *sweet* damsel in distress. With those big doe eyes of yours, it should be easy. When we have an assignment, we use other members of the Red Court as part of our plans to give the ones organizing it some distance and keep suspicion of our involvement down. In this case, we're breaking up Chase Merriman and his girlfriend. You know him?" She dug around in the canvas tote bag she used in place of a backpack as she spoke.

Ugh. Of course I knew Chase. He was the kind of guy who everyone knew. Though not particularly athletic, he had friends on every sports team. His popularity transcended cliques, and he was a perennial favorite of every teacher. At last year's academic awards ceremony, he was called on stage so often he took over MC duties. He was just *that* guy. And my rival for top of our class.

"Who doesn't?" For some reason, revealing the depth of my unspoken rivalry with Chase seemed too personal. "I don't remember who he's dating right now. Who's his girlfriend and who asked for them to be broken up?"

"Don't know, don't care. This is for another team. We're

just helping carry out their plan. From the sound of things, the girlfriend has some insecurities dating Chase. We just need to give her a little push to call things off."

That sounded awful. My stomach gave another uneasy pull. *Keep it together, Ember. You knew you'd be breaking a few eggs. Revenge doesn't come cheap.*

We'd reached the gymnasium and Haley ducked behind a pillar, motioning for me to join her. "So, you need to quickly devise a way for Chase to put his arm around you. I suggest fake crying, something to give you an excuse for him to hold you and for you to bury your face in his shoulder. I'll be taking a picture." She waved a cell phone in front of me. "But I don't want to see your face."

She turned away to better position herself behind the pillar. That couldn't be the extent of her direction.

"Umm..." I hesitated. "Chase and I don't exactly get along." We didn't do anything to *not* get along, but there was an understood animosity between us that I appreciated. I knew where I stood with Chase.

Haley turned back to face me. "Like I said, Ember. This is your initiation. I think I'm right about you and your potential, but you need to prove that you can think on your feet." She looked down at an incoming text on her phone. "Chase is going to be coming out of the gym in about ten seconds, so think of something quickly."

With that, she gave me a little shove, a stiff nod, and a grim smile. Must have been her idea of reassuring behavior. But considering she was a seasoned member of the Red Court, she probably had all the same personality quirks (read: character flaws) I did.

A stream of students was flowing out of the gym to the locker rooms. I walked slowly toward them, pretending to be looking in my bag while covertly surveying the mass of bodies for Chase. He was handsome, I'd give him that much, with sandy hair and a strong jawline. His stock photo cuteness had always irked me, and it only bothered me more that I cared at all.

Where was he? Had I missed him? A moment of panic seized me along with the fear that all my work had been for nothing when I saw him breeze out of the gym wearing his Heller High Athletic Department tee and sweatpants.

In one terrified moment, I decided to collapse to the ground and start sniffling, praying that he would stop. My face was in my hands and I squeezed my eyes shut, willing a couple of tears out. Risking a peek through my fingers, I saw him glance in my direction and then around the hall, which had emptied of everyone but us.

He cleared his throat, clearly straining against the impulse to leave me there or kick me while I was down. "Hey, um, what's wrong with you?"

"I—" I faltered. I hadn't thought this far. "I'm ok. I just had a really tough conversation with my sister." April was never far from my thoughts, and she was the first person who popped into my mind.

"Oh," he said. For a second, I thought he would leave it at that, but he continued, "Is she ok?" The words were forced through stiff lips. This wasn't going well. He looked down the hall again, trying to find an escape.

"She's a wheelchair user, and has been for a while, but she quit physical therapy." April was a wheelchair user, but she was a star at physical therapy. I didn't feel right lying about her. My sister was the one who was always on my side when I argued with my parents. The one who used to sneak me dessert when I didn't finish my dinner. She was my soft center that I protected with a fence. An electric fence. Topped with barbed wire. I'd even considered adding a moat with crocodiles around it for good measure.

Something shifted in Chase's expression, and his mouth tightened to a thin line. My lie stripped him of his normal bravado.

"My older brother was in a car wreck last year. He went through something similar. Not nearly as serious, but he tried to quit PT, too. Said it was too hard." His sincerity was astounding. What universe was I in that Chase was *nice* to me? When we had to recite Shakespeare soliloquies in English last year, he was the only one who didn't clap for me. We clapped for everyone; it was required.

I sniffled loudly for effect. "What did you do?"

He paused for a beat and flicked his eyes to mine before looking away again. "I was getting my license at the time, so I offered to drive him. When he said he wouldn't go, I told him I would only practice driving with him. He knew how badly I wanted to drive, so he agreed. Twice a week, I drove him to PT and back." A wide smile stretched across his face, and his eyes unfocused like he was seeing into a memory woven by his words. "He was with me when I passed my driver's test last week."

My own grin crept onto my face until I was smiling as broadly as Chase. His plan was hopeful, and just a bit devious. I could appreciate both aspects equally. Also, my own birthday was two weeks ago. I was a week older than him and that made me feel warm, almost happy.

I thought back to my lie and my smile faded to a frown. "I already have my license," I murmured.

Chase's attention snapped back to me and a blush crept up his neck. "I...I wasn't suggesting you do the same thing or anything like that. I don't know anything about your sister. It's just... It's just that sometimes you have to pull people outside of themselves. Get a different look at things, you know?"

"Thanks," I said.

Chase nodded and began to walk away. I suddenly remembered that our exchange was supposed to result in a staged photo and scrambled to think of something else to say.

"Chase!"

"Yeah?" He had the barest hint of a smile. I'd never said his name before, only cursed it silently.

"Did he get better? Your brother?" I stalled for just a bit more time.

My hand went absently to fiddle with the ends of my long brown hair, pulled into a no-frills ponytail. One nervous tell I hadn't been able to stifle.

His smile turned fond. "He did. He's going to school to be a physical therapist, actually."

He turned to go again, so I stood up suddenly, gave a yelp of pain, and reached down to my ankle.

Alarmed, Chase jogged back and reached out to steady me at the waist. I put some weight on my faux-injured ankle and let it buckle. Chase's grip tightened and I pulled him close to me for the briefest second before righting myself and letting go. He smelled warm and spicy, better than a boy should smell after gym.

"It must have gone numb from sitting on it wrong. Please go. I'm sure you're already running late for something."

He gave the slightest suggestion of a shrug. "I don't have anything that won't keep for another minute. Are you sure you're ok? I'd hate to leave you here with a hurt ankle. You'll be trampled when the bell rings." Was that a joke? Were we *friends* now?

As if on cue, the bell rang, signaling the end of the day. I put my foot down again and made a show of testing my ankle's strength.

"It's fine, really. Go." Suddenly, I couldn't bear to be next to him. Even though he'd just finished gym, I was the one who needed a shower.

"Alright, Ember. I hope you and your sister work it out."

We turned at the same time to head in opposite directions. It was only after I peeked over my shoulder to see him ducking into the boys' locker room that I realized he'd said my name. It gave me a small shiver of delight.

A hand shot out from behind a pillar and jerked me back. I forgot Haley was stationed there, so I quickly joined her behind the pillar and glanced at her face. She looked triumphant and held up a cell phone with a picture of Chase and me. He had both hands on my waist and my face was tucked neatly into his neck. It could have been innocent, but what really sold the whole thing was his expression. He had this relaxed, confident look on his face that said there was nowhere else he'd rather be. It was perfect.

"Ember!" Haley gave me a small but rough shove. "You

nailed it. I couldn't hear what you said, though. How did you get him to do it?"

Something told me not to divulge the details of our conversation to Haley. I didn't think telling her about my sister would do me any favors in the long run. April said she never told anyone who caused her accident, that as far as the Red Court and the rest of the school knew, she believed it was just bad luck. My attitude with Haley had to be beyond reproach so she never doubted my intentions about joining. Everything depended on it.

"I just told him some sob story." *Keep it close to the truth.* "He ate it up, too. Seems like he's not the worst guy after all."

Haley waved a hand dismissively in my direction while she tapped out a text one-handed, sending the incriminating photo off to whoever was running this assignment.

"Now what?" I needed more details about the process.

"Now nothing. Our part is done. That's all we had to do. The team running point on this one will make sure the photo makes it back to Chase's girlfriend. From there, it should be smooth sailing."

For everyone but Chase, I thought.

"This is for you." Haley handed me a cell phone. It was a compact smartphone, but certainly nothing to write home about.

"Er...thanks?"

"It's your burner. There should be zero Red Court communication on your other phone. There's no such thing as privacy on a phone you don't pay for. This one has my number in it. It's how you and I will stay in touch."

"Oh!" I exclaimed, understanding her meaning.

I opened the contacts tab and saw a phone number, Haley's, and another contact labeled "Fire Alarm."

"What's this 'fire alarm'?"

"If you ever get in trouble, get caught, or find yourself cornered by someone who thinks they know what's going on, text that number with your location. It's our fail-safe, but you only get to use it once and only when there is no other option. There is no pseudo-emergency. If you pull the fire alarm, help will come, but you better need it."

Haley made the whole thing seem so dire. I could only bob my head in response and whisper, "Got it." And then because I couldn't stop myself, I asked, "What happens if you pull it twice?"

"Whatever happens, you face alone. We don't know you and you don't know us. Better get moving." Haley gave me another shove, this time into the growing mass of students in the hallway. "And, Ember," she said, "welcome to the Red Court."

CHAPTER 5

I RACED HOME in my Jetta, which was certainly not my MO for driving. My license was only a couple of weeks old, and I was a speed-limit-is-my-friend kind of girl on any other day, but today was special. All the pent-up adrenaline from receiving my playing card, to meeting Haley, to being part of my first assignment, coursed through my veins. The Red Court was exhilarating. It was hard to admit, even to myself, but I buzzed with genuine excitement. I was a part of something now that made my pulse race like no track meet or debate tournament could. These were high-stakes games, and I wanted all in.

I pulled up to our house, a cookie-cutter copy of our neighbors', and ran to the door. Fall in Colorado had turned from seasonal and pleasant to chilly and unforgiving quickly this year. Shutting the door against the wind and rustling leaves,

I called out a quick greeting to see if either of my parents were home early from work. Met by silence, I made my way down the hall to my sister's room.

"April!" I shouted as I entered.

"Yes?" She didn't look up from her laptop.

April's brow was furrowed in concentration as she worked on the midterm for her psychology course. She was a single point of focus amid the chaotic stacks of papers and textbooks surrounding her. If you asked her, she'd know precisely what was in each stack.

After her accident, April elected to change her college enrollment to online from on-campus so she could work as a volunteer coordinator at her physical therapy center. April's mind for details was the perfect fit for the role, but I worried that she was driving herself into the ground. Between her classes, rehab schedule, and full-time job, it wasn't unusual for her to work late into the night. The dark smudges beneath her eyes worried me.

"I'm in," I said. I felt my chin lift in a moment of pride.

April's head snapped up from her work. "What?"

"I'm in," I repeated. "The Red Court. I'm officially a member."

April ran a hand through her cropped hair. We had similar petite frames and the same fair skin and hazel eyes, but her hair was lighter, like our mom's. Her mouth parted to speak, but she didn't say anything. I wanted her to be excited for me, but I knew better than to expect it.

April had more reasons than anyone to want the Red Court destroyed, but she didn't carry the same anger I did. She'd moved on, past the pain and the prognosis that her chances of walking again were slim to none. She'd found her place along the new path she'd forged for herself. It was me who couldn't forgive, couldn't forget that the Queen of Hearts was out there planning to hurt someone else's sister.

A fresh pang of shame shot through me for my earlier thrill at being named a member of the Red Court. My resolve strengthened. I was going to find the Queen of Hearts and blackmail her into submission. Her remaining days of running Hell High were few.

"Part of me was hoping you wouldn't get in," April whispered.

A small stab pierced my heart. Did she not have any faith in me?

"Ember, you're so talented. I hate that you're investing your time in this. You could do so much better, give your time to something so much more worthwhile. And I know you don't want to hear it again, but you could get hurt." There was a hint of regret buried beneath the sweetness of her voice. I was her little sister; she was concerned for me, like any big sister would be.

I grasped her hand. "Don't worry about me. I'm not missing out on anything." Maybe it was the desperation for her approval I was wearing like a second skin, but her face softened.

"I'm proud of you for wanting to change things. What the Red Court does to people is terrible. I only wish that I had done something about it earlier. If I'd been less focused on myself a few years ago, I might have been able to put a stop to them myself." April gave me a sad smile. My chest contracted in response. It was everything I needed to see to know I was doing the right thing.

"You could never be selfish."

Unlike me.

My selfish need for revenge was what had fueled me through my exhaustion during finals and pushed me to run for captain of the debate team. It was basically my own renewable energy source, which was good because I would need it now more than ever.

"You'd be surprised." April loosed a small, reluctant laugh before sobering. "You don't have to do this for me. You know that, right? I'm not waiting for the Red Court to end to get on with my life."

Though she seemed tired like usual, April's features lacked the restlessness I knew I radiated. Maybe she was truly happy, but something in my mind refused to quiet. It was like a record skipping across the same thought and had been every day since I learned about the secret society that hurt April. The Red Court still existed, independent of my sister and what happened to her. She was only one person they hurt. If it didn't stop, there would be more.

"I know *you* don't need me to do this, but *I* do."

"So, how did it happen?" She set her laptop down and shifted to make space for me on her bed. I made to help and lift some of the clutter out of the way. "Don't mess with my system," she insisted. "I can do it."

Typical April. Adamant that she could take care of everything. A stubborn strength rested in her bones. If she'd been interested, the Red Court would have jumped at the chance to have April. The thought left a sour aftertaste in my brain, and I shoved it away.

I recounted my day for her, trying to include all the small

details. When I mentioned Haley was the Red Court member who recruited me, a flicker of something I couldn't identify crossed her face.

"Do you know Haley?" I asked. April was nearly four years older than me, so I didn't know many of her friends when she went to Heller.

"I knew of her. She was a sophomore when I was a senior. She's, like, artsy, right? Even as a freshman she had some piece in an art contest and won some big prize."

"Yeah, that's her." I paused, unsure if I should share my apprehension. "I'd be lying if I said I wasn't at least a little nervous."

"I'd be lying if I said I didn't regret telling you about the Red Court in the first place." Her voice wavered. "In case you need to hear this, you can walk away. It doesn't have to be you, Ember."

Time seemed to slip backward to my earlier conversation with Haley, when she made a similar offer. I did have a choice, and I would choose to do the right thing, no matter what it cost me. "If not me, then who? Who else knows what I know and is willing to try?"

The Red Court took and took, and it was time for them to start paying. Who better to end them than someone who has seen the impact of their cruelty up close?

The front door opened and my dad's voice called out. "We're in here," I called back.

My dad came down the hall and poked his head through the door. "How are my two best girls?" he asked. He was a classic college professor with his dark hair neatly combed. In class at the University of Denver he was all business, but outside of school he was prone to whimsy in a way that his two daughters never were. Case in point: naming his children after their birth months.

"What about Mom?" I asked with an eye roll.

"Shhh," he whispered conspiratorially and added an exaggerated wink for effect. "Don't tell her."

"We're fine, Dad." April smiled.

A crease appeared across his forehead. "Ember, I got an email from the school about this morning."

My stomach bottomed out. "This morning?"

"I know the administration is taking steps to address the culture of bullying among students. If you ever want to talk about it, we're here."

I shot an uneasy glance at April before saying, "Thanks, Dad. I'm fine."

The school district should receive an award for the spin job they put on Red Court hits. Bullying didn't even begin to cover it.

He nodded. "Tacos for dinner tonight?"

"I'll be out to help in a minute."

April busied herself neatening the stacks of notes around her. "I'm actually headed out tonight. Going-away party for someone at work."

Dad eyed her. "Aren't those sorts of things usually at bars?"

April rolled her eyes. Hard. "It's at a restaurant. Relax."

My sister had been rolling her eyes at any attempt by my parents to actually parent her since she was eight.

"Ok, then," he said, and knocked twice on the door frame.

After he left, April turned back to me. "It's in the bar at the restaurant."

I shared a secret smile with my sister and stood to go help Dad with dinner. "Sounds fun."

"Ember."

April's tone sent a shiver down my spine. It was a plea and a warning and something else I couldn't name.

"I wanted to tell you...to be careful. If it gets to be too much, we'll get you out. Together."

"Of course."

Lie.

There was nothing that would stop me.

CHAPTER 6

WALKING THROUGH SCHOOL the next day, I tried to look like I wasn't harboring a big secret, and then tried even harder to look like I wasn't trying. My life over the past year had been straightforward: work hard and earn positive attention for accolades. I worshipped at the shrine of my routine, border-line fanatical about each element. Now that I had achieved my initial goal of gaining access to the Red Court, there was no routine, and it was freaking me out. Haley texted once to let me know that she'd be in contact again only when she had something to say. So much for our hair-braiding sessions where I got her to spill everything she knew.

Gideon woke up with a cold and tapped out for the day, so I was free to waste my off-hour feeding my caffeine habit. After I put in a few minutes of face time with Mr. Carson to make up for my lapse in participation the day before, I swung

by my locker to nab a jacket. When the locker door popped
open, I found myself staring at a Queen of Hearts.

My own heart seemed to still for a long moment. I considered the card, trying to puzzle out its meaning before I picked
it up. Why would Haley need to leave another card for me? I
lifted the card from its perch on the top shelf and noticed the
script on the back was neat, almost girlish, and not the block
lettering from yesterday. Someone else had left me this message.

Welcome to the Red Court.
I expect great things from you.
Make me proud.

Unlike the invitation yesterday, this playing card didn't
have a signature. Only a small red heart drawn below the
text. My hands began shaking. It was a note from the Queen
of Hearts. I held something of hers, and that fact made my
place in the Red Court feel real, feel like something was
happening. And it reminded me the Queen of Hearts was
watching me probably as much as I was looking for her. Behind the note was a stack of playing cards. My own personal
supply of threats.

As slyly as possible, I slipped the Queen of Hearts playing
card into my wallet, leaving the rest. The card Haley left me
yesterday was safely tucked away in my dresser at home, but
this one was special. It needed to be kept close. Grabbing my
coat, I bolted for the nearest exit to find some coffee and my
footing in this new landscape.

★ ★ ★

I stood at the counter of my favorite coffee shop in what felt like a waking dream of queens and playing cards (how was this my life?), chatting with Damien, aka Maker of the Best Lattes, when Chase Merriman breezed in the front door. It seemed fate wanted to rub my nose in my own misdeeds. I was hoping to avoid him for at least…forever.

He immediately joined the line but hadn't looked up to see me. This was a good thing, since I was staring at him in a way a normal person probably wouldn't be. After our little heart-to-heart yesterday, I couldn't decide if he was a decent person or if I hated him more for knowing something so personal about me.

Damien noticed my gaze and smothered a grin. I scowled at him and went back to discreetly watching Chase for a few more moments. His breaths seemed strained and his blinks took just a hair too long. Noticeable bags had taken residence under his eyes. He was like a walking advertisement for why humans needed to sleep. Chase was the undeniable kind of handsome that even sleep deprivation couldn't touch. Because, of course.

Chase shifted his weight just before he glanced in my direction. Crappers. I didn't have time to look away or think of anything else to do but wave lamely and turn around to place my order. As I moved to the far end of the counter, a girl came up behind Chase and they chatted amiably. She was from our school and had the kind of looks you couldn't forget, with a warm brown complexion and striking brown—almost amber—eyes. She'd be the sort of girl Chase would date. She leaned forward and placed a hand on his arm.

I wondered if she was the jealous girlfriend when another guy walked up and placed his arm around her waist. Chase gave them a friendly nod as they left. I tried to watch him out of the corner of my eye as he gave the cashier his order and came to stand near me.

"Hi, Ember," he said when I didn't acknowledge him.

"Oh, hi," I responded. So. Very. Lame.

"How's your sister?" His tone was polite, and not at all intrusive, but that didn't stop me from bristling.

"The same as she was yesterday," I responded, letting acid soak my words.

He stepped away from me like I'd physically pushed him. Regret hit me with a jab to the stomach and frustration followed with a hook to the jaw. The foot-in-mouth one-two punch. Chase didn't do anything to me, other than edge me out last year with a higher weighted GPA. I was the one who told him about April...as part of an elaborate ruse to trick his girlfriend into thinking he was unfaithful.

God. Already my part in the Red Court was blurring lines unexpectedly.

"I'm sorry," I muttered, and then louder, "I'm just not used to people asking me about her."

"It's ok. I shouldn't intrude. I was only making conversation."

I stared at Damien behind the counter, my eyes pleading with him to hurry. He caught the look and slowed his movements.

REALLY?

The uncomfortable silence grew until it was unbearable. I broke first.

"How are you? You seem tired today."

"You mean I look like shit?" he asked with a laugh. It was a nice laugh, easy and good-natured. I couldn't remember hearing it before. At school, he was always the one making the jokes instead of laughing at them. Like he wouldn't deign to chuckle at sophomoric humor.

"No, you don't look like shit. You look like you pulled an all-nighter. Big test today?"

"I wish." Another laugh, but rueful and a bit more reserved. "Actually, I was up half the night talking to my girlfriend. Well, I guess she's technically my ex-girlfriend now. We broke up."

"I'm sorry to hear that?"

Why did that come out as a question?!

He shrugged, clearly shooting for nonchalance and not pulling it off. "I think she has some trust issues to work through. She kept accusing me of being with other girls, which is ridiculous since I was with her nearly all the time."

"Wow," I said. What else do you say to the guy whose relationship you were part of a plot to destroy?

"I'm oversharing, aren't I?"

"Not at all. You were so…nice to me yesterday, listening to my problems. The least I can do is listen to you, but you should know that my fees are pretty steep."

He smiled. Cracking jokes with Chase was not part of my routine. My eyes lingered on his mouth and his lips that seemed too soft for a boy. Not in a bad way, but in a kissable way. Why was I noticing his mouth and thinking about kissing him? *Focus, Ember. Get out of this conversation.*

"I'm glad I did. We've never really had a real conversation

before. Now twice in two days. It's kind of weird that we keep running into each other."

"Yes, but that's life. Weird and unpredictable." I scrambled to get the conversation back to safer territory before he thought to ask why I had been wandering the halls crying during class. "This breakup sounds like it's a good thing. I couldn't imagine being with someone who didn't trust me." *Because I was SO trustworthy.*

"You're right. It is. It'll just take some time getting used to it. I was with Madison for over a year. Our moms are close, so that will be tough around Christmas."

"Don't stress. Lots of people have awkward holidays. My grandmother comes over every Thanksgiving and performs this elaborate taste test where she literally tries every dish and gives a critique like we're on *Iron Chef*. It's pretty terrible."

Silence with a side of awkward descended on us again, but this time Chase broke first.

"I didn't set the curve for our last Lit test even though I got a ninety-six. Was it you?"

My smile escaped before I could put a leash on it. I absolutely set the curve; I missed only one question. "That's too bad. Maybe next time."

Damien finally called my name and I snagged my Americano off the counter, swallowing back a snarky remark. "I better run," I said to Chase, lifting my coffee in salute. "See ya."

"Until next time," he said. I didn't know if he meant the next time we saw each other or the next time we competed to set the curve on an exam. Both options sent shivers down my back.

I climbed into my car and heard an unfamiliar ring tone coming from my bag. It was my new Red Court cell phone.

I raced to dig it out and glanced at the display. It was Haley of course, though her name didn't come up, only the number that had been saved alongside the mysterious Fire Alarm contact.

"Hello?" I answered, then added, "This is Ember."

I heard a sigh. "Listen, Ember. I know you're new to this game, but stay away from Chase Merriman."

My mouth popped open and I looked around. I had no idea why because it wasn't like I expected to see someone standing in the shadows with a sign that read "Red Court Spy," but instinct prevailed and I closely examined everyone in the parking lot. A girl from my Geometry class was standing in front of the coffee shop texting. Could she be Haley's eyes? She was something of a slacker, so not likely. But still, she could be watching me if she owed the Red Court a favor.

"How did you know I was talking to Chase? And it wasn't like I planned to run into him. He was just there. And he started talking to me first." My defense was thinner than tissue paper, even to me.

"You can't see my face right now," she drawled, "but it's not impressed by your excuses. And never mind how I know. Do I need to remind you that you helped break up his last relationship? Not even helped. You were the reason they broke up. Once his girlfriend saw that photo, she went *b-a-n-a-n-a-s.*"

My skin prickled. "How do you know that? I thought you said we don't get to meet any of the other teams."

"I don't have to know them to hear how their assignments

go. I don't usually care enough to follow up, but this was your first job and I wanted to see it through."

I huffed, disappointed by the completely reasonable response.

"Anyways, that's not why I called. We've got a job. I'll be in the theater room. Meet me after school."

CHAPTER 7

AFTER CLASSES ENDED, I changed into my running clothes and made my way back to the performing arts department. I wasn't sure how long this meeting would last, but it had been days since I was on the track and my legs were aching for a good workout. Despite the cold wind, I knew track would be the calmest part of my day. No matter what storm was raging around me, there was peace in running.

"Hey." I jogged into the theater room and dropped my stuff. The theater room had a damp basement smell that was becoming familiar.

"Hey yourself." I'd known her for only a day, but Haley had the kind of barbed exterior that made you wonder if she was shielding herself from getting hurt or warning others to stay away from damaged goods.

She had a fancy tablet balanced on her knees and was fully engrossed in whatever was on the screen.

"What kind of action are we getting?" I asked impatiently after a few moments of silence. In addition to my run, I had hours of homework and some debate team work to do. Gigi, the ambitious freshman from debate, had asked me to review notes from our last meet to help her improve. I did not have time to wait here while Miss High-and-Mighty ignored me.

She gestured toward the stack of playing cards next to her on the sofa, a royal flush. I'd brushed up on winning poker hands the night before.

"It's an election rigging for Homecoming." She finally tore her gaze away from the tablet and looked at me. "My favorite." Her eyes were legitimately sparkling like the Grinch's after he stole Christmas.

"Do you do a lot of elections?"

"The last two Homecomings, one prom, and one student council election." There was a fierce note of pride in her voice.

"Impressive."

"Come look."

Haley moved to the floor and set her tablet down. She also took out a couple of notebooks and spread them out.

Sitting next to her, I examined the screen on the tablet. "What's all this?"

"This is what we use to start every assignment. Once I'm dealt a hand, I know to log in to this special email account for the job brief. It contains everything we need to know to get a job done."

"Why even get the playing cards?" It had been irking me ever since I received my Red Court–issued phone. The cards in the locker seemed like an oddly analog move in an otherwise digital game.

"It's tradition. Plus, there's something exciting about opening my locker and seeing a hand all laid out."

That was true enough. I'd felt the thrill of seeing a playing card in my locker twice. "Does the Red Court usually get more than one request for Homecoming? How would we decide?"

Haley shrugged. "From what I understand, no. We get far fewer requests than you might think for something this big. Most students who are popular enough to win don't need our help. It's only the really desperate ones that come knocking. If we do receive more than one request, the Queen of Hearts decides which way we go, but we never let anyone know that their favor hasn't been accepted ahead of time. They'll figure it out eventually, but by then it's too late."

I mulled this over. Getting yourself elected to Homecoming Court probably required more resources than other jobs, like breaking up a couple. The open look Chase had worn when we talked in the hallway flashed in my mind, but there wasn't time to consider why it bothered me so much. Haley and I had work to do.

She continued, "Anyway. This is what we get for every new job. It explains the goal of our assignment. In this case, it's getting Maura Wright elected Homecoming Queen. I also have a list of assets available to us."

"Like supplies?"

"More like people. When you said that favors don't cost money, you were right, and I told you that we collect on our debts in other ways. We couldn't do everything ourselves. We ask those who owe us to perform small parts in other assignments. That's how the Red Court has been able to continue for as long as it has, by parlaying one favor to the next. We have a lot of influence on our own as members, but it's multiplied by ten when you consider how many people we have control over."

The thought both sickened and intrigued me. "Can I see it?"

"Eventually. When it's your turn to start running your own jobs, you'll be granted access to the ledger. But you still have some work to do to prove yourself."

A thought occurred to me. Did this ledger have record of April's takedown? Could I find the person who'd requested a hit on her? I'd always been more focused on the game and not the players, but finding a name would be gravy on top of the Red Court's destruction.

"Is it everyone since the beginning of the Red Court? It would have to be thousands of names long."

Haley shook her head. "This list is only of current students. It's the primary pool we work from. We keep more detailed records, but only the Queen of Hearts has access to them."

My shoulders sank, but mindful of Haley's calculating gaze, I moved the conversation in another direction.

"Aren't you nervous that one of these people might turn on you?"

"No. If they did, we'd turn on them. If anyone came forward, it would be mutually assured destruction. And no high school student is willing to risk social ruin."

She said *high school student* like she wasn't one. Like *I* wasn't one. The other kids in our school had morphed into a "them."

"What's mutually assured destruction?"

Haley smirked. "If you get Clark for US History, you'll

hear all about it. It's this thing from the Cold War. Basically, it means that if anyone on this list sells us out, we take them down, too. We have so much dirt on everyone. It would be wholesale slaughter of the entire school's reputation. Even the administration is too scared to acknowledge we exist. I mean, how would it look if we laid everything out?"

"It seems like a dangerous line to walk."

"We wouldn't be here if we didn't at least get a small thrill from the danger of it all." An uncomfortable sensation of being seen tickled the back of my neck. This, at least, I knew I shared with Haley.

She clapped her hands together. "Let's start planning." Haley continued to outline the process for me as we went along.

At the top of the list were ten highlighted spaces. "What are these blank spaces for?"

"These are for the other members of the Red Court. Most teams will use two or three girls. Bigger jobs might need as many as six. We mark these spaces with what we need and the Queen of Hearts does the rest."

Ten other Red Court members. If you counted the Queen of Hearts, Haley, and me, there were thirteen of us total. I added this fact to my mental inventory to share with April tonight. Every piece of information could be valuable later.

"How many will we use?"

Haley grinned. "I don't need help. It's easier for me to do things myself than explain how to do them correctly to someone else."

"I know how that feels." I returned her smug smile and was surprised that it was genuine. I was beginning to like Haley, for all the problems it might cause me later.

We fell into companionable silence as we examined the rest of the brief. It read like a giant list of people the Red Court had influence over, including teachers, coaches, and members of the school's administration, all potential angles we could play to get our girl elected.

I knew Maura a bit; we had an elective business class together, and her family lived in my neighborhood. She was pretty and popular, but she also struck me as nice. The kind of person that would never sell herself to the Red Court.

"Did Maura request this?"

"Hmm? Oh, no. She didn't." Haley scrolled to the top of the dossier. "We got the request from Reece Jordan."

"That's Maura's boyfriend." I'd seen him waiting for her after class almost every day. Which came across as sweet, and a tad nauseating.

"Since Maura didn't ask for this, will we be collecting from her?"

"Nope, she's really just a bystander in the whole arrangement. For elections, it's rarely the targeted winner that asks. It's almost always a boyfriend or girlfriend or someone hoping to become a boyfriend or girlfriend asking on their behalf."

"He must really love her if he's willing to get in bed with us to make this happen." There was nothing that could make me ask the Red Court for anything.

"Or he's really stupid." Haley's sneer should win some kind of award. "Half the time they break up and then try to back out of the bargain when we come to collect. They just don't get that there isn't an expiration date. You make a deal, you pay up. Period."

Despite Haley's protestations, I really did think Reece loved

Maura. All you had to do was see them together to know that. He was doing this because he loved her and wanted her to win. Love could make even the most sensible person do ridiculous things, which was why I would not be falling in it anytime soon.

Haley roughly pieced together a plan and I marveled at her strategy. She'd broken the job up into three parts: getting Maura nominated for Homecoming Court, methodically dismantling the competition, and securing the votes.

Haley's gift for election rigging was beyond evident. She had talent and she used it well. We had the added advantage of Maura's preexisting popularity. Haley mentioned that it wasn't always so easy, but with Maura already having some notoriety, no one would question her nomination and subsequent win.

"Do you ever fail at a job?" She shot me a dark look, and I cracked a smile. To a stranger, that look would appear capable of peeling paint off the wall. I was slowly learning that Haley just had a dark sense of humor; I would bet my life that she meant that glare as a joke. My reaction was awarded with a quick smirk.

"I've never failed at a job. It's been known to happen, but the Queen of Hearts won't accept something we have no chance of succeeding at. Our assignments are typically challenging, but never impossible, which is why there is no opt-out clause for jobs. If you're in, you're in all the way."

I nodded. "That makes sense. What should I do now?"

Haley reviewed the pieces we'd need to put in place for the first part. She cautioned me to never tap the shoulders of anyone we needed to collect from until the last second to minimize risk or acts of conscience.

My first task was to secure copies of the nomination forms, which we would be using to stuff the ballot box in Maura's favor. Based on Haley's experience, a hundred should be enough to name her a finalist.

"We've got Max Stanley on student council. Write up a note telling him to leave a hundred copies of the nomination form in his locker by the end of the week." She handed me the locker skeleton key and sent a text with his locker number.

When we'd been at it an hour, and my legs wouldn't stop bouncing from anxiety, Haley told me to get out of her sight.

"Should I text you after I place the note in Max's locker?" I asked on my way out. She nodded without further acknowledging me. "Ok, bye."

"Ember." She shut off her tablet. "Don't do that."

"What? Say goodbye?" I thought for sure this was another joke of the ill-humored, but she leveled me with a stern look.

"We're not friends, Ember. We don't wave to each other in the halls. We don't grab coffee on the weekend. We're a team doing a job together."

My traitorous face must have looked hurt, because she eased her sour expression the tiniest bit. I cleared my throat. "So, the Red Court is telling me who I can hang out with now?"

"Stop. I'm not trying to be cruel. You go everywhere with Gideon already, and you should still do that. Everything has to look like business as usual for you. But we're not supposed to be in contact outside of Red Court work, and this makes it easier. We don't want to slip up if we run into each other. It would be suspicious. We weren't friends before, and it would make zero sense for us to be close now."

I nodded, and she went back to her work. I watched her

for a moment and realized that I didn't even know her last name. This girl who knew everything about me, who could apparently have me followed without my noticing it, was still essentially a mystery. If I was going to get more information about the Red Court, it would have to come from her. She was my only link. And if I was going to do that, I needed to get close to her.

CHAPTER 8

"WHAT ARE WE doing here?" Gideon whisper-hissed at me. He'd already tried striking up a normal conversation, but I'd shushed him.

We stood in front of locker 1018, Max Stanley's, as I struggled to fit the skeleton key into the combination lock without seeming like I was breaking and entering. The sickly orange carpet in the hall where his locker was gave me hives; I couldn't get this job over with fast enough. Keeping Haley's comment about appearing normal in mind, I brought a reluctant Gideon along with me with the promise of an explanation. We were always together during our free period. Gideon already wasn't a fan of my role in the Red Court, and I hadn't thought of a way to explain what I was doing that made it seem less awful. Maybe because blackmail wasn't supposed to be nice.

"I'm leaving a love note." I added a glare to complement the thick undercurrent of sarcasm.

"Because squeaky clean StuCo boys are totally your type. Is this Red Court work?"

Gideon mentioning the Red Court—even in hushed tones—caused my heart to pound erratically. Who needed cardio when your best friend casually tossed out the name of the secret organization you belonged to?

"Keep. Your. Voice. Down," I gritted out through clenched teeth. And then because I couldn't not sass him, I said, "Not all of us are lucky enough to fall for a tortured artist who hocks lattes all day."

"Don't talk about Damien that way!"

I shushed him again and finally jimmied the locker open. As quick as I could, I dropped a playing card—the Jack of Spades, which was used to collect all debts—with a note written on the back on the top shelf and shut the door. According to Haley's instructions, I gave Max Stanley three days to leave me copies of the nomination ballot in his locker.

Gideon and I turned to leave as casually as we could manage, though we probably failed. Subtlety was neither of our strong suits.

When we reached the quadrangle outside the foreign language hall where Max's locker was, Gideon pulled up short. "Spill it, Ember. I'm not playing along with your games unless I know the rules."

Haley hadn't mentioned how much I could say to others about my membership in the Red Court. It must have been because sharing anything was forbidden. And beyond being forbidden, having this conversation in the hallway was a risk I didn't need to take.

Gideon was staring at me impatiently. "Let's go to my car," I said.

"Don't try to turn this into a coffee trip. I'm not going anywhere with you until you start talking."

I rolled my eyes hard enough for it to hurt. "Fine. Let's at least go somewhere with a door."

We walked down the hall until we found a janitorial closet that had been left ajar. I made a mock sweep of my arm to usher him inside.

"Do you know Maura Wright?" I asked once I closed the door.

"Sure." His eyebrow quirked upward, which he only did when he was very interested. Like he couldn't be bothered with the effort unless it was good enough.

"Well, I'm going to get her elected Homecoming Queen. Me and my partner. Max owes us. I'm collecting."

"Wow. You and the Red Court are already an 'us.' Assimilated that quickly, huh?"

"Stop it." I fixed Gideon with a look. "Don't give me a hard time. It's the last thing I need, especially from you."

Chastened, Gideon dipped his chin. "So, what are you collecting?"

"Homecoming nomination ballots. Max has until the end of this week to leave them for me to collect out of his locker. Are you satisfied now?"

He nodded and I opened the door to the closet. "Good, because I'm getting high from the fumes of whatever is in that bucket." I gestured to the corner where some industrial-strength cleaner sat. "There's somewhere else I want to go."

We walked to a nook next to the library where the student art showcase was set up. I'd been meaning to go ever since I met Haley.

I paused in front of the first painting that struck me. It was an abstract piece, a style I'd never gravitate toward ordinarily. Most abstract work was too untidy, but this one was... compelling. Red, gold, blue, and purple met in a purposeful collision, a flame caught on canvas, and I was the moth drawn to its light. It looked like I felt at my most desperate—on fire and burning to escape.

I checked the title card and saw that it was painted by Haley Bitmore-Stanton.

"That's my partner," I whispered to Gideon, who was touching the edge of a sculpture.

It was like seeing Haley again for the first time, but through her art instead of the hard exterior she armored herself with. There were other pieces she'd created in the showcase, but my eyes kept trailing back to the flame. There was something about it that reminded me of Haley, while still feeling like it reflected a piece of me. Haley and I shared some common ground, but did that make us similar? The thought shook me. I had a purpose in the Red Court, and it wasn't the power that appealed to me. But I didn't know what had drawn Haley to the Red Court's doorstep. If I was going to get closer to her, I needed to find out what had motivated her to join in the first place.

"I was thinking of submitting a piece for the Winter Showcase this year," Gideon said.

I lifted a brow in imitation of him and waited.

"I think some of the black-and-white shots I took are good. Maybe one of them might be good enough to win." His tone was reserved. Entering something into the art showcase was a big deal. From the way he wasn't exactly making eye contact, I could tell he was anxious.

Gideon was as intelligent as they came, but he was also a talented photographer. During a recent trip into Denver's industrial RiNo neighborhood, Gideon had spent hours wandering the streets and taking photos. He saw the world so differently from me and captured images of tumbledown buildings or stray dogs rummaging through the trash with the sort of naked honesty that made them painful to look at. The incident with the stray dogs led him to volunteer at an animal shelter. That's what I loved about Gideon most. There was beauty to be found almost anywhere, but he also saw the ugly parts of life and never looked away. He did something about it.

"Which one are you thinking?"

He half shrugged. "Not sure. Next time you come over you can cast your vote."

I grinned as wide as my face would let me. Gideon was asking my opinion about photography. This development deserved a parade.

"Don't go congratulating yourself just yet. I said you can vote. I still have veto power."

"If you want my expert opinion, it'll cost you. My time is very valuable. Or I could try to rig the showcase vote in your favor."

Gideon's good mood vanished instantly, and I cringed. He

was already nervous and making a dumb comment like that probably took a piece out of his confidence.

Way to be a supportive friend.

"I'm sorry. That was a stupid thing to say. I can't make a joke to save my life. You're so talented. You won't need any help. Please forget I said anything."

He pursed his lips, chewing on his words. "Do you feel guilty about rigging the Homecoming election?"

I rolled with the question, wanting to distance myself from my dumb comment. "Please. In ten years, no one will care who won."

The guilt I felt about Chase and his girlfriend weighed heavier on my conscience, but I'd deal with that later.

"True fact. But what about the kid with the locker? You don't feel any remorse in screwing with him and getting him involved in your scheme?" Gideon was checking his hair in the reflection of a glass trophy case, ensuring that each lock was placed where it should be. A needless exercise since he and his hair had a telepathic relationship wherein it did everything exactly as he requested.

I grabbed the end of my ponytail. "I know it seems callous, but no one is forced to make deals with *us*. Everyone knows the price and they still ask for favors."

Gideon's reflection rolled its eyes. "Whatever you say. Just thought someone needed to Jiminy Cricket you before it was too late."

"No worries. I don't think I'm in any danger of turning into a donkey." I chuckled.

"You might make an ass out of yourself yet, but that's not what worries me."

My laughter cut off abruptly. "What do you mean?"

"This whole thing. The revenge part, too. You might win the game but lose yourself."

I turned away with a dismissive wave so he couldn't see my face. My need to take down the Red Court seemed to occupy most of the space inside my body. Didn't he know I'd lost myself to it a long time ago?

I dragged my journal out of my bag as we made our way to the library.

October 3
When you're made of fire, do you feel guilty watching other people burn?

CHAPTER 9

THE TRACK WAS empty most Saturday mornings. I got up extra early to make sure I was the first one there. This time of year, the air was particularly brisk around dawn, but I let it clear my head as I started my warm-up lap on the track that wrapped around the football field. With my earbuds tucked in my ears, and the sun barely peeking over the horizon, I could pretend I was the only person alive. Some might be disturbed by this fantasy, but I found it comforting. There wouldn't be anyone else to worry about except me.

I was hitting my stride and softly singing along to the music blasting from my earbuds when I saw an unexpected familiar figure walking toward the track. I'd arranged to meet Haley at school later to work on our assignment. I would have time to shower and grab coffee beforehand.

"Hi," Chase said as I came to a halt in front of him. It was hard not to as he was standing in the middle of my track. Did he think he owned the track? He didn't. *I* owned the track.

"Hi. What are you doing here?"

"I'm thinking about going out for track in the spring. Thought I should get some practice in."

"Of course you are." Track tryouts were open to anyone in good academic standing. Maybe I could sabotage his grades and that would keep him off my track. I added that to my list of things to look into. If there was one thing I was certain of, it was that getting closer to Chase was a bad idea. Why couldn't he do me a favor and go back to low-key hating me? My agitation was showing, but I couldn't seem to tuck it behind the mask of indifference I once wore in front of him. "And why are you in my way?"

He laughed his easy laugh. "Right now or generally?"

"Both." I stepped around him and started to run in earnest.

He was smiling his stupid, handsome smile and jogged to catch up. "I can't help myself. I just love being the thing standing between you and something you want."

"You know, you really shouldn't run without getting warmed up first." Gawd, that sounded obnoxious, even to me. Why couldn't I just be polite and normal around Chase? He would leave me alone if I didn't let him push my buttons.

"I know. I'm risking a lot to talk to you, so maybe you should just stop so I don't get hurt."

What was I supposed to say to that? Throw me on stage at a debate meet and I worked every event, but in front of some cute, infuriating guy, I was totally tongue-tied. I settled for a sneer and pushed my pace.

After a few moments, he said, "I've been thinking about you."

This pulled me up short and I stopped to gape at him. *Shut your mouth, Ember. You are not a fish.* I snapped my teeth together with an audible click.

Chase looked so unsure, so unlike his normal confident self. "The other day, in the hall, there was something, wasn't there?"

There certainly was. It was me playacting to get his girl-friend to dump him.

He continued, "I thought I knew who you were, and after we talked, I realized I didn't know you at all, but I wanted to."

"You followed me here?" I asked, half–creeped out and half-flattered. Good thing I had pepper spray on my key chain in case Charming Chase turned out to be Creepy Chase.

"No! Well, maybe. I saw you out here by yourself a few weeks ago when I came to watch a soccer game. I was hoping to catch you."

I was officially confused. "I thought you hated me," I blurted out. "Don't you want to beat me at, like, everything we do?"

Chase almost laughed but held it back at my glare. "True, but I also don't hate you. I like competing with you. You make me want to be the best."

The Red Court made me dangerous to know. I wished I could reset my relationship with Chase and send us back to a week ago when we were rivals and nothing more. "This makes no sense. We're enemies. Act like it."

He scrubbed a hand over his face. "I'm explaining it all wrong. You're smart and talented and...beautiful."

And a liar, my mind added before I could shut the thought out. Haley's warning came back to me. She would have my head if she knew. Hell, she probably already did. I'd bet I was somehow microchipped, and she was on her way to strip me of my Red Court membership and then bury me six feet under the bleachers as punishment.

"I'm sorry, but this—" I gestured between us "—isn't in the cards for me."

Literally. Not in the cards.

"Oh," he said and took a step back. "I'm sorry. I didn't— I just thought maybe—God, I feel like such an idiot."

"Don't," I said and, for some reason, reached out and squeezed his hand. It was warm and I wanted to keep holding on to it, but I let go. "My life right now is insane. And this can't happen for me." And then because I had a death wish, I added, "Right now."

There was no going back with Chase. As much as I didn't want to admit it, I was glad.

He smiled hopefully and nodded his head. "I'll let you get back to it, then."

He headed to the field on the other side of the bleachers so we wouldn't technically be working out on the same track. I popped my earbuds back in and continued running, but my peace was shattered. There was no way I was going to find any rhythm with Chase in such close proximity and the knowledge that he thought I was beautiful knocking around in my mind.

CHAPTER **10**

MY MEETING WITH Haley was abruptly rescheduled with
a terse text.

> **Haley:** we need to meet somewhere else
>
> **Haley:** there was some kind of leak in the theater room

The Heller basement was known for occasional flooding.
There never seemed to be enough in the budget to permanently fix anything.

I considered our options. I couldn't invite her over. Too
many questions from my parents. And I wasn't sure how April
would react if she saw Haley, knowing who she was.

> **Me:** We could meet at the coffee shop. It wouldn't seem
> out of place if we had books out.

Haley: too risky

Haley: my parents will be out tonight if you can come to my house at 6

Going to Haley's was the perfect way to learn more about her. I silently thanked whoever decided to underfund Heller's maintenance department.

Me: I'm missing out on lasagna night, but I can make it work

Haley: ok

The drive to Haley's took me to the edge of town. Here the houses were small but sparse. Apparently, the cookie-cutter neighborhoods like mine hadn't reached this far to swallow the land and spit out tidy grids of streets and two trees per lawn. Haley's house sat on a trim square of grass, somehow a comforting piece of civilization in the untamed prairie landscape.

I triple-checked the address before getting out of my car. The unfamiliar surroundings put me on edge. I didn't know what I was walking into, and I mentally prepared for the un-expected.

Haley answered the door before I could lift a hand to ring the doorbell. She had probably been watching me look from my phone to the numbers on the mailbox and cackling at my unease.

"Thought you'd never get out of the car. A little too coun-try for you?"

I scoffed. "Hardly. I just don't enjoy ringing strangers'

doorbells. Probably residual PTSD from selling Girl Scout cookies to weirdos."

"You would be a Girl Scout."

Haley ambled to the kitchen without further invitation, so I removed my shoes and coat and set them neatly on the hall bench near the door before following. The smells coming from the oven awoke my inner hunger monster and it let out a growl via my stomach. Notes of garlic and butter hung in the air, calling to me like sirens.

"What are you cooking? It smells incredible."

"I'm trying out a recipe for zucchini rollatini. We'll see how it goes."

The walls were covered in staged family photos and antlers. There wasn't a trace of Haley's personality anywhere. For someone so talented, it was odd that none of her pieces were displayed in her own home.

"You can have some if you're hungry."

My stomach leapt for joy. "That would be great."

The framed photos grabbed my attention. Why were there so many different families, but so few of Haley's own?

Haley noticed my confusion and said, "We have a lot of extended family that sends my mom photos. She likes to hang them on the wall, since we don't have any recent ones." She focused her attention back on her meal preparations. I added this fact to the list of things I knew about Haley for further consideration.

I thought of my own house covered in a timeline of photos of me and April. We didn't have any family portraits from the last few years, either, but even my embarrassing school pictures kept finding their way onto the mantel no matter how hard I tried to hide them.

An awkward silence descended, growing more palpable by the second. I cleared my throat. "I can't believe the theater room flooded again. I was wondering why we meet there and not the art room. You don't do any performing arts, do you?" I asked.

"Nope." Haley brought a pan out of the oven. "The art room is taken. So is the gym, the lab, and the library. Teams are assigned workspaces so we don't interfere with each other."

My mind began to spin. Had I ever noticed anyone odd in those spaces? Not really. It was a school and groups of students were clustered everywhere, working on team projects or studying for tests. Even most Saturday mornings the school was open thanks to play practice or business club meetings. The Red Court was hiding in plain sight and doing a damn fine job of it.

"I inherited the theater from my partner when I was an underclassman. She was a theater geek. Next year it will be yours, when I'm gone. Do you have a problem with that?"

"Not at all. It's just funny being there again. I used to go there all the time when my sister was a student."

Haley nodded and pulled some plates down from a cabinet. "April, right?"

My heart stuttered. "You know my sister?" I skated over each word smoothly, like it was a sheet of ice thin enough to fracture, pulling me down into the icy depths.

Did Haley have anything to do with her accident? April was a senior when Haley was a sophomore. There was a chance it could have been Haley. A chance, but I didn't want it to be.

The official story of April's accident was in the news. Heller went through massive safety evaluations after the fact. My family was even present when the official reports were given to the school. As far as anyone knew, April's accident was the fault of unsecured rigging in the theater catwalks.

"Not really. I was sorry to hear about her accident. My art class made cards for her when she was in the hospital."

Would someone responsible for April's accident make her a card? I had a hard time believing even Haley could be that callous. But I didn't know her that well.

"How's she doing?"

"She's a psychology major and works at the physical therapy center. She's doing really well." *Despite what the Red Court did to her.* I was doing my best to temper the instinct to close off where April was concerned. It was a struggle to wrest even the smallest tidbits into conversation through the protective layers of loyalty to my sister.

"My first day at Heller, when I was a freshman, some guys were giving me a hard time and April stepped in. She helped me out. I'll never forget that." Haley dropped the guarded expression I'd come to expect. She looked so genuinely sorry. Was it an act or, for once, was I seeing her truth?

She looked away and I moved us to safer ground. "Why is none of your art on display? Don't you want to set up your own showcase?"

"It's all in my room. Food's ready."

Haley plated rollatini, salad, and crusty pieces of garlic bread and set them out for us on the counter. I settled on a stool and inhaled deeply.

"This looks amazing. Thank you." I took my first bite and flashed her a cheesy thumbs-up.

Haley looked at me like she was waiting for the other shoe to drop.

"You're supposed to say 'you're welcome,'" I whispered.

She rolled her eyes. "Whatever."

"Good effort."

From what I could gather, Haley's whole life seemed to be art and the Red Court. Basic kindness shouldn't have been anything major. Haley didn't seem to have many people she could count as friends.

We had just finished eating when headlights flashed through the windows.

"My mom and stepdad are home early." Haley's stricken voice told me that this was not good news. I steeled myself for whatever was about to walk in, but still startled at the bang of the door flying open.

A man, late forties by the look of his receding hairline and paunch, teetered in. "Who are you?" he asked when he caught me in his gaze. The sneer he directed at me felt foreign. Parents usually liked me.

I did a double take at the wild-haired woman who came in next. She had to be Haley's mom, though she could pass for an older sister. The only feature she carried that Haley didn't was a deep parenthesis around her mouth from the frown she wore.

I cleared my throat awkwardly to respond. "I'm Ember Williams. I go to school with Haley."

Without clear direction from Haley, I didn't know if it was better or worse to identify myself as a friend. My being at their house might go over better if we were study partners working on a French project.

"Is that right?" the man asked with yet another sneer. Did the sneer come out on its own as he talked? It seemed involuntary. Maybe it was some incurable condition. Or maybe he was just a jerk.

I rubbed my palms against the rough fabric of my jeans. I wanted to bolt. Something about the way he looked at Haley unsettled me—like she was a kid about to lose her lunch money to the school's biggest bully.

"Hot date tonight, huh?"

I glanced at Haley, uncertain where this was going. Did she have a date to go to? Then his words clicked. He was asking if I was Haley's date.

Haley looked ready to burn down the world but held her tongue as she stared at her mom, who was shaking her head and pleading with her eyes for Haley not to respond.

There were layers to this dynamic I didn't understand, but my presence didn't seem to be helping. I needed a way out.

I cleared my throat again. "Actually, I'm doing a feature on Haley's art for the school paper. She said most of her work is here, and I asked if I could come see it."

Haley's mom eased forward and took her husband by the arm. "Dave, why don't you go sit down and I'll grab you a glass of water?"

He reluctantly allowed Haley's mom to lead him into the living room.

I looked back to Haley. "Do you mind if I go check out the pieces in your room you mentioned? I don't want to inconvenience you further."

Skating away, I waved to Haley's parents. "So...nice to meet you." As I passed her, I gave Haley's mom a tight smile, although part of me wanted to shake her and tell her to GTFO.

After peeking in a few rooms, I found Haley's and settled myself on a stool next to an easel. The room was tiny but had two giant windows that must light the space like a Hollywood soundstage during the day. Haley wasn't kidding about her room having all her work in it. Every square inch of wall was covered by canvases and artistic black-and-white prints of the landscape that I recognized from my drive here.

When Haley came in, I shot to my feet, ready to apologize for the lie and ask if I should climb out the window. She held a hand up to silence me and quietly shut the door.

"It's fine. I'm sorry he was such a dick."

"What happened?"

"My mom said he had too much to drink at dinner again and they couldn't make it to the movie. He passed out on the way home but woke up when they got here. I wish he would have just stayed asleep in the car."

"Should I leave?"

Haley was irritatingly imperious about most things, but this was one area where I wanted to take her direction. There was a lot I didn't know about alcohol and addiction, but it was a sickness that could implode and bring down everything around it. Regardless of her place in the Red Court, I didn't want to make this situation worse for her. I couldn't— wouldn't—add fuel to that fire.

"He won't remember, anyway. He'll be out in fifteen minutes." Her eyes were distant as she spoke. She was locked away in a place inside herself where no one could reach her. I'd seen

April do the same just after her accident; she disappeared, and I had to find a way to get a message to her through the walls she constructed to keep herself safe. It took some time, but she found her way out.

"Can you show me what you're working on?" I asked Haley.

She seemed to jolt out of a trance and looked around. "Yeah, this is my piece for the Winter Showcase in December."

Haley walked over to a large canvas with a drop cloth draped over it.

"Yeah? Gideon's entering a photo. Why is it covered?"

Haley considered me for a moment before pulling the cloth away. I could tell this was a part of herself she guarded closely. "Because it was mocking me. There's something missing, but I haven't been able to decide what that is."

The piece was unresolved smears of black and white paint. I knew nothing about art, not really, but I could almost see what Haley meant. The painting seemed like it was reaching for something, but not quite able to grasp it.

"Your muse abandon you?"

"No, it's just sometimes I start a piece thinking it's going to go one way, and then I find out that it's taking me in a different direction. It develops into something unexpected."

I nodded.

Haley paused and looked at me with a puzzled expression. "You paint?"

"No, I mean I can relate to the painting. Sometimes I feel like I'm on a path and going one place, only to discover the road has changed somewhere along the way and I'm hurtling toward someplace else. It's never what I expected."

"Is it ever?" Haley mused. After another moment, she said, "Thanks for not being weirded out by the date comment. I'm not hiding anything. I just don't have very many people I'm close enough with to share my relationships."

I smiled. "Really? I'm surprised you're not gabbing over girls with good ol' Dave."

Haley scoffed and let the drop cloth fall back over her painting.

A blue-and-green piece in the corner of Haley's room piqued my interest and I walked over to examine it. "Tell me about this one."

"Just something I had to get out of my head. I saw this green hill cut across a clear sky. It was like a stock photo, it was so perfect, and I wanted a version of it for myself. To remember it."

The whorls of blue were so thick they held texture and contrasted against the swipes of green. It was almost like I could see through the paint to the memory Haley captured, could sense the movement of the grass in the wind.

"I think this one is my favorite." I noticed the various writing utensils and stacks of Homecoming nomination forms on a chair. "Should we get to work on the ballots?"

Haley shrugged, slipping back into Red Court mode. "Sure. We need to cast a hundred or so votes for Maura." She sat on the floor and began divvying up the ballots and pens.

"Doesn't sound so hard."

"It's not, but it is tedious. Max now knows that the Red Court will have a hand in the results. Until it's done, we don't want him to know who we're getting elected. Once it's over, he won't have any reason to pipe up. We'll be writing our nominations in various pen and marker colors with a hundred different handwriting styles."

"Got it, Coach."

Haley's cat eyes narrowed to slits, but she didn't object to the nickname.

I took note of the precautions in our plan. It seemed like Haley had thought of everything. As I filled out nomination forms, I thought about how little I knew about the Red Court, information I'd need to bring it—and its members—down. I sat on the floor and took a gamble at asking Haley another personal question. "Why'd you join the Red Court?"

She stopped working and glanced up at me. "For the favor. I admit it's not the most inspired reason."

I didn't respond, waiting for her to enlighten me.

"The favor. You know?"

The implication that I was missing something obvious poked at a personal sore spot. I wouldn't have asked unless I didn't know, and I hated not knowing. "No, I don't know."

"It's the pot of gold at the end of the rainbow? The supersize favor?"

"What?"

"We don't ask for favors like everyone else because we're guaranteed the biggest one of all. Before you graduate, you get one very big favor. No debt to pay. It can be anything you want. You write up the assignment and the Queen of Hearts will review and accept. She's never turned down anyone. I've heard that she'll make suggestions, but whatever you want, you get." She paused and cocked her head at me. "If you didn't hear rumors about the favor, then why did you join?"

Shoot. I chewed my lip for a moment. "Control," I blurted out. "A lot of my life is dictated by other people or activities. It's nice to be the one pulling the strings."

Haley squinted at me in appraisal and then went back to her forms. "That's what my first partner said. She liked the thrill of working behind the scenes. I think the protection aspect must hold a lot of appeal to other members, too."

I gave a mental sigh of relief. I needed to be more careful. I couldn't paint myself into any corners with Haley, open any conversations I didn't have a way out of. I already got the feeling that she sensed something was off about me. Maybe April and I had done too good a job setting me up to be Red Court material. I was honed and sharpened for this role, formed to be exactly what they would need.

"Have you already asked for yours?"

She smiled slyly at me. "Indeed, I have."

"What is it, then?" Haley's favor would give me the answer to my biggest question—why was she part of the Red Court?

"That's for me to know, but it's going to be epic." She raised her brows at me. "Start thinking about what you want, Ember. Your senior year will be here before you know it and you'll need to have your plan all worked out by then."

I pasted a devious smile onto my face but knew my eyes were still uneasy. "Sure thing."

For the past two years, there had been only one thing I wanted, and I was getting it. But sometimes, getting exactly what you want feels like the worst thing to ever happen to you.

CHAPTER 11

"**HAPPY BIRTHDAY!**" I exclaimed in chorus with my family and Gideon the next day.

My mom blushed and quickly deflected our attention. "It will be April's birthday before we know it. How do you think it will feel to be out of your teens, sweetie?"

April's gaze moved from her phone back to Mom. "What?" Her glazed expression spoke volumes of the toll midterms were taking on her.

Mom's smile turned brittle. She and April were never very close, but over the last couple of years it seemed like they could never quite sync up, even in casual conversation. "I asked how you think being out of your teens will feel."

"It'll probably feel the same." April's tone wasn't sharp, but resigned. "I really need to get back to my budget spreadsheet for the work retreat I'm planning."

"Of course, let's cut the cake," my mom murmured.

It wasn't that she was a bad mother; she and April were just so different. Our mom was up when the tide was high and left low when it went back out. April was steady, nearly unshakable.

I scrambled to think of something to say when Gideon chimed in. "Just think, April, soon you'll be able to score us booze." He winked at my mom.

"Oh, Gideon," my mom said through a laugh, pulling herself back from the edge of her melancholy. Inexplicably, Gideon was my mother's favorite human and thus he was invited to every family gathering.

She picked up the cake to carry it into the kitchen and asked Gideon for help slicing it. He shot me a look that said I was both welcome for his help and I would probably be buying him coffee for the next two weeks.

My dad was busy fiddling with his phone, trying to put on some festive music over the portable speaker he'd bought for these exact occasions, so I sidled up next to April.

"Are you ok?" I asked.

"I was on Facebook, and I got a reminder with a photo from Mom's birthday a few years ago. It was a picture of me and Alec."

"Oh." April's bleak outlook made sense. Alec, the exboyfriend, and the most taboo topic.

I remembered that day. We went to Armando's, our favorite Italian restaurant, and Alec serenaded our mom with an over-the-top version of "Happy Birthday." April loved it. I gave it a five out of ten.

"I clicked on his profile because I'm an idiot." Tears were

building in her eyes, though I couldn't tell if she was sad, angry, or both.

"Has he gained twenty pounds and started to lose his hair?"

April laughed. "No, he still looks like Alec. He has a new girlfriend. She goes to his college. I'm happy for him."

April's "I'm ok, promise" voice was out in full force. It was full of light, but it was more like the bright light of a tanning bed and just as fake.

"It's ok to be sad. You're allowed to be angry or upset."

"Who says I'm angry? I'm fine."

"Fine" was not a feeling. It was the absence of happiness.

She went over to Dad to help him with his phone and I was left with a familiar hollow feeling in my stomach. As I sat by myself, my mind wandered back to the night of the accident. I was only fourteen, and I'd watched my sister get ready for a party that night. I could still taste the air flavored with April's favorite gardenia perfume and a hint of texturizing spray. There was no one in the world I looked up to more than her.

That night she snuck out past curfew to meet some friends for a party to celebrate the end of the school year. I saw now that getting her out late, already breaking a rule, was part of the Red Court's plan. If she was too focused on not getting caught, then she wouldn't notice that she was being lured into a trap.

From what she told me, someone in her group had the bright idea to pull a prank at the school. The senior prank the year before had been epic, involving leading cows up to the third floor of the high school from a nearby field. (Fun fact: cows go up stairs but won't go down them. Each cow had to be loaded into the elevator, one by one, to get them down.) They went to the school to hang a banner up in the theater, but when one of them tripped the security alarm, they all scrambled. April never saw who clipped the catwalk's rigging to her belt loop, ensuring she'd be the only one left to take the blame.

When the security guard found April, she was lying immobilized on the stage. She had been trying desperately to free herself and escape when the rigging failed, and she fell. She broke her femur and fractured her back when she crashed into the set pieces for the spring musical below. After the dust settled from two surgeries, April was left with an incomplete T12 spinal cord injury. She had sensation in her legs but wasn't able to walk; she'd been a paraplegic since.

Over the years, a single frame from the blur of my memories has haunted me. I wasn't allowed to see April until she'd come out of her first surgery. I was so anxious to see my sister that I sprinted ahead of my parents to get to her room. When I think of that moment, the antiseptic hospital smell fills my nostrils, turning my stomach. April had been sleeping or not quite out from under the anesthesia, and she was alone in a large, two-person room.

When my eyes landed on April, I skidded to a stop, my sneakers squeaking. She looked so small in the bed, like a doll. In that moment, I'd never felt more helpless. I wanted nothing more than to be the big sister and take April home, away from the hospital and pain.

She stirred when I settled beside her, mumbling something in her sleep that didn't make sense until much later: *what goes around*. At the time, I dismissed it as the residual effect of whatever pain medication she was on. Amid the flurry of events after April's accident, I didn't devote much brainpower to what she'd said when she was only half-conscious.

There was only so much I could do to help my family at the time, and I tried making meals and cleaning the house while my parents were occupied. Not that anything I did seemed to ease the stress of the situation. As the weeks bled on, April's pain—physical and emotional—fed the helplessness until I was drowning in it.

Gideon breezed back into the dining room and sat next to me. "Your aunt just called. Your mom said it would be at least five more minutes before we can eat. Whoever decided that red velvet should be a cake flavor should be forced to consume all the food coloring that has ever been used to dye a perfectly good cake red."

I barked out a laugh. "And not like a nice red, either. It's an unsettling shade of crimson. It's probably a vampire's favorite cake."

"Maybe it's the Queen of Hearts's fave?"

Gideon was called back into the kitchen and I mulled over his comment. I didn't want to think of the Queen of Hearts having a favorite anything. That made her sound so…normal.

The quiet of the room closed back in around me, shrouding me in memories. It hadn't been until the end of the following summer, after she'd left the inpatient rehab program, that April told me the whole story. How she hadn't known she was a target of the Red Court until a playing card floated down from the theater catwalk when the security guard had left her to get help. She was barely conscious, but the card, a Joker, had almost landed on top of her. She picked it up and examined it and saw her name written on the back. It was then she knew she'd been set up.

April's story was all it took for me to pick up the mantle of the Red Court's destruction. Her words from the hospital floated back to me, the fog of confusion lifting away.

"What goes around," I had murmured to her when she was finished.

"What did you say?" April asked. She looked shaken and her pale complexion turned waxen.

"It was something you said after your surgery before you were really awake. What goes around. You were talking about getting revenge, right? You want to get rid of the Red Court for good."

April bit back tears and nodded. "The Red Court has done terrible things. You have no idea how much they've done." She shuddered a deep breath, steadying herself. "They're going to keep doing terrible things until someone stops them."

That was when my helplessness found a new outlet: revenge. As April found her equilibrium, I began to plot. At my coaxing, she told me how the Red Court exposed your worst secrets, how students entered into bargains for favors and ended up owing a debt that could never be repaid.

"How can I stop them?" I'd asked her.

By then she'd grown reluctant at my obsession with the Red Court. April couldn't have known that my early questions were building blocks to a much larger plot. She was making progress at therapy and was doing well in school. But every time I thought about abandoning my plot, a cold feeling of dread would settle into my stomach. I wanted them to suffer, craved it.

"You'd have to find the Queen of Hearts. She's the only one who knows who everyone else is."

I had nodded eagerly, writing down what would become the promise that defined me. Gain access. Find the Queen of Hearts. Make her pay. Dismantle the court from within.

By the time April confronted me about my obsession with the Red Court, it was too late. I had a promise that turned into a plan, and there was nothing my sister could say to deter me.

I folded up my anger like a note and slipped it away as my mom and Gideon returned from the kitchen with individual slices of cake, each bearing a single candle. In the Williams household, everyone blew out a candle and made a wish, no matter whose birthday it was. My dad started it ages ago, but only to placate his two young daughters who demanded to blow out candles on his birthday. In the dozens of birthdays since, it's come to mean so much more. It's our way of sticking together. When one of us is celebrating, we all join in. And when one of us is hurting, we all feel it, too.

I'd made a promise a long time ago, and I was finally, finally going to fulfill it. There wouldn't be any wish for me this year. I was going to get what I wanted. I pictured the Queen of Hearts and blew out my candle. I was coming for her, and she'd better watch out.

CHAPTER 12

THE FOLLOWING TUESDAY at school, I noticed a large display next to the cafeteria. There were names and pictures plastered all over the walls. It was the nominations for Homecoming Court. Each grade had its own representation for Lord and Lady, Duke and Duchess, Prince and Princess, and, finally, King and Queen.

There, under Queen, was Maura Wright. Her bright, smiling yearbook photo seemed to shout at me in glossy relief next to the two other contenders. Didn't anyone else notice that her photo seemed just a bit bigger than the others? Or that her picture looked cropped and zoomed in, like she appeared more prominently than the other girls?

I was having a private "Tell-Tale Heart" moment, and any second I was going to start ripping my hair out and screaming like a madwoman.

I skulked away before someone noticed my guilty look and pulled my journal out.

October 9
Is there such a thing as a victimless crime? Or are we creating victims that will never know they've been wronged?

I heard a throat clear softly and I slammed my journal shut.

"Is that a diary?" Chase asked with mild amusement.

"No, it's a journal. I don't write long, rambling essays on unrequited love."

"Then what do you write?" He seemed genuinely interested and made a grab for my journal.

I danced backward to keep it out of his reach. "Just how I'm feeling in a particular moment or what I'm thinking about a specific situation. It's a short record more than a journal. I'm not about remembering specific details of my day-to-day, just how they make me feel."

After our conversation on the track, I wasn't sure where we stood. Chase didn't hate me and there was no point in lying to myself any longer about hating him. I didn't hate him, but my feelings weren't fully resolved into any one, categorizable emotion. I TBD'd him.

"Don't you need details for them to make sense later?"

"No, because that's not really the point. The point is that I feel a certain way at that exact moment in time. That something moved me enough to stir up some emotion or make me ask a question. I'm out in the world living my life, and this is my proof."

"That's kind of badass."

I laughed. "Journaling is badass?"

He shrugged. Chase was dressed in jeans and a thick gray sweater that I wanted to steal and envelop myself in. "Ok, maybe not badass. It's cool that you record the pieces that matter this way."

I tried to quell the blush flooding my cheeks. I was unsuccessful.

"I, uh, think someone over there is trying to get your attention," Chase said, looking past me at some point over my shoulder.

"Hmm?" I asked, a bit dazed. I shook my head to dislodge the dreamy fog that had taken up residence in my brain and turned to see Gideon looking conspicuously away from us.

When Gideon saw he had drawn our attention, he gave up his ruse and came over to speak to us.

"There's something I want to show you." His words were only directed at me.

"I'm talking to Chase," I said and motioned toward him.

Gideon turned to look at him as if he had just remembered Chase existed and added, "You can come, too."

Gideon snatched up my hand and began to lead me to the math hallway with Chase trailing behind, looking so entertained I wanted to smack him.

"Oh no. What's going on?" I asked the question without needing to because it was obvious to everyone watching. I was witnessing another Red Court takedown.

Taped all along the hall were photos. They were all different from the looks of it, but they all featured the same guy. A good-looking senior I recognized but couldn't name. Though it was a series of unrelated candid shots, the narrative was pretty clear.

A mixture of day and night images, close and faraway, showed that this guy had more than one girl in his life. In some shots, the more public ones, he was pictured holding hands with a petite blonde girl. In more of the night images, he was with a taller brunette.

The photos themselves weren't scandalous, but I could only guess that what they revealed would be the cause of death for this guy's relationship.

"Was this that group, then?" Chase asked. His face was one-part pity, two-parts disgust.

Gideon's expression mirrored my own feelings of distaste. He only pulled us farther down the hall. I felt sick to my stomach knowing what I'd find. Proof positive that this was a Red Court job. That it was perpetrated by members of an organization I belonged to.

We stopped in front of an alcove and I made myself look up at what was in front of us.

"'You never stop owing us,'" Chase read the sign aloud. Taped to it was a simple playing card—a Joker.

"The Red Court," Gideon said. "Who else?"

"What kind of person do you have to be to do this kind of thing?" Chase's hardened voice caught me off guard, and shame washed through me.

"I'm not sure." Gideon kept his face turned toward Chase, but his eyes flicked to me.

I wanted to grab him and shake him. Hard. I wasn't like this; I wouldn't do this kind of thing.

Except I would. In some ways, I already had. This was the kind of person I was and seeing it from this angle revealed a harsh truth.

Reeling, I turned from both of them and mumbled an excuse about the bathroom. I made my way back down the hall without looking up at the photos and ran smack into a petite frame.

"Ouch!" I muttered. "I'm sorry, I wasn't looking where I was going."

The girl I bumped into hadn't moved a muscle. She just stood staring at the photos, tears sliding slowly down her cheeks. She was pretty and familiar, but no one I knew. I followed her gaze and saw that she was staring at a picture of the faithless guy wrapped up with a girl.

Oh. It's her. That's why she looked familiar. She was the girl in the photos, the one he'd been cheating on.

"I'm sorry," I said again. Though this time my apology was more like my condolences. She hadn't done anything wrong, but she was the one who ended up in tears, humiliated in front of the whole school. It was so unfair. Why did she have to suffer for someone else's mistakes? However, her boyfriend— or ex-boyfriend, I guessed—deserved all this and more.

The girl yanked at a chain hanging around her neck hard enough to snap it. "Me, too," she whispered and dropped the necklace on the ground before walking away.

I stooped to examine the silver charm on the broken chain. It was a flat polished disk with a date engraved on one side from just over a year ago. An anniversary present? More like an unwanted token to remember a lie. I pulled away and kept walking down the hall, leaving the necklace where it belonged.

This was all so messed up, but I was in too deep, and there

wasn't anything to do about it. Out of habit, I reached for my journal again, and jotted down the first thing I thought of.

October 9
There's no way out but through.

I wasn't in this thing to make friends. I shouldn't care what Chase Merriman thought of me. I knew why I was doing this, and that was enough. My plan was sound. I just had to stick with it, but my unease grew with each takedown I witnessed. If I was caught, what would the Red Court do to a traitor? Whatever it was, I had no doubt it would make the hallway scene look like a fun trip down memory lane.

No matter. It was time for the Red Court to pay. My job would be less difficult if I embraced the part of myself that enjoyed the work, just to make the next month or two or however long it took easier to bear. It was a dangerous line to walk. If I leaned too far into the parts of the Red Court that called to me, I risked not being able to pull back. But I could do it. I had to. There wasn't any other way.

Perhaps I could even minimize the damage to innocent people wherever possible. Having someone like me was only a good thing to the students caught in the line of fire. I wasn't here for them; I was here for *her*.

A glimpse of familiar curls flashed at the corner of my vision. Haley. I was glad there was nothing written on my face but determination.

Though we didn't acknowledge each other, waves of approval rolled off her. She must have seen me dodge Chase and the cold resolve that followed after my run-in with that girl. A normal person would probably have had some kind of reaction, and not the detachment I was allowing to swallow me. I quelled the rising sense of satisfaction at having pleased her. Being a perfectionist meant I wanted to do everything well, even when that meant impressing others with my heartlessness. Succeeding as part of the Red Court meant failing at being a decent human being. I'd have to sort through all that later.

When I walked to the sink in the girls' bathroom, I was surprised at who I saw staring back in the mirror—the girl I'd called up and embraced from some dark part of myself. It was a girl without a shred of empathy. It was an echo of Haley. It was a Red Court girl.

CHAPTER 13

"IT'S TIME FOR part two," Haley said as she plopped down next to me. It was another Saturday and another day of plotting back in the theater room at school. The carpet was dry, but the damp smell had intensified. Haley brought a Tupperware container with veggie lasagna for each of us. My high praise from dinner at her house must have won me an encore. I'd hit the track again that morning, but Chase was nowhere to be found. Maybe it was a small mercy, but I was still disappointed he wasn't there. I hadn't spoken to him since the day we saw the takedown photos.

"I heard that guy from the photos had his car egged every day last week," I ventured as I ate my lunch. Seeing the outcome of another team's work firsthand had me wondering if there was someone in the Red Court as good at takedowns as Haley was at election rigging. I was desperate to find out who it was that ran that job. Maybe they had a hand in April's accident, too.

"Not surprising. When we run a takedown, that kind of thing is often the result." Haley had already inhaled her meal and was popping her neck and rolling her shoulders out like a prizefighter preparing to enter the ring.

"It was definitely us, then? The pictures?"

She gave me a look that said I should stop asking questions. "We didn't take them if that's what you mean. We probably pulled a lot of strings to have that many photos taken. It was nice work. Very poetic."

I chewed and bobbed my head, thankful for a mouth full of lasagna to spare me from responding. A few fitful nights' sleep didn't help sharpen the focus on my mission. Reconciling my goal to take the Red Court down with the firm belief that some people get what's coming to them was not going well.

"The next phase is twofold, and it involves securing votes for our girl and dismantling any momentum the other two candidates have."

"Go over that first part," I mumbled around another mouthful and waved my fork at her to continue.

"You and I will focus on inflating support for Maura. It only takes a handful of well-placed rumors to make it seem like she'll run away with the election. We each only need to plant three or four of these, and then we sit back and watch them spread like wildfire. Once those start to go, these elections tend to work like self-fulfilling prophecies. The expected winner typically comes out on top because people like to bet on a winning horse."

I tried to ignore the comparison of Maura to a horse. "Sounds easy enough. What's after that?"

"Next, we call in a handful of favors. We're looking for people with a certain amount of influence to lobby against the other candidates."

"We just went through all that trouble last week filling out the ballots so what's-his-face student council kid wouldn't know who our nominee was." I was indignant at wasting a Saturday. Time was my most valuable commodity. "Won't these kids figure out what's going on?"

"Not necessarily." Haley's tone was patient; she did love to flaunt her evil genius. "We went cloak-and-dagger with Max because we can't count on someone on the outside of the Red Court with his kind of involvement in the election not to ruin the whole thing in a fit of morality or accidentally spilling his guts. The people we pick for this part of the job will only focus on tearing down one candidate. Besides—"

I cut in before she could finish. "I know. Mutually assured destruction and all that."

She nodded primly and pulled up the list of kids we could work with. We began reviewing each of them and identified which would be best suited for this job. All of the names on the list linked to separate documents that had descriptions of each of the assets' strengths and weaknesses as well as a brief summary of the job we ran for them and all the other favors we had collected. It was an organized criminal's dream.

"Do we ever stop collecting favors at some point?" I asked.

"No one is ever really free until they graduate. And sometimes even then..." She trailed off cryptically.

"How do you collect once a student has left? What if they go to college across the country?"

"Sometimes the ones who leave are the ones who need a clean slate the most. It's easy to keep tabs on people when you know their pressure points."

The clinical calculation wasn't easy to hear, but it all made sense. I reminded myself that each of the names on the list wanted something bad enough to make a deal. We weren't leading lambs to the slaughter. If anything, they'd walked themselves over willingly.

"Do you ever feel bad calling in debts and collecting from these people?"

She made a dismissive noise. "No, and you shouldn't, either. Everything has a price."

That kind of thinking made the bitter pill of Red Court work easier to swallow. Besides, I wasn't there to help the people who'd made bargains. I was there to stop the Red Court from hurting innocent people like my sister. The rest could burn for all I cared.

I cleared my throat softly and held my phone, my actual phone, up to my ear.

"I don't know," I declared loudly. "Jenny says that Maura Wright is going to *run away* with it this year."

Step one: site cryptic source with common name who has inside information.

There was no place more crowded than the girls' bathroom during a passing period, and this was my third passing-period bathroom trip today. I continued to recite my side of the fake conversation.

"Well, I'm only telling you what Jenny told me. Of anyone, she'd be the one to know."

Step two: provide air of credibility to cryptic source.

My face was strategically turned from the mirrors and stalls toward an alcove with a spartan bench. This piece of information had to be attributed to my fictional friend Jenny, not me, so it was imperative that no one noticed who was relaying the information.

This part of the plan relied on high schoolers' propensity for gossip and providing fodder for the rumor mill that was too good for any eager ears to pass up. Whispers from behind me started speculating on the Jenny in question. Jenny the head cheerleader? Jenny the sophomore student council secretary? Jenny the lunch lady? All possibilities. Not that it mattered. The ball was rolling and Maura Wright was the Homecoming Queen front-runner.

As I exited the bathroom on my way to World History, I texted Haley.

Me: Done.

Haley: good

Haley: you need to deliver a note to mia gary

Mia Gary was the Favored we had dismantling Maura's biggest competition, Teagan Bradley. A tall order since Teagan had won a Homecoming crown all three years and was going for the sweep.

Me: It won't be a note congratulating her on a job well done, will it?

Haley: no...she's been too enthusiastic in her work

Perfect. Haley directed the saboteurs to be subtle. There wasn't such a thing as subtle enthusiasm.

Me: And I'm delivering this note to her why?

Haley: you're my underling

Me: ☹

Haley: relax her locker is 1124 two down from yours

Haley: do you need a jack of spades

Me: No, I have a deck.

My gift from the QoH. It's been in my locker, waiting for its chance.

Haley: mia is saying that teagan is purging to fit into her homecoming dress

Haley: if we don't lock this down teagan will end up with pity votes

Me: That's awful.

Haley: sometimes the favored go off script and take things too far

Haley: we need to remind her that we are in charge

Me: Consider it done.

Mia deserved to have her cage rattled for spreading a nasty rumor like that. She was only supposed to talk about how unfair it would be if Teagan won again. This task certainly showed Mia's true colors, and they weren't flattering.

No matter what the Red Court dictated, things could always get out of hand because too much hinged on the Favored playing their parts just right. I wondered if April's accident happened because someone the Red Court tasked to take her down went too far. The thought flew circles around my head, dizzying me with the repercussions. If one of the Favored was at fault, I'd never know, never be able to make them pay. But there was someone else within reach. Mia was about to get her due.

I was looking over my texts with Haley when I almost ran headlong into Gideon.

"What are you doing down here?" I knew Gideon's schedule by heart and his next class was Lit on the third floor. The history hall, located on the ground level, was completely out of his way.

"Looking for you, Em."

He'd been acting strange since that day in the hall, when we saw all of the photos.

"I've barely seen you recently. Even my dad is noticing."

There was a desperate edge to his voice that I hadn't picked up on before, and behind that, there was an undercurrent of resentment. It was true that the Red Court was keeping me busy. Between our current task, school, track training, and debate, I hadn't had time for much else. The realization left me with a guilty conscience, which wasn't a feeling I appreciated since most days felt enough like an emotional roller coaster and I didn't need anything else adding to the ups and downs.

"I'm sorry. I know I've been MIA, but I need you to understand what I'm trying to do. Of everyone, you're the one person I need to be ok with. Every other relationship in my life is complicated except ours. I take that for granted. I know I do."

"Then make it up to me." The muscle along his jaw ticked as he fought for composure. "If you're going to go around advertising that I'm your best friend, then be my best friend. I get your crusade. I don't agree with it, but I can see that it's important to you. But you haven't even been to my house to help me pick which photo I should submit for the Winter Showcase. Just know that I'm not a fan of being an under-study in your life."

I fought through a fresh wave of guilt. "I will. How about movies on Friday at your house? I'll bring everything, come to you, and that way your dad can see that I'm still alive and haven't abandoned you. We can look through your top options, and I'll tell you which is the best of the best."

Gideon gave me a smug look, which meant that he accepted, and turned to go to class.

"Better move your ass. You're going to be late!" I called after him.

He shook said ass at me.

After school ended and the halls emptied, I pulled a Jack of Spades from the deck in my locker to write Mia a little note. Last year, Mia's best friend had a serious boyfriend and was pulling away from her. Fortunately for Mia, the Red Court had the resources to make sure that relationship met an untimely end. What could I have her do so that fact never came to light? Probably anything. The thought was chilling.

If knowledge was power, then secrets were its currency; the Red Court had both in spades.

I moved down to Mia's locker and, channeling my best Haley, I wrote a note in stark black lines. It was as unlike my handwriting as I could manage.

> *Your job is to do what we say, not improvise.*
> *Secrets only stay secrets if you play along.*
> *Try again.*

I pulled the skeleton key from my bag and jimmied her locker open. I looked over my note again and smiled. The cards made sense now. There was something personal in the delivery, something of mine carrying the weight of the Red Court behind it. I kissed the Jack and placed it on the top shelf.

Sealed with a kiss. You've been outmatched, Mia.

CHAPTER 14

"EMBER!" GIDEON'S DAD called out delightedly as he opened the door. "Gideon said you were coming by. Come in, come in! It's been so quiet without you around."

If Gideon was my mother's favorite person, I was his dad's surrogate child. We used to joke that we could just move into each other's rooms and our parents would probably send the rest of our things in boxes to follow.

"Hi, Brent," I said and gave him a hug. He was a fast-forwarded version of Gideon, with the same shock of dark hair. Brent's had a silver streak shot through one side that made him look quite dashing for a dad, even in an old Cal tee from his days at Berkeley. From what Gideon said, Brent's Match.com profile was the talk of the single ladies in their neighborhood.

When you met his dad, Gideon made even less sense. How

could such a soft-spoken, kind person make a Gideon? He was raised by his well-adjusted dad in a supportive environment. Granted, Gideon's mom was out of the picture, but not in a bad way. Gideon's parents met in college, and she was a free spirit who had decided shortly after Gideon was born that a quiet life in the suburbs wasn't for her. Gideon's dad preferred stability for their son, so they parted ways. I liked to joke that even though he didn't have her hair, he sure acted like a fiery redhead. She kept in good contact, had never missed a birthday or Christmas, and came to visit whenever her travels brought her through town. She was a pretty cool lady, and Gideon agreed.

The abnormality of Gideon's good relationships with both of his parents, ones built on trust and honesty, only added to the mystery of it all. Regardless, I couldn't help but be grateful for whatever strange alchemy shaped the truest friend I'd ever had, snarky attitude and all.

"I'm upstairs," Gideon called from his room.

I slipped off my sneakers and placed them in the spot of the shoe rack reserved just for me.

"Stop by before you head out and we can catch up. I have some leftover *bulgogi* you can take home. You need to fill me in on everything that's been going on," Brent said as I started up the stairs.

"Excuse me?" Surely Gideon wouldn't have told his dad about the Red Court, right? That was the kind of thing parents frowned on. Mafia-like hits and blackmail weren't polite dinner conversation.

Brent stared at me for a beat, also confused. "School? Track? Debate? You have to let me know how things are going."

Sagging with relief, I said, "Sure. Will do!"

I pivoted back toward the stairs and bounded up the flight to Gideon's room.

"Finally," he said when I dropped onto his couch next to him.

Gideon's room was like a thesis in Gideon. Posters, framed photographs, and sculptures in varying shades of gray were all strategically placed, and all had special meaning. Gideon didn't buy anything, make anything, or accept any decor as gifts without heavy consideration. The things he selected were an extension of some part of himself, something he loved.

"Please," I said. "I'm right on time. As always."

I set my stuff to the side and scooted forward to examine the prints he'd laid out. "Which is your favorite?"

They were arranged in a row so we could look at all five side by side.

He squinted one eye in consideration. "I'm not sure yet. The theme for photos is 'Past, Present, and Future' and I think these are the best options."

Each shot was beautiful, even to my untrained eye. The way Gideon caught the edge of a building to give the main subject a better sense of place without taking away from the shot's focus was brilliant.

After a few minutes, he nudged the corner of one of the prints. "This one fits the theme, but I don't want to pick it if it's not my best."

I considered the photo, seeing what he meant. The image captured a small abandoned auto-repair shop with the windows boarded up. It was cast in the shadow of a new office building under construction, and behind them was Downtown Denver. He'd managed to capture a sense of change and uncertainty. It was stunning. "That's the one."

A flash of a smile was gone almost before I registered it. "Thought so. Submissions are due in a couple of weeks, but I think this is ready to turn in on Monday."

I grinned and unloaded my bag of goodies, handing Gideon his. Mine were a bit more sensible, but his tended toward junk food.

"What else did you bring?"

I'd downloaded two movies to my laptop to mirror onto his TV. One I hoped he would pick, and one I knew we'd end up watching.

"I have *The Notebook* and I have—"

"Gosling," he said without waiting to hear my other option.

"But—"

"There is nothing that could dissuade me from Ryan Gosling."

"It could be another Ryan Gosling movie for all you know."

Gideon hooked my laptop up to his TV and signaled to me to start the movie. "Could be, but it isn't. It's probably a Bond movie or something like that."

It was a Bond movie, actually. Gideon had zero appreciation for a good spy movie. Even though my life was full of subterfuge, Bond still held a lot of appeal. His version of spying and righteous might seemed a lot cleaner than what I was dealing with. Odd, considering he was constantly killing people.

Gideon dug into the snacks I brought and sighed contentedly when Allie and Noah's love story began. We'd seen it dozens of times, but it never failed to strike a chord with my friend. Maybe he only pretended to be jaded and was really the normal one. Liking happy love stories was the kind of thing regular kids did.

"I hate Rachel McAdams's face." He tossed a buffalo ranch chip at the screen.

Or he just really liked Ryan Gosling.

Watching a cheesy romance wasn't my thing, never had been, but watching movies with Gideon definitely was. As busy as the last few weeks had been, I hadn't realized how much I craved some normalcy. Now that I was here, back to our old Friday night routine, I almost wanted to cry from relief. On the other hand, having things I cherished also reminded me of how much I had to lose. When you were in a high-stakes revenge game, losing had the potential to destroy not just my life but those of the people I loved as well.

Hold on a little longer. You're almost there.

"Hey," I began when Ryan Gosling was off-screen. I didn't dare talk while Ryan was gracing us with his presence. "Are we good people?"

"What?" Gideon's eyes swiveled reluctantly away from the screen to meet mine. I repeated my question.

"Depends on your definition of 'good.'"

"If you have to qualify what 'good' is, then I think that answers my question."

He paused the movie and turned to me. "What's all this? Since when do we care whether or not we count ourselves among good people?"

"Since I got involved in some shady business and realized how good at it I am."

"You only joined to dismantle them. A lot of people would qualify that as a decent sort of thing to do."

Gideon studied me in a practiced way, reading my face and pushing past any pretense I might be using to hide behind. I both loved and hated that he could see so much of what the rest of the world overlooked.

"But I'm doing some bad things along the way."

"It sounds like you're asking me if motivation matters. If motivation can determine whether or not a completely justifiable act is a good one."

I nodded. Gideon could reach into my head and pull out the exact thought I wanted to share when words failed me. This I unquestionably loved. There was so much doubt in my life right now, but Gideon and I understood each other and that made the uncertainty of other things bearable.

"I don't know, Em. Determining whether the ends justifies the means is above my pay grade."

I sighed. I'm sure Gideon knew the answer I wanted to hear, and that was why he wouldn't give it to me. He was forcing me to face the part of myself I'd seen in the mirror after the photos in the hallway surfaced. It was the version who enjoyed threatening Mia, the one I pulled up from the darkness I kept carefully hidden inside. Would this small fraction of who I was take over entirely before the Red Court fell? There was no way to know, but I had a feeling I would need to embrace more of that sliver of my personality to get revenge. And soon.

After movie night, I reluctantly slogged home. My dad was parked on the couch watching the evening news. For some reason, his welcoming smile snapped my brittle nerves and tears escaped onto my cheeks.

His eyes widened. "Ember, honey, what's wrong?"

I walked over to him and allowed myself to be enveloped in a hug. I didn't often let him hug me, but his warmth was comforting, and I sank into his side.

"I'm just having a rough day," I mumbled into his chest.

"Do you want to talk about it?"

I shook my head, hoping the strength of his hug was enough to hold my broken pieces together. There were no explanations to give when you were out for blood.

"Ok. Then maybe I could talk to you. I was hoping for some help."

I sniffled and roughly brushed my tears away. If my dad needed me, I would be there for him in any way I could. He asked for so very little from me or anyone else. My independent streak had to be a Williams family trait, passed down from one stubborn parent to their child.

"What's up?"

"I was thinking I could take your mom out someplace special for our anniversary."

I laughed. "Dad, that's, like, five months from now."

"I know! I really need to get moving."

He shifted so he was looking down at me, all earnest expression and guileless smile. "Do you have any suggestions?"

I tried to think of what my mom would like, of what she perhaps wished for when she blew out her birthday candle. She wasn't into designer labels or fancy restaurants. The only thing my mom ever seemed to want was all of us together. Family was the most important thing to her. That must be another thing I inherited.

"Maybe we could do a weekend away in the mountains. All of us together," I said to him. "I can help plan it."

Sadness touched my dad's hazel eyes. "I don't want to put anything else on you, honey."

"No, Dad, it's ok." I placed my head back on his shoulder. "Taking care of the people I love is the most important thing to me."

CHAPTER 15

THE FOLLOWING DAY was my last "working" Saturday with Haley. Homecoming was the next weekend, so we had only a few more days to wrap up our plan.

Haley ran through the details from step two. Our rumors of Maura winning combined with the work of our smear campaigns against the other nominees should be enough to get our girl elected.

"That brings us to phase three," she said, tapping her nails against the screen of her tablet.

I swallowed a large bite of the hummus and veggies Haley had brought. "Finally. Alright, let's hear it." I was ready for this job to end. I needed to direct my attention to the real prize.

"Thursday night we sneak into the school."

I gaped at her.

"I know. It's a tall order, but it's the only way to be certain."

"All this work. We're guaranteeing her a victory with everything we've done."

"No, we're putting her in a place to win. There are no guarantees of victory. We've laid the groundwork for her win to be possible, hell, probable even."

I let my snacks fall to the ground with a thud. "I can't believe this. We've put in weeks and weeks of work only to change the final result if we have to?" I was incredulous. Beyond incredulous. I was angry.

"Ember, the Red Court is about subtlety. I know it's hard to understand now, but this is the way of things."

"Like that takedown in the hall. That was real subtle." I snapped my jaw shut hard enough to grind my teeth.

"You saw the sign in the hallway. He owed us and didn't feel like paying up when the time came. Typical popular-guy attitude. No one is out of our reach, and the cleanup crew loves their work."

"What, we have janitors in the Red Court?"

Her lips thinned into a straight line, a sure sign Haley's patience was running low. "We have a team that is dedicated to making the people who don't play nice pay for it. You have to really love that kind of work to do it all the time. It wasn't like it was me, so what's your issue?"

Not even this new bit of Red Court truth could deter my disgust. The broken expression of the girl with the necklace played on repeat in my mind. "It doesn't matter that it wasn't you. You're part of the group that committed the act. The perfect example of guilty by association."

"Look in the mirror, little girl. Everything you just said

applies to you, too. You joined knowing full well what you were getting into."

I huffed. There was no retort I could give her without my real reasons for joining the Red Court spilling out, too. My emotions were making me sloppy.

Get it together. Forget about the girl. Forget about Chase's accusing eyes when he looked at the Red Court's work.

"If you'd like to step down from your soapbox, we can get back to the plan. I think we did enough legwork that when the student council tallies the votes Thursday afternoon, we'll be ok. The results will be delivered Friday morning to the administrative offices. All we need to do is get into the student council room and check their files. Even if we do need to change the tally, we can have Max back us up with a phony story about finding extra ballots."

I opened my mouth to object, but she held a hand up to stop me.

"This is only a contingency. We don't take chances, so we plan for this in case we need it. But it's like I said, we should be fine."

"It's the 'should' that worries me."

"I know. Let's go over how we're getting into the school Thursday night."

"Breaking and entering?" I snapped.

Haley rolled her eyes. "Very funny. There's a service door by the furnace room next to the gym. It's easy to jimmy the lock and there's no alarm there."

"Sounds convenient."

"Quite convenient. We may have had it disabled some time ago. And there may have been some encouragement to the principal to overlook this flaw in the system. We also have the password to access the computers in the StuCo room."

I felt ill. All of this was too easy. I couldn't imagine what they had on Principal McGovern. He was Heller's de facto mascot with his shock of white Einstein hair and adorable bow ties. For the first time, I considered my ultimate goal and felt the magnitude of it. How was I going to take them all down? What could I do that would dismantle the years of work it took building the Red Court to what it was? What would it cost? The last question left a tremor of unease quaking through my core because the answer was the one I dreaded most: *everything.*

"What do you think?" Haley asked after reviewing the details. "You ready?"

My nerve was close to failing me. I'd never wanted to do something less. But giving up wasn't an option. Not when I was so close.

"Not remotely, but this is most likely as good as it will get."

The day of our B and E arrived sooner than I would have liked. Every time I paused for a minute, my stomach would tighten into knots and my palms itched so badly that I resorted to using cortisone cream. To distract myself, I put extra effort into my usual routine. I was ahead in every class, had made it to the track for extra practice, and prepared for my next debate meet.

At 10:00 p.m. on the dot, I parked my car a few blocks from the school and pulled on a dark gray hoodie. If I was taller, I might have even intimidated an odd passerby on the street.

As it was, no one seemed to look twice at me as I stepped quietly through the evening streets.

Once out into the open parking lot, I yanked my hood over my head to shield myself from the blustery October night. I spotted Haley near the door to the utility room on the side of the building and ran the last hundred yards to her.

"Here. Put this on." She handed me a dark baseball cap by way of greeting. "And keep your hood up."

My hand trembled as I reached for the hat. We were breaking into the school, committing an actual crime. Playing cupid or queen-maker wouldn't land us in the kind of trouble that follows you for the rest of your life. This wasn't riding the coattails of the chess club on Saturday mornings to gain access to the school. If tonight went sideways, we could end up being arrested.

Haley slipped her hat on and tugged the bill low over her eyes. She noticed my nerves and quirked a smile. "I've done this before. It's all going to be fine. We get in, we get out. Now, let's go." She pulled the handle to the service door up and out in a practiced yank.

To my shock, the door popped open without any sirens blaring. We ducked in quickly and pulled the door shut behind us.

"We have thirty minutes before security gets here for their rounds," Haley said.

"And the cameras?" I eyed the black half orb protruding from the ceiling.

"Keep your face down," Haley whispered. "The security system is really old, and the recording is erased every morning unless there was something to report, which of course there won't be. But don't look directly into the camera."

We made our way silently through the school. It was eerie to be there without the hum of thousands of students surrounding us. I attempted some deep breathing to bring my heart rate down from critical levels.

The student council room was an old teachers' lounge that had been converted a few years ago when the new wing of the school opened and the teachers were given a bigger space. It had a mini kitchen and couches that had seen better days but was large enough to afford the StuCo kids a few round tables. Even in the blue emergency lights, it felt warm and lived-in. Instantly, I was more at ease.

"Let's get to it." Haley marched over to a computer in the corner of the room and sat down at the desk.

Time seemed to still around us as the ancient computer booted to life; I could have run ten laps around the track in the time it took for the screen to stop showing us the spinning wheel of death. With nimble fingers, Haley typed in a username and password. She smiled widely when the "welcome" screen lit up the display. I moved to stand behind her and peered over her shoulder.

"Do you know where to look?"

"Not for sure, but I'm going to start in this folder labeled 'Homecoming.'"

She opened the folder and we both scanned the documents list for something containing the winners.

"Bingo." She double-clicked a spreadsheet file named "Royalty."

We both held our breath as the spreadsheet opened, then

let the air out in unison when Maura Wright's name was at
the top of the list with the highest vote count.

"Well done us." Haley clicked the X to close the document.
"Now what?"

"Now we celebrate."

Haley stood abruptly and pushed her chair toward me. I
took a step back to avoid it but tripped and crashed backward. Something solid hit my back and then gave way with
a blast of frigid air. A loud siren wailed overhead. I'd opened
the emergency exit.

CHAPTER 16

"RUN!" HALEY URGED as she hauled me to my feet. She turned to shut the computer down manually and gave a yelp as she knocked her knee hard into the desk.

The sound of footsteps echoed down the hall along with a man's voice, probably a security guard. He was early.

"Shit. Shit. We can't stay here." Haley moved to shuffle me out the door, but her progress was slow and she reached down to rub her injured knee. There was no chance she could run on it. We were going to get busted.

"Let's split up. You go out through here, and I'll go back through the school."

"Absolutely not. That's an awful idea," she whisper-shouted.

"Don't worry. I'm fast. He won't catch me."

Without waiting for Haley to argue any further, I bolted out the door into the main hallway. Just as the guard was rounding one corner, I sprinted around another and pushed my pace.

Feeling faster than lightning, and certainly faster than a high school security guard, I chanced a look back. There was no way he'd catch me now. I was nearly past the atrium windows that looked down into the library when I ran into a solid mass. Two hands grasped my shoulders and held me firmly in place.

"Let's go have a seat in the office while we wait for the police," a gruff voice said.

A black hat emblazoned with SECURITY in bright yellow letters shadowed the older man's face. Another security guard? How much security does one suburban high school need?

I silently complied and allowed myself to be steered toward the main office, keeping my chin tucked. What did they do to students caught breaking into the school? Suspension? Expulsion? A hundred scenarios burst through my mind like fireworks, each worse than the last. What would my parents say?

The idea of my mom and dad having to come pick me up at a police station was horrifying. The second guard had me situated on one of the hard plastic chairs in the waiting area and was on his cell phone with the security company by the time the other one showed up.

"God, you're fast!" The guy was younger than I would have expected. He nodded appreciatively at me but stopped when the one who caught me, who looked to be in charge, cut him a sharp look.

"Track," I replied simply.

The older guard got off the phone and excused himself

to secure the door I'd opened, leaving me alone with the younger guy.

"I'm Tim." He couldn't have been older than April, but I didn't recognize his face.

"Minnie Mouse," I mumbled. Feeling sorry for myself, I let my head fall into my hands and wallowed in the helplessness threatening to overtake me. Of every emotion, helplessness was the one I avoided most. Shifting, I felt the burner in my pocket dig into my side and remembered my fire alarm. If there was ever a time to ask for help, this was it.

"Could I have some water?" I asked Tim. I played up my dry throat and gave him a weak cough.

"Yeah, sure."

He turned toward the water cooler at the far side of the room. I pulled out my phone and opened my list of contacts. When I got to "Fire Alarm," I started a new message window and remembered Haley's instructions to send my location.

Me: Help! Hell High main office

A reply came back within seconds.

Fire Alarm: 5 mins

I wasn't sure what that meant, but I didn't have time to write a response as Tim turned back to me.

"Here you go." He passed me a small plastic cup of water.

"Thank you."

"What were you doing here, anyway? Don't seem like the usual sort we see busting into the school late at night."

He observed me with what looked like concern. A small pucker formed between his bushy eyebrows.

"I—"

The sound of a door slamming echoed from down the hall. Tim whirled around, looking bewildered. "Is there anyone else with you in the school?"

"Nope," I said, grateful it was the truth. Haley had to be long gone by now.

"I need to check this out."

A flicker of hope shot through me, straight to my fingertips, as Tim made a move toward the door. They caught me once, but I wouldn't let it happen again.

He paused, considering me. "I hate to do this, but I can't leave you like this."

Tim reached into his utility belt—a glorified fanny pack if I ever saw one—and pulled out a zip tie. My hope crashed down through my feet. He secured my wrist to the metal arm of the chair.

"I'll cut you loose as soon as I get back in here. It will only be for a minute." He gave me an apologetic grin.

As soon as the sound of his footsteps down the hall faded, I began tugging at the binding. The hard plastic cut into my wrist as I used all of my strength to wrest my arm free.

"Arg!" I grunted. There was no way I was pulling my arm free.

Time was passing and my window was narrowing. If I didn't get out of here in the next minute, there wouldn't be another chance. I felt the certainty of this truth in my bones. This was my shot.

Casting about, I looked for anything that might cut through

the bond. I saw a pair of scissors on a desk across the room. If I could lift the chair, I might be able to get there.

Before I could make my move, a figure ghosted into the room.

She was in black Lululemon leggings and a hoodie. Basically, my outfit, but nicer.

Take that, Haley.

A ski mask shrouded her features, but I didn't need to see her to know who she was. The Fire Alarm.

"We don't have much time," she whispered urgently. "You need to run out of the first set of doors at the north entrance. You know which ones?"

I nodded. My mind was too occupied trying to process what was happening to give me the ability to speak. She slipped a pocketknife from her black boots and began sawing at the zip tie.

I was in the presence of another Red Court member. And not just any member. The Fire Alarm. Now that my brain had caught up with the moment, I began cataloging everything I could about her, which wasn't much. She had a slim build. The raspy whisper didn't give any clues on her voice. I needed more information.

"You got here fast."

"Haley called me when you didn't come out. I came right away to pull the plug on the security cameras. I was nearly done by the time you texted me."

The zip tie gave way with a snap and my hand tingled from the rush of blood flowing to my deprived fingertips.

"Thank you," I breathed out.

The Fire Alarm dismissed my gratitude with a wave of

her hand. "We need to get out of here. Did they get a good look at your face?"

She glanced up at me and I caught a flash of familiar light brown—nearly amber—eyes before she stood and moved like a wraith to the door.

"Umm, maybe? I tried to keep my head down."

"I'll see what else I can do to smooth this over. The school doesn't usually broadcast this sort of thing. The administration has taken enough heat the last few years. We've lost the service door for good, though."

"I'm sorry."

She ignored me and leaned her head out the door, looking in either direction before motioning for me to follow.

"Go," she said quietly. "Run and keep running until you're clear of the school."

Without another word, I took off in a sprint toward the north doors. Halfway down the hall, I looked behind me to see a flash of movement disappear around the corner at the other end.

As I ran, the memory of the coffee shop the day after I joined the Red Court came racing back. The girl who was talking to Chase. Her eyes were the same unique shade of brown. It had to be her. Shauna. Her name surfaced from the long-term memory pool of things I didn't need to access on the reg.

I got to the north doors and burst out into the night, gladly greeting the cold air. The night was a disaster, but it did have one redeeming factor. I had the name of another Red Court member.

CHAPTER 17

ONCE I CLEARED the parking lot and made it into the neighborhood across the street, I finally sucked in a full breath of air. My pulse was racing, but I felt...good. Like I'd accomplished something. By totally screwing something else up.

I checked the clock on my phone. The last twenty minutes seemed to have simultaneously passed in both a matter of seconds and over the course of hours. Shaking my head to clear the last of my anxiety, I walked quickly to my car. A figure stepped out from the shadows next to it and my heart seized with fear.

"Oh my God!" Haley exclaimed and bounded toward me. "What happened? I thought for sure you were busted. What were you thinking taking off like that?"

"I don't know, but I was busted."

She paled. "What?"

"I got caught by security. Pulled my fire alarm."

The adrenaline that bolstered me through the last hour ebbed and exhaustion coiled around me like a heavy chain, weighing my shoulders down. I wanted nothing more than to crawl into my bed and sleep for days.

Haley studied her shoes. "Me, too. I thought we'd need an assist with the security cameras."

"That was a good call. I'm glad one of us was thinking ahead."

"What was she like? The Fire Alarm?"

"Kind of bossy. She was wearing—"

She held up her hands to stop me. "Never mind. It doesn't do anyone any good to hear specifics about other members."

A thought occurred to me. "She's not the Queen of Hearts, is she?"

Do I know who the Queen of Hearts is?

"The Fire Alarm? No, she's a specialist."

"More special than us?"

"Yeah, what she just did for you, whatever it was she did, is all she does. She won't take any assignments like us. She keeps tabs on the jobs we run and gets us out when we need it."

"I can't believe I called her on my first assignment. I'm a total failure."

I did feel a little like a loser, but I was more interested in how much Haley was sharing than my loss of the Red Court's only safety net. I mentally revised the total number of Red Court members from thirteen to fourteen. This was the most she'd ever divulged about the way the Red Court operated at one time. I'd been fed an appetizer and now I was hungry for the main course.

Leaning my back against the side of the car, I let out a shaky breath and purposefully swayed, but just a touch. *Careful, Ember...*

Haley joined me against the passenger door and studied my face. In the sickly glow of a nearby streetlight, I probably looked worse than I felt.

"You ok?"

When in doubt, stick close to the truth. "I think it's all catching up with me. I thought I was going to get hauled off in a police car. Do you think we still need to be worried? Are they going to investigate this?"

"She'll take care of it. She knows people in the right places to make this kind of thing go away." She let the words settle between us, then brightened. "Come with me."

Haley drove us in her car along a small road east of the school. The area where we lived east of Denver was recently developed, so there were wide-open fields and rolling hills only five minutes past Heller. Sometimes, it felt a bit like living at the edge of the world. Only it was Kansas on the other side of the void.

"Are you going to murder me and dump my body under a bridge?" I was kidding. Kind of. I didn't come out this way often, but something about the lack of anything brought out my paranoid side.

"No, if I wanted you out of the picture, I'd hire us to do it." Haley laughed a short, barking scoff. I thought she was kidding, too. Kind of.

We drove in silence while I fretted about being out so late, which was ridiculous since neither of my parents were likely to check on me. I was a good, curfew-abiding daughter. The post-adrenaline crash left my skin feeling too tight, and I fidgeted trying to get comfortable in the vinyl seat.

Haley mistook my discomfort for judgment. "It's my mom's car. Kind of a beater, I know."

"It's not that. I'm trying to keep it together right now. I'm still a little shook up."

She smiled a new smile. It was softer than the razor-edged smirk she usually produced, more like a butter-knife grin.

Eventually, Haley pulled to the top of a ridge and put the car in Park. "We're here."

"Where is here?" I strained to see in the weak light of her head beams if we'd come to an actual destination. Didn't seem like any place special.

"This—" she seemed to struggle finding the right words "—is my place. It's where I come when I need to be reminded."

"Reminded of what?"

"That this moment, this day, this year, is just a blink of an eye when you consider the vastness of the universe." Her voice had a faraway quality to it. Haley had never been so open with me, and I couldn't shake the feeling that she was showing me something most people never got to see. My first impression of her as someone who'd destroy me without a second thought didn't fit anymore.

"That sounds very depressing. Not like something you should drive twenty minutes to remind yourself of. Just look around you at school."

"School is part of the problem. It's easy to get sucked into it all and feel like it will never end. Never get better. When

I'm out here—" Haley gestured to the darkness cocooning us and the sky's canopy of stars "—I'm reminded that nothing, not even the moon, is permanent."

I was beginning to understand. "You come here when you feel bad about something you've done. Red Court work."

She nodded, her face a painter's palette of emotions—sadness and anger and hunger. Somehow, they all worked together to form a determined look, like when you mixed three colors together and got something totally new.

"I understand." I turned to stare into the distance. The lights from my neighborhood were visible, or at least I could see the way the sky reflected their glow. "I'm a bit relieved, actually. I was thinking that I was the only one our work affected."

"You'd have to be made of stone not to let it get to you, even just a little, but it gets easier every time."

I couldn't let an opening like this pass me by. "Do you think the Queen of Hearts feels that way?"

She chewed her lip. "It's better not to think about questions you'll never get the answer to."

Haley's guarded attitude reminded me of the way I acted when someone spoke ill of Gideon or even mentioned my sister. It was almost as if she was defensive, like I was talking about someone she knew, someone she cared about. Did she somehow know the Queen of Hearts?

The conversation was striking a nerve. I had to pull back or I'd risk all of the ground I gained. There didn't seem to be a safe way of asking about the Queen of Hearts. What I needed was to find a way to get Haley to open up more and trust me.

"You said school was only part of the reason you come out here. What's the other part?"

Her jaw locked and something dark came over her face. "My stepdad."

Neither Haley nor I had mentioned her stepdad's drunken behavior the night I was at her house. "Dave. He seems like a real gem."

She huffed through her nose. "He married my mom five years ago. At first it was ok, but eventually I saw through his act. He's just one of those guys who makes himself feel bigger by pushing the rest of us down."

"What does your mom say?"

"Nothing. She's always making excuses for him. Spineless."

We watched the car's headlights shine into the endless night. It was like the track at dawn. Nothing and no one around. Maybe Haley found the idea of being the last person left alive comforting, too.

"I can't wait to get out," she whispered fiercely.

"Where will you go?"

"Art school hopefully, but I'd need a scholarship to pay for it."

She let her words hang in the air until I understood the pause. "The favor."

"The lady in the postgrad office? Her sister is on the scholarship review board at the art institute I want to go to."

"But how will that work?"

"The same way all of this works. Until then, I have this place. I like the openness of it."

"Me, too. Thanks for taking me here. I feel better." My mind ached to wander through our conversation like a gallery and dissect every moment as though they were still-life photos. I found myself thinking of Haley's painting from school, the flame, but I couldn't say why.

I turned to her. "I bet you won't even need the Red Court to get the scholarship. Your paintings in the art display are great."

"Thanks," she whispered without looking at me, like she wasn't used to compliments on her work.

After a few more minutes, Haley drove me back to my car. I went home without incident and pulled out my corkboard and an old yearbook. The corkboard remained empty on my wall unless I needed it. It was only pulled out for big projects as a place to put all my thoughts before I could arrange them into logical threads. I often tacked ideas or articles or pictures to the board. Something about looking everything over at once helped me put together the bigger picture, like everything on the board was an individual puzzle piece. I just needed to find where it fit.

I set up a wheel with thirteen spokes—one for each member of the Red Court. On three of the spokes, I wrote the names of the Red Court members I knew: Haley, Shauna, and me. I added Haley's and Shauna's yearbook photos to each of their spokes. When I wasn't dead on my feet, I'd begin adding details about them, but this was a start. At the center of the wheel I added a red cartoon heart I foraged from an old sticker book. I flipped it around so the work was facing the wall and the blank backside was visible.

Still in the cat burglar uniform, I crawled into bed. As I drifted to sleep, I realized why Haley's painting had come to mind earlier. Looking at her work had given me the oddest sensation of looking at a reflection of myself. Listening to her speak tonight had given me the same feeling, like I was looking into a mirror.

★ ★ ★

The next day, the Homecoming Court names were announced and not even a whisper of the break-in and subsequent bust was to be heard. To no one's surprise but her own, Maura was named Queen. I watched from down the hall as she teared up in front of the display decreeing her royal in silver glitter and distributed hugs to her friends and boyfriend. No matter what else happened, I was glad Maura won. She looked genuinely happy, and I was proud of my role in that. From the corner of my eye, I caught a swish of blond curls and a grim smile that reminded me I had work to do.

Before heading home for the day, I stopped by my locker to dump some notebooks I didn't need over the weekend. Waiting for me on the top shelf was another Queen of Hearts. Did the QoH have dozens of card decks lying around without one of their queens or did she somehow order them à la carte? The familiar swoopy lettering covered the back of the card.

> *A job well done deserves a reward.*
> *Leave a card here with a request.*
> *You have until Monday after school to decide.*

If I had until Monday, that meant the QoH would need to come collect that afternoon. For the first time, I knew where she would be and when. She was as good as mine.

CHAPTER 18

THE MORNING OF Homecoming dawned clear and cool. At least it would be sunny, if not quite warm.

"Thank goodness it's going to be a nice day," I said to my mom at breakfast. "If the debate team had to do another car wash in the cold, I was going to call in sick."

She looked at me over the top of her laptop, doubt evident in her quirked brow.

"Ok, I wouldn't have called in, but I would have worn a waterproof suit of some kind."

My dad walked into the kitchen and placed kisses on the tops of both our heads.

"Should we bring a car by for you guys to wash? We're pretty good tippers." My father could have written the handbook for cheesy dad remarks.

Hmm. My parents at the car wash fundraiser? No, thanks.

"Umm, that's ok. I'll call you guys if no one shows. Otherwise, we should leave room for non–debate team families. It will raise awareness for our program in addition to money to send the team to Nationals."

Neither of my parents were fooled by my flimsy excuse. I got the double-brow-quirk treatment from the two of them. Did they have to practice that to do it in unison?

My dad gave me an indulgent smile. "Sure thing, honey. Whatever you need."

He went about making a breakfast smoothie for himself, but I felt his words like a shot to the heart. Didn't my parents know how hard I tried every day to *not* need anything? Ever since our talk a week ago, my dad had been extra attentive, so I was on my A-game at home. He didn't need me to add to his worries.

A car horn sounded from the driveway. "That's Gideon."

"Doesn't he want to come in for breakfast?" My mom's forehead creased. She was crushed at missing out on some quality Gideon time.

"We don't have time. Maybe he can come in for a bit after the carnival."

With my mom slightly mollified, I darted out the door to meet Gideon.

"Hey," I chirped when I climbed into the passenger seat of his dad's car.

"Hey yourself."

Gideon's hair was styled with a deep side part. A pair of black Wayfarers and a faded tee advertising Palisade peaches added to the retro vibe.

"My mom misses you."

"Who wouldn't miss me?"

He didn't miss a beat.

We pulled out of my neighborhood and headed toward Hell. The annual Homecoming carnival was set to start at ten. I was in charge of the debate team's car wash and had to arrive early to set up.

I'd been prepared to tell Gideon about my latest card from the Queen of Hearts, but the words lodged in my throat. I'd promised to stay honest with him about the Red Court, but I was beginning to think he was safer the less he knew.

Counting the previous card from the QoH, which I'd never mentioned, this note was the second secret I had kept from Gideon. Soon there wouldn't be anyone in my life I could be fully honest with. I grabbed my journal to put my thoughts to paper.

October 27
You reap what you sow. I dread my harvest of secrets.

I tucked my journal away and looked to Gideon. Journaling was one of the few things beyond his scrutiny. He knew what it meant to me, how important it was to my sanity.

"Remind me why you're coming to the car wash?"

"I have nothing to do today. And something interesting always happens at the Homecoming carnival."

This was true. Whether it was someone getting too aggressive at the pie-a-teacher-in-the-face booth or seniors commandeering the dunk tank for an impromptu pool party, the Homecoming carnival provided enough gossip to keep the school going until the end of the semester. The administration would have canceled it years ago if it didn't fund half the clubs and teams for the rest of the academic year.

The coup de grâce was of course the parade. The debate team's float was a car covered in what looked like soap suds to double as an advertisement for our car wash. School families and alumni all turned out to support the Heller High community. Everything wrapped by early afternoon to give us time to get ready for the dance, or to watch movies at Gideon's again, whichever.

Gideon steered his way through the mass of students zipping around the parking lot getting booths set up and carrying supplies. He parked as close to the car wash as possible, which was on the other side of the school. Last year, half the team had come down with a stomach flu, and I was left to run everything. This year, trusting no one else, I volunteered to steer the ship as team captain. When we picked our way through the melee, I was shocked to find Gigi barking orders to everyone, including several senior boys.

"Nice work," I said as Gideon and I surveyed the orderly way everyone was lined up, supplies ready to go. Some of the debate team members eyed us warily, and I looked to Gigi for an explanation.

Gigi, who stood all of five feet, beamed in my direction. "I may have implied that you'd randomly draw a name for someone to be kicked off the team if you got here and found a mess."

Gideon barked out a laugh and tried to disguise it as a cough.

"I appreciate the initiative, but we need everyone's help if we're going to meet our goal for this year."

Gigi had the kind of tenacity that surprised people, if only because of her small stature. She was a spitfire, hungry to impress and eager to win. After only her first debate meet, she asked me to start coaching her. When I looked at her drive to succeed, I saw myself mirrored, the better parts of myself.

Gigi excused herself to terrorize some juniors who were tossing buckets of frigid water at each other. The idiots were going to get hypothermia. October warm was not July warm.

I had just tossed my bag down when my phone started to buzz. I grabbed it and stared at the screen. Nothing.

"I think it's your other phone." Gideon's eyes were wide with meaning.

I scrambled to grab my burner from the depths of my bag, ignoring the itch plaguing my palms at the thought of doing Red Court work today of all days. There had to be a better place to store my other phone so I wouldn't get confused at which one was ringing.

"Hello?"

"Hey, we have a situation."

"What kind of situation?" Having this call in front of Gideon felt too much like my worlds colliding. The two were not supposed to meet.

"The kind where something went wrong with another team's job and they need us to clean up."

"What do you need me to do? I'm working the carnival today. It'll be hard to get away."

"I know, I know. I'm going off the script. I have an idea you should be able to complete during the carnival. Just keep doing what you need to and be ready. I'm going to herd them to you."

"What are you talking about? What sort of job is this?"

She huffed, obviously annoyed that I couldn't keep up with her evil plan. "It's a setup. We need to put two people together and hope they stick in time to go to the dance tonight."

"Are we matchmakers now?"

"Sometimes." She sounded distracted. "This is not my kind of thing. I'd rather anything else than this, but no one else could pull it off today."

I'd never asked what happened when you failed at your assignment. If work well done earned a reward, the opposite must be true. Whoever screwed this up was bound to be punished.

"Ok. Just tell me what I need to do."

"That's the spirit."

Haley clicked off the line and left my snappy remark to die on my lips.

"What's happening?" Gideon asked.

That question had at least a dozen answers, most of which Gideon wouldn't care to know.

"I'm to play cupid in some desperate fool's attempt to find a date for Homecoming."

Gideon smirked in a self-satisfied way. "I told you. Something interesting always happens at the carnival."

CHAPTER 19

THE CARNIVAL WAS well underway by the time Haley texted me with instructions. Despite the nice weather, the debate team's car wash wasn't shaping up to be the fundraiser we needed. Our team even wore coordinated red tees that read "Will get dirty for dollars."

> **Haley:** u need 2 come by the main stage in 20 mins
>
> **Me:** Fine. What do I need to do?
>
> **Haley:** crash the stage and steal the microphone
>
> **Me:** Pardon? You must have made some typos.
>
> **Haley:** nope
>
> **Me:** ...
>
> **Haley:** crash the stage and make a pitch for the car wash
>
> **Haley:** I can do the rest

What was Haley thinking? Me, crash the stage? There were probably things in the universe less likely to happen, but I couldn't think of any.

Gideon had wandered off to find some funnel cakes for us, so I handed the reins to Gigi and took off to think of a plan. The main stage was at the center of the carnival and the source of noise that could be heard for miles around. Each year, student council hosted a battle of the bands to raise money for some part of the school that was crumbling—the weight room was this year's lucky recipient. Most of the money seemed to go to athletic equipment.

"Ember!"

I turned to see Chase walking up, arms laden with the cheap stuffed animals that lined the game booths.

"Hey," I said. "Do you think you have enough teddy bears?"

Chase's grin stretched across his whole face. "I have a gift for ring toss."

Being friendly with Chase still left me feeling like I was in an alternate universe, even as my heart skipped enough beats to be dangerous each time I saw him. "You can say that again. What are you doing with all of those?"

"My little sisters love them. I was commanded to come home with no less than six this year."

How much did he have to spend on ring toss to win— I counted—seven bears? "Looks like you have an extra."

"Actually, this one is for you."

Chase handed me a white bear with a little red rose in its hand.

"Thank you," I said softly.

A cute boy giving me a bear he won at the ring toss booth. It sounded like something that happened sixty years ago to couples in old movies. It was also unbearably sweet. The kind of thing that should have me gagging but instead put a strange pressure in my chest, like the air in my lungs was trying to escape through my heart.

Chase looked away with a pleased, shy expression. He shouldn't have given me the bear. He should have found someone else who could say more than thank you. Someone who could tell him yes when he asked her out on a date.

"I can't accept this," I murmured and tried to hand it back.

He gently stopped my hand and shook his head. "I insist. You'd be doing me a favor. I have two sisters and seven bears. That's bound to cause a fight when one ends up with four. They'll probably agree to split the bear in half, so you're really doing it a favor, too."

I chewed on my lip, wanting to hold on to the bear and knowing I shouldn't. "Ok, thank you." A buzz in my pocket reminded me I had somewhere to be. "I better get moving. Lots to do today."

Chase fell into step beside me as I continued toward the main stage. "Where're you headed?"

"I'm going to make an announcement for the car wash."

Chase looked questioningly at me. "I didn't know they did announcements for that kind of stuff during the battle of the bands."

"They don't," I muttered. "We've got a good team and several of us have a decent shot at Nationals. We need to raise enough for everyone to go."

"Do you have a plan?" Chase asked, amusement sparking in his brown eyes.

"I'm thinking of one."

"Are you going with anyone to the dance tonight?" Chase's gaze was firmly fixed on the ground.

Was he asking me? "I'm not really the 'dance' type. I'm just hanging out with Gideon, watching movies."

His shoulders relaxed. "I'm not, either. Well, not much of a dancer, I guess."

"Are you saying you can't dance?"

Chase's cheeks tinged pink, but he didn't respond. Interesting. Something Chase Merriman couldn't do.

We came to the main stage at the center of the carnival. One of the bands was in the throes of a song on the stage, guitar and drums raging. I cringed at a discordant shriek of feedback coming from one of the amps. These guys needed some serious help. Not even the Red Court could rig a win for them.

Once the song came to a close, none other than Max Stanley came onto the stage to thank the band and announce a ten-minute break as the next act set up.

"Now or never," I said to Chase and stormed the side of the stage after finding a safe place to stash his gift.

I leapt up the stairs and took a deep, steadying breath before I strode out from behind the makeshift curtain and stood next to Max.

"You got this," a voice next to me said. Chase had followed me up the stairs and stood next to me, grinning at the crowd. He'd left his burden of bears on one of the amps.

A few hollers from Chase's friends carried over the noise

and he gave several waves and shout-outs to his admirers. Max only stared at us, dumbfounded by our appearance.

I plucked the mic from his grip and spoke. "I just wanted to remind everyone that the debate team's car wash is going on in the faculty parking lot. Each wash is free, but please be generous. Our team is working hard to get to the national competition, and…"

No one was listening to my ramble. Worse, I couldn't see Haley anywhere. She hung me out to dry without any help. What was I doing?

Chase leaned in and picked up where I left off. "Come on and help the debate team raise some money. If you don't want a car wash, I'll stand up here and sing the Heller fight song until we get enough donations for me to stop. No one wants that."

Chase started to sing—his singing voice was terrible, like two tone-deaf raccoons shrieking—and more whoops reached us along with a few whistles. Some of his friends tossed bills and change onto the stage for his efforts. I finally spotted Haley on the outskirts of the crowd, arms folded across her chest, talking to someone with a serious expression. The girl she spoke to wore a beanie pulled low over her brows, nearly covering her eyes. With her face angled away, I couldn't make out any distinguishing features. As she turned to go, the mystery girl pulled a phone out of her pocket. One that looked just like mine, a Red Court burner.

The crowd in front of the stage thickened and I lost sight of the girl in the gathering mass. Part of me wanted to jump off the stage and follow her. The Queen of Hearts. It had to be her. Could Haley have been lying this whole time about not knowing her identity? Was the QoH watching me to see if I could complete the job? My thoughts refused to organize amid the noise of the crowd and Chase's off-key rendition of the Heller fight song.

A guy came up the steps on what looked like shaky legs. He marched purposely over to where Chase and I stood, and he held his hand out for the mic. His cheeks were flushed red against fair skin. He wasn't StuCo, that much I knew. Honestly, it looked like he was about to be sick.

Chase took this cue and gave a bow before handing the microphone over and stooping to collect his earnings. He grabbed my hand to lead me off the stage. My feet dragged and my eyes lingered on the guy. What was he doing? Beyond him, I noticed Hell's activities director giving Max a hard time for letting us on the stage.

Damn.

I didn't want him to get in trouble.

"Umm. I wanted to say something to Ella Keyshaw," the would-be Romeo said. "Well, I wanted to ask her something. Ella, will you go to the dance with me tonight?"

I stumbled over some cords on the stage and gave a yelp, but that didn't drown out the resounding "yes" that came from someone in the crowd. Ella had her date to Homecoming.

I disentangled myself and tugged free from Chase's grip. "Thank you for your help. I would have lost it out there without you."

Chase gave me his brightest grin, one that made his eyes crinkle in the corners and my heart stutter. "I couldn't let you go out there alone."

I seriously needed a CT or ECG or whatever it was they

used to monitor heart function when I was around him. Maybe they could give me a pacemaker for when my heart eventually gave out under all the strain. He dug out the bills and coins from his pockets, an impressive amount for such a short performance, and handed them over.

Behind the curtains, with the rush of adrenaline in my veins from the high of Red Court work, I felt bold. Bold enough to reach up on my toes and place a quick kiss on Chase's cheek.

"I better get back." I barely recognized the breathy voice as my own.

"I'll see you around."

I gathered my bear and walked back to the car wash in a daze, thinking about the girl I saw with Haley, trying to match her face with any in my memory, but snapped back to attention when I noticed the dark-clad figure shadowing my steps across the crowd. When I found a quiet spot behind a concession stand, I stopped and waited for the shadow to emerge.

"That was interesting," Haley said when she appeared around the corner.

"Something interesting always happens at the carnival."

She made a noncommittal noise. "And Chase?"

"Things didn't go exactly as planned. But you have to admit it all worked out in the end. I even got fifty bucks for the car wash."

No use telling Haley that Chase came on the stage with me on his own and was not actually part of my scheme.

"How did you do it?" I asked her.

"The other team did most of the work. Our lovebirds just needed one last shove to send them over the cliff."

Haley made their date for the dance sound about as appealing as actually being sent over a cliff. I waited for Haley to fill in the rest of the story. Finally, she relented.

"I merely mentioned that the two of you appearing on the stage was bound to result in you getting asked to the dance, a 'promposal' or whatever they're called, and how that was the best idea ever. When that didn't happen, our boy decided to steal the show."

It was amazing how little effort the Red Court had to expend. So much of what we did were tiny moves here and little corrections there to set things in motion.

"So glad I could help you out. What would you have done if Chase hadn't gone up there with me?"

"I'd have figured it out. I always do."

"Did I see you talking to someone in the crowd? Was she in on the job?"

Haley narrowed her eyes. "No, not really. I was talking to a lot of people. It's hard to push through a crowd and be polite at the same time. I was probably apologizing for stepping on her foot when she wouldn't budge."

I snorted. Haley wouldn't give up anything so important as the identity of the Queen of Hearts that easily. If anything, her cagey response was encouraging. There was something there; I just had to find the right thread to tug and watch it unravel. "I better go."

"Ember," Haley said when I brushed past her. "Did you get a card in your locker yesterday?"

My feet sank into the pavement, trapping me where I stood.

Something in Haley's tone triggered warnings in my head. I glanced back at her pale face and wild hair. She looked like the goth ghost of Christmas past. "Why?"

"Sometimes the Queen of Hearts leaves us notes after our jobs. Sometimes she even offers us favors."

"Favors?" I kept my voice light, betraying only a hint of interest.

"Just be careful what you ask for."

Haley turned her back to me and ducked around the corner on quick feet.

"I'm always careful," I whispered to no one. The lie caused a sudden pang in my chest. As much as I wanted to find out the Queen of Hearts's identity to bring her down, I also felt something else when I caught sight of the girl in the crowd. I wanted to please her.

CHAPTER 20

AFTER MOVIE NIGHT at Gideon's, I spent the rest of the week-end considering the favor I would write on my card for the Queen of Hearts. Did I need to write a real request if I was planning to bust her when she picked it up? I wasn't sure what I was going to do when she showed up. If I wasn't able or ready to confront her, I'd have to have a real favor on the card to buy me some time.

The problem was finding something that wouldn't hurt anyone if the Red Court acted on it. Who would even se-cure something for me? It couldn't be one of the other teams. They'd know I asked for something, and if they thought to check, my name wouldn't be on the list of people who owed favors. We weren't in the Red Court because we were slow on the uptake.

So it would have to be the Queen giving me what I wanted.

My head swam at the thought. I could have the Queen of Hearts herself doing my dirty work. Would it be the girl from the carnival?

With nothing to go on but the quickly fading image of her face in my mind, I flipped through my and April's yearbooks. After an hour of scanning page after page of school pictures, I was no closer to putting a name to her face. I turned to some light Instagram stalking, checking through followers from some of the more notorious Hell High students, including Chase. Even though it was public, it felt like an invasion to scroll through his photos. He still had some posted with his ex-girlfriend, and I had to click away before I transformed into a green-eyed rage monster. With any luck, I wouldn't need to track down the girl in the beanie. She would be coming to me.

When I walked into school Monday morning, the whole place was abuzz about the carnival and the dance. Who showed up with whom. Who wore what and who copied them. All of it seemed a million miles away from my reality.

The hallway next to my locker was noisy and crowded. I used the cover of voices and crush of bodies to my advantage and opened my locker unnoticed. It was time to leave my own note for the Queen of Hearts. The playing card, an Ace of Spades, felt like a brick in my pocket, awkward and heavy. I'd chosen the card on a whim. It didn't have any special meaning, but maybe putting my request on it gave it meaning, made it mine.

I palmed the card and reached up to place it on the top shelf, where all the Queen's notes appeared.

"What are you doing?"

Gideon startled me and I dropped my card. It floated slowly down before Gideon neatly grabbed it from the air.

"Don't!" My fingers grasped the edge of the card before Gideon pulled it away and held it in the air where I couldn't reach it. "Don't be a child. Give it back!"

I would not jump to reach it. I would not jump to reach it. I would *not* jump to reach it. Desperation got the better of me and I jumped like a five-year-old with my hands in the air.

Gideon gave a wicked laugh. He so delighted in reminding me that I was short. "Calm down. I'll give it back. I just want to see it."

His laughter stopped when he looked at what he held in his hand. His eyes scanned back and forth across the card, soaking in the words and their meaning.

"I can explain," I said. The noise in the hall was loud enough that a conversation would have to involve shouting. I so didn't want to do this right now. "Later. Let me explain later."

Gideon handed back the card. "Sure. Whenever it's convenient for you."

"Please trust me. I know what I'm doing."

I took the card and placed it on the shelf. Shutting my locker with more force than necessary, I turned back to Gideon. He was already gone, swallowed by the sea of bodies coursing through the hallway.

Gideon wasn't waiting for me after second period. He wasn't waiting for me in the library. He didn't respond to my text messages, either.

I decided to wait for him at his next class. If I blocked the door, he couldn't avoid me. I'd make him listen. I needed him to understand.

I sat in the hallway and pulled out my journal. There wasn't anything to say. I couldn't remember a time when there wasn't something to write, something I needed to get out of my head. Frustrated, I jammed it back into my bag.

I rolled my head around, attempting to release the tension in my neck. My favor was a good one. The only thing I could think of that wouldn't hurt anyone. In fact, I was helping. When I'd tossed around ideas of things I could do, I remembered Max was in trouble because of something I did.

Word had spread as far as the car wash that after my stunt, Max was in detention and at risk of losing his spot in StuCo. Apparently, the faculty advisor didn't believe that Max wasn't in on the antics. If I could do something, I wanted to help him. So I asked for him to keep his spot in StuCo. The detention wouldn't do any harm in the long run, but losing his spot as junior class secretary seemed extreme.

The bell signaling the end of third period rang and I watched students pour out from their respective classrooms. A few minutes passed, and a familiar dark head surfaced in the mass of students.

"Hi," I said when he got close enough. "Can we talk?"

"Now's not a great time." Gideon tried to sidestep me, but I moved into his path.

"You said whenever it was convenient for me."

Gideon's lips twitched in an almost smile. "Fine. Speak."

I grabbed his hand and guided him down the hall to a more secluded spot. As secluded as you could get in a crowded hallway.

"My favor is gratis."

"Pardon?"

"The Queen of Hearts gifted that favor to me. I decided to use it to help Max because my stunt got him in trouble at the carnival."

"So, you don't owe anything for it?"

"Nope. I already paid up."

Gideon didn't seem pleased, but at least he was talking to me.

"I don't remember seeing this in your plan. You promised not to keep anything from me. I can't watch out for you if I don't know what's happening."

"This *is* part of the plan." I weighed the potential danger I'd be exposing him to by telling him against the idea of him pulling away from me. Selfishly, I didn't want to lose my friend. "The Queen of Hearts is coming to get the card from my locker at the end of the day. Phase two is now in motion. Do you want to join my stakeout?"

His face brightened at being included in my scheme for sabotage. "I don't have any plans."

"Great. Meet me after school by the girls' bathroom on the main floor."

At 2:45 p.m., Gideon and I bustled over to the pillars in the hallway by my locker. Short of being an ideal hiding place, it was actually pretty terrible. But there wasn't much cover in the hall. We could have hid in the trash cans, though there wasn't a sum of money large enough to convince me to squat in those petri dishes.

By 3:15 p.m., Gideon was quickly losing patience. "Where is she?" he demanded.

"Shhh! I'm sure she's waiting until everyone goes home before breaking into my locker."

The clack of heels on the tile silenced us both. We adjusted our positions so we were out of view from the direction of the noise. My line of sight was partially obscured by the other pillars. I held my breath as I glimpsed a pair of feet stop in front of my locker.

"Stay here," I whispered to Gideon.

"No way!"

"She can't see you. What if it goes wrong? You can't have a target on your back, too."

The distance between pillars was only a few feet. I moved quietly from one to the other, trying to get a better look at who was there. I peered around the corner and saw an auburn head bent close to the locker door. I leaned forward, trying to get a better look. She was taller than the girl from the carnival.

She was also visibly shaking. Why would she be shaking?

And crying. She was crying.

The Queen of Hearts would never...

It wasn't her.

I looked back to Gideon. He was making frantic shooing motions, urging me to confront the girl at my locker.

I nodded, but I wasn't about to confront this girl. She wasn't who I was looking for.

I stepped from my hiding place and approached the girl.

"Hey," I said.

She spun around and threw her back against the locker.

"Hey," she replied and swiped at the tears on her face.

"Are you—"

"I'm fine."

"Clearly." I raised my brows like I was Gideon, a borrowed tactic that always got me to break.

"No, I'm fine."

The silver of the locker master key glinted in her hands.

"What's that?"

She shoved the key into her pocket and looked everywhere but at me. "Nothing. Did you need something?"

"I only wanted to see if you were ok, but I see now that you're fine, so I'll leave."

"I'm sorry," she mumbled, eyes cast down.

Great. I made it worse. I had to say something, to let her know that she'd be alright. Eventually, anyway.

"Don't be sorry. Whatever's going on, you're going to be ok." I tried to look encouraging, but my smile felt more like a grimace.

"Thanks." She sniffled and turned around, going back to her lock picking.

I strode back over to Gideon and he followed me out of the school and toward my car.

"What happened?" he asked when we were safely stowed in my Jetta.

"It wasn't her. I'm such an idiot. She doesn't do anything herself. Why would she do this? She makes people who owe us favors do things for her."

Gideon muttered a curse.

"I let myself get too emotional over this. If I had stopped for a minute to think about things, I would have seen it."

"So, what have we learned?"

"That the Queen of Hearts is well protected. I need a more direct path to her."

There were only two other girls I knew to be part of the Red Court. I hadn't made any progress with Haley. Still, I couldn't shake the feeling that the girl she'd been talking to was somehow important. I wasn't ready to close the door on the possibility of that girl being the Queen of Hearts.

Until I made any progress there, maybe it was time to focus my attention on the only other option I had.

The Fire Alarm.

CHAPTER 21

THE NEXT DAY, I woke up with renewed determination. Shauna, aka the Fire Alarm, was as well connected in the Red Court as the Queen of Hearts herself. If she knew who all the members of the Red Court were, did she know the Queen of Hearts, too?

From a few unassuming questions to classmates and members of the debate team, I learned Max Stanley was off the hook with the administration. Though I didn't ask for it, his detention was also canceled. Everything magically disappeared, easy peasy. The lack of an MO was the Queen of Hearts's MO. Her work was flawless.

Over the next few days, I tried to catch a rare glimpse of Shauna during passing periods. As a junior, she didn't share any of my classes. She also tended to flock with a more popular set than would ever deign to glance my way. The only exception was Chase, who seemed like the exception to every rule.

After my behavior at the carnival, I was studiously avoiding him, rushing out the door after each class with an apologetic smile. When my mind stopped worrying furiously over the Red Court, my lips would tingle in phantom remembrance of the way his cheek felt when I kissed him. Each time, I shivered at the memory of the October chill that clung to his skin and how it was scented with his usual spicy warmth.

By Friday of that week, I was losing my edge to the lack of progress. Shauna was panning out to be another frustrating dead end.

"Hey, Ember." Chase stepped in front of me as I was escaping from Carson's Lit class.

I huffed, upset at missing an opportunity to follow Shauna. "Didn't we talk about you getting in my way?"

He flashed a cheeky grin. "That was before you kissed me."

I felt a scarlet flush heat my face and glanced around for any listening ears, ones that potentially belonged to the Red Court.

Recovering quickly, I said, "Don't you have somewhere to be?"

"I do, but I wanted to talk to you before you ran away again."

My face had to be as red as the Queen of Hearts playing card in my wallet. I vowed to make Chase freaking Merriman suffer for this. If it was the last thing I did, I would pay him back.

"I'm not running," I said through gritted teeth.

"It's just an expression. I have something for you."

He held up his closed fist and unfurled his fingers to reveal an origami heart. I reached for the neatly folded paper, but he snatched his hand away like a five-year-old. "You have to say please."

"Please," I crooned with mock sweetness. My curiosity was piqued.

His self-satisfied smirk irritated the ever-loving crap out of me, but he handed over the heart. Chase's origami game was strong and the symmetrical heart impressed me with its crisp edges. He leaned close, his lips almost brushing my ear as he whispered, "Have a nice day, sweetheart." Brushing past me, he left the room without another word.

Once he'd gone, I opened the heart, careful not to crumple the clean, sweeping lines so it could be refolded. It was our last Lit exam. Well, it was Chase's graded copy, the one Carson handed back before the end of class. He got a 95 percent and had set the curve. I knew my paltry 92 percent wasn't going to cut it this round, but the blood in my veins still heated that Chase was pouring salt in my wound. Just below his score, he'd written a note to me.

Maybe next time...
Chase

My own words from the first time we met at the coffee shop had come back to bite me.

I relished the satisfying rips of the paper as I shredded it into confetti and tossed the pieces into the trash. A snicker from the far corner of the room reminded me I wasn't alone.

I turned to find a grinning Carson looking at me with amusement from his desk.

"A little competition might be good for you two," he said.

"Good for me, you mean. When I beat him."

I turned on my heels and marched out of the classroom.

Game on, Merriman.

I found Gideon waiting at the bottom of the stairs that led to the third floor.

"Do you want to go for coffee?" he asked.

"Excuse me? I think I might be dreaming." Coffee was never on the menu if I was even ten seconds late to meet Gideon. His punctuality was a greater enemy than the Queen of Hearts.

"Whatever," he shot back. His face was a lazy mask of boredom, but I knew him too well to buy the act.

"Aren't you worried about being late?"

"We'll be quick." He turned on his heels to head toward my car. "I just need to get out of here for a minute."

Before I could dig any deeper, the very person I'd been looking for appeared across the hallway outside the stairwell. Shauna was kitty-corner from our position with her back pressed against the wall.

Shauna shared our off-hour, but I had yet to catch her by herself. She was usually encircled by at least three other girls, all laughing like they hadn't a care in the world. Despite her well-crafted image, I couldn't seem to see anything but her eerie calm when she rescued me. That seemed like the real Shauna, not the giggles and girlfriends. She held an important role in the Red Court. She was the Queen of Hearts's right hand. She was the embodiment of what the Red Court was all about.

I snagged the edge of Gideon's shirt and pulled him backward behind the corner and out of sight.

"What the—"

"Shh. Shauna is right there."

True to my word, I'd filled Gideon in on the details from my failed reconnaissance mission before Homecoming. He'd been stunned by my close call and morbidly curious about Shauna's role in the Red Court. Much to my annoyance, he insisted on "helping" me follow Shauna around.

Staying hidden as much as possible, I peered at Shauna where she stood studying her nails, the picture of ennui. The sound of someone coming from down the hall caught her attention, and her head snapped up. The person approached out of her line of sight and stopped around the corner from Shauna.

After a beat, Shauna snapped, "What were you thinking?"

A petite dark-haired girl I didn't recognize trembled with her arms wrapped around her middle.

"I'm sorry. I freaked out." The voice was unfamiliar, but the contrite tone was unmistakable. She'd pulled her fire alarm.

"You know the rules. You call, I come."

I looked back to Gideon and found his eyes wide with understanding. Another member of the Red Court was talking to Shauna. Neither girl had eyes on the other. To anyone passing by, it didn't appear as though they were having a conversation.

"I know. It's just that I think he knows, and I was told to call you if someone knows."

"Calling me isn't the problem. Panicking for no reason is the problem. You don't call me all hysterical because your boyfriend might suspect something. You find out more and handle it."

Even though I wasn't on the receiving end of Shauna's wrath, my face burned at the acid in her words.

"Don't you dare cry, Gretchen."

"I'm s-s-sorry." Gretchen gave a great sniffle and took a deep breath. "What are you going to do?"

"What's his name?"

"Sam McCormick. You're not going to do anything to him, are you?"

Shauna rolled her eyes. "We'll keep an eye on him. In the meantime, you are on probation. No jobs, no meeting your partner."

"But I have to meet her. I got the photo of—"

"Stop right there. Do not tell me. I can't believe you made it through initiation as careless as you are."

Gretchen scrunched up her face, obviously fighting tears. I didn't think I handled my encounter with Shauna as gracefully as I could have, but at least I didn't cry.

"Sorry. Could you leave this in her locker, then?" Gretchen placed an envelope on the ground.

"Stop apologizing already and pull yourself together. It's going to be fine."

Shauna had already lost interest and was focused on her phone. Gretchen shuffled away like a scolded puppy. I'd learned my lesson about judging books by their covers with Haley, but this sad, quiet girl seemed to lack the qualities that Haley once told me about. More than anything, she didn't seem to have an ounce of confidence in herself. What on earth was she doing in the Red Court?

Just as Gretchen ducked out of sight, Gideon's phone started blaring. Shauna's head lifted and I ducked back around the corner to shove Gideon roughly up the stairs.

"Stop trying to answer it and get moving!"

Gideon gave up on silencing the phone and bounded up the stairs two at a time. I followed as fast as my legs could carry me. I didn't dare look behind me as we hauled ourselves to the top of the stairs and around the corner into the girls' bathroom.

Gideon finally shut his damn phone off and we stood side by side against the wall, gasping for air. A few minutes passed, and it seemed like we were in the clear. Shauna, for whatever reason, didn't pursue us.

"Why was your phone on?" I demanded.

"I was waiting for a call." Gideon met my eye and quickly looked away.

"From who?" What could possibly be so important that Gideon would leave his ringer on and risk losing his phone for the day? Hell High had a generous phone policy compared to most other schools, but an incoming call during class was a guaranteed way to lose your phone and land in detention on a Saturday.

Gideon looked sheepish.

"I'm waiting."

"Damien," he answered quietly.

"Seriously?! Is that why you were so desperate to go for coffee?"

"I don't do desperate." He shot me an icy glare that could give Shauna a run for her money.

"Since when is Damien calling you?" Despite my annoyance, and almost getting busted by Shauna, I was nearly giddy for my friend. He didn't open himself up often or fall into crush after crush. Gideon was hard to win over, but he was worth it times a million when you did.

"He was going to meet us for coffee. We've been texting a little bit. I wanted you to meet him officially and without a counter between you."

I clasped his hand and gave it a squeeze. "I'd be honored. I'm sorry my Red Court nonsense got in the way."

He shrugged. "Being a spy was kind of fun." The edge of a smirk appeared at the corner of his mouth.

"It was, wasn't it?"

Still holding on to Gideon, I dropped my head back against the wall. My heart beat at a gallop and adrenaline was singing inside me. My feelings toward the Red Court—bitterness and anger and exhilaration—were all tangled up in a heady mix that gave me a high like no other.

And I was officially addicted.

CHAPTER 22

THE QUESTION OF Gretchen dogged me through the weekend, a shadow constantly at my heels. I couldn't outrun it on the track or distract myself with homework or reading assignments enough to avoid it. She was a puzzle I couldn't solve, and I didn't know why that bothered me so much. It was enough of a distraction to pull me away from the mystery of the girl from the carnival.

I looked Gretchen up and added her to one of the empty spokes on my corkboard. Her last name was Goldberg. She was a sophomore like me, but we didn't have any classes together. That wasn't too unusual with a class of over six hundred students, but I thought I'd at least recognize other kids in my grade.

Overestimating yourself again, Ember.

"Do you know anything about Gretchen Goldberg?"

I asked Gideon the next Monday in the deserted section of the library. Gideon was covertly texting Damien that our coffee date was rescheduled for next week.

"Sure," he said, not looking up from his phone.

"And?" I prompted when it became clear he wasn't planning to participate willingly in our conversation.

"She's in my math class. She's really smart. Doesn't tend to do homework, but she aces all the exams and that saves her ass from failing."

I made a noncommittal noise. Smart but lazy did not Red Court material make.

"Is that who we heard in the hallway last week? Talking to what's-her-face?"

"Yeah, and I can't understand why she's in the Red Court. I get me, obviously. I even get Haley and Shauna, but Gretchen's different. She seems…"

"Nice?"

"Not to put too fine a point on it, but yeah. She seems nice. And the rest of us aren't. What does she want so badly to make her turn to the Red Court?"

"That's the million-dollar question," he quipped before returning to his phone.

A text from Haley had me hauling to the theater room after school. It had been over a week since Homecoming and I'd received nothing from my partner since the carnival.

"What's going on?" I said after kicking the door open in my best Haley impression.

She sat perched on the sofa, unamused by my antics. "We

have some work to do." Her expression was bordering on pissed off. Well, more pissed off than usual.

I was instantly on guard. "Ok. What kind of work?"

She sighed. *Seriously, what the hell?*

"The kind where we need to do some cleanup."

"Again? Sheesh. First the carnival and now this? Are we the only competent ones in the Red Court?"

"You did get busted when we broke into the school."

"Fair enough. How can I help?"

"Another team was working on this, but we'll have to step in to finish."

I thought of Gretchen and her probation. Was this her job? Haley handed over a folder with some notes on a student that graduated two years ago. Someone who still owed us a favor and hadn't paid up when we called it in.

"Oh," I said, "I know him."

It was April's ex-boyfriend Alec, the one who'd moved on to a happy life without her. Not that the breakup was his choice. But still, his memory caused April pain on an ongoing basis.

"I know. I read in his file that he used to date your sister. He's going to college in Denver now."

"Lucky him. Shiny new life. Shiny new girlfriend." Whatever we'd be collecting from him would be my absolute pleasure.

Haley studied me, perfectly still. It seemed like her version of the Gideon arched brow. Something I'd done interested her. Maybe it was the malicious light that was undoubtedly glowing in my eyes. "Shiny new fiancée, actually. They just got engaged." Haley paused a beat to let that fact settle in.

"He never had to repay his favor while he was still here, but as you know, no one ever really stops owing us."

"What did we do for him?"

"Seems like we helped him land the lead in the musical a few years back." Haley was back to business, scanning through her tablet for additional notes.

I remembered my mom's birthday and Alec's need for applause and attention. Ugh. Gross.

"And what do we need from him?"

"To repay the favor in kind. Auditions for the spring musical are in a week, and we have a request to help a certain someone get a role.

"All we need is for Alec to make a phone call to Mrs. Conrad, his old teacher. Ask her to look out for a new talent. Fortunately for you and me, a lot of work has already been completed. This should seal the deal."

I flipped through the rest of the dossier. A printed photo of Alec meeting with my sister was the final page. They were sitting across from one another, hands linked over a table. Because I knew April, I could see the tension in her expression, but I doubted anyone else would notice it. The jump from friends to something more would be an easy assumption to make based on the photo.

"What is this?" I looked to Haley, whose face was carefully blank.

"The only leverage the other team was able to get on Alec to use against him."

This must have been the thing Gretchen had to deliver her partner. The missing piece for her job.

"But that's my sister. And this picture is recent." April was using her new lighter-weight manual wheelchair, which she'd gotten only a month ago. Haley had to know who was in this picture with Alec.

"I know who it is, but we have a job to do." Haley was all business.

"So, what's your plan?"

"Deliver this to him in person along with a note telling him he has twelve hours to call Mrs. Conrad or this picture will be delivered to the future Mrs. Alec."

I nodded.

"Remember, he owes us, and either he pays up or he pays for it."

"Right, no one stops owing us."

Haley stood up and dusted off her standard all-black outfit. There seemed to be patches of plaster dust clinging to her.

"Sculpture unit," she said by way of explanation.

Before she left, I asked, "Why didn't the Red Court collect from Alec while he was here?"

Haley lifted a shoulder. "Sometimes there isn't anything we need."

I twisted my mouth. Alec was decently popular and had some influence in the performing arts department, obviously, since we were cashing in on his equity two years after he graduated.

"Also, I think he was pretty broken up about what happened to your sister. He was kind of out of it for a long time."

"And the Red Court showed him some mercy? That sounds like something we'd do. Right after our annual charity project."

"Or he was useless because he was so upset after everything that happened."

"Last I saw, he was doing just fine."

I refused to give an ounce of sympathy to Alec. He made a bargain and it was time for him to hold up his end of the deal. "What goes around," I said quietly.

"What was that?" Haley asked sharply.

"Umm...nothing. Just thinking out loud. Alec's getting what's coming, you know?"

Haley nodded and left the theater room without another word.

Whether she knew it or not, April was about to be an accomplice in a Red Court job.

I left the theater room and headed to debate practice, my head swimming. The day was far from over, and now I had an unscheduled trip to Alec's. The timeline for musical auditions didn't broker any room for a night off, even though the stack of homework in my bag was literally weighing me down.

"Hey, Ember," a bright voice called from the main office as I passed.

"Hi, Gigi. How are you?"

"Good, good. I'm excited for the next meet." She bounded up next to me, buzzing with energy, and looked back to her mom. "Bye."

"I'll come by the debate room in an hour," Mrs. Martin said. "It's good to see you, Ember."

I gave her a friendly wave. Martin was my assigned guidance counselor. I hadn't had much cause to occupy the couch in her office. Direction was the only thing I didn't need. I knew what I needed to do.

"I'm excited for the next meet, too. Only a few more practices left. Saturday will be here before we know it." I gave her as bright a smile as I could muster, which I think was about half its normal wattage.

The anticipation of an upcoming debate meet used to get my blood thrumming, but I'd moved on to harder stuff.

"I've been reading through your notes, and I can't thank you enough. I think I'll place this time."

A softer smile formed on my lips. "I bet you will, too. You work harder than anyone else." Gigi's commitment reminded me of myself.

"Thanks. I'm really trying. I want debate to be my thing. The thing that I'm good at, you know?" She peeked up at me with a shy grin. Gigi wasn't typically bashful; she must not share how much her success on the debate team meant to her very often.

A strange impulse struck me. I wanted to guide Gigi, be the person who gave the advice that got her where she needed to go. Just like my work with the Red Court, I was in a position to help someone else. And help I would.

"You know what? I'm feeling pretty prepared for the next meet. How about you and I work together today?"

A high, girlish giggle sounded from farther down the hall. I turned to see Shauna, Chase, and a few of their friends on their way out to the parking lot.

Chase looked in my direction and gave me a sly grin. He'd managed to stay clear of me since his little stunt with the heart note.

Wise choice, Merriman.

Little did he know that Carson approved a special extra

credit project for me to do independently. When I would be finding time to do it was a problem for Future Ember.

I shook my head at him, my own sly grin snaking its way across my lips. He was going to be eating his words. Topped with whipped cream and sprinkles. An eat-my-dust sundae.

Shauna gave Chase a playful shove and continued laughing on her way out the door. I almost didn't catch the glare she shot my way. She had to know it was Gideon and me spying on her the other day, and it seemed like we were caught in a bizarre game of "I know that you know that I know." My only hope was that I'd end the Red Court before she decided to act on what she knew.

"What was that about?" Gigi was staring at me.

"What was what?"

"That smile that Chase Merriman just gave you." A slight teasing edge tickled her words.

"We're pretty competitive, and he was just reminding me that he set the curve on our last Lit exam."

Gigi made a "humph" noise, clearly not buying my story.

I rolled my eyes. "Come on."

It shouldn't have surprised me that even Gigi knew who Chase was, either personally or by reputation only. Even more reason for me to avoid him. Being around Chase would only get me noticed, and not in a way I'd like. If only my foolish heart would stop stuttering every time I saw him.

CHAPTER 23

I WAS BACK in my ridiculous cat burglar outfit, creeping in front of Alec's house just after dark. Hopefully, the ensemble didn't prove unlucky a second time. If it did, I was going to toss it into Gideon's fireplace and light it on fire to exorcise the demons. A patch of scrubby ponderosa pines across from Alec's house provided good cover for my stalking. Only the puffs of white from my breath were visible in the golden glow of the streetlight. I shuffled farther back, hugging myself to conserve as much heat as I could.

Waiting alone in the dark left my mind time to wander. How could April not have told me about meeting Alec? Just over a year ago, April had tried to rekindle things with Alec, but he'd moved on and told her to do the same. She'd dated a couple of guys since then, all of whom were a hundred times better than Alec as far as I was concerned. Was that what this

coffee date was about? I was her sister. She could have con-
fided in me. Although I would have done my best to talk
her out of meeting Alec. Maybe that was why she didn't say
anything.

A text drew my attention away from the stakeout.

Gigi: Thanks for helping me today! I feel so much better
about Saturday.

Me: Of course. You're going to do great!

I smiled to myself, happy to help someone like Gigi. I had
the odd sense that she reminded me of the person I could have
been if my life didn't revolve around revenge.

I tucked my phone away and shifted in position for a better view of the street. Alec may have graduated from Hell
High, but he was still living at home, two neighborhoods
over from my house. The picture of Alec and April weighed
heavily in my pocket, along with the note instructing him
that his fiancée would be receiving a copy tomorrow unless he called Mrs. Conrad to recommend some silly freshman for a role in the musical. Never mind that I didn't think
Alec's word was worth anything. Apparently, the Red Court
thought differently.

The flash of headlights spooked me as a car came around
the bend. I recognized it as Alec's truck. Haley's plan dictated
that I should leave the note on Alec's car or wrap it around a
rock and chuck it at him if I was feeling less charitable. But
neither option was very appealing.

I imagined the look in Alec's eyes when I showed him the
photo. I wanted him to see me and know that I held his fu-

ture in my hands. This wasn't high school. It was the rest of
his life I could be affecting. My pulse was already racing at the
implication of what I was doing, catapulting me to a whole
new level of Red Court high.

As Alec gathered his bag and coat from the front seat, I deserted my hiding place and crossed the street.

"Alec?" I called out.

He turned and squinted into the darkness. "Hello?"

His confusion turned to surprise when he recognized me.
"Ember? What are you doing here?"

Ruining your life.

"I have a delivery for you, actually."

"From April? Listen, I can't accept any gifts or notes. I *tried*
to tell her over coffee the other week. I'm engaged now."

He held up his left hand like he was wearing the engagement ring. So dramatic.

"That's not what this is." I gave him a withering glance,
my best Gideon and Haley hybrid.

"Oh, ok. I was sorry to have to tell April I didn't want to
get back together. I know things haven't been easy for her."

"They haven't, but if you ask me, she's a whole lot better
off without you."

I yanked the picture and note out of my pocket and shoved
them at Alec's chest.

"Ow! What's this?" He looked down at the note and photo.

"The Red Court wanted me to give that to you."

"I don't understand."

Alec's fingers clenched around the paper. If I had to hazard
a guess, I'd bet he did understand. This was his reckoning.

A past mistake finally catching up to him. He should have run farther.

"The Red Court says that if you don't call Mrs. Conrad by tomorrow morning, like they've asked, your fiancée will be receiving a copy of that photo."

Alec's chin lifted and he narrowed his eyes. "So?"

He just *had* to be difficult. The Red Court wouldn't have given me the photo as ammunition unless it was capable of striking a killing blow. "Does your fiancée know that you met your ex-girlfriend, one who broke up with you, for coffee? Recently?"

His eyes flicked quickly to the left, but I caught what they said, even if Alec wouldn't admit it out loud.

"If you were going to meet April for coffee just to tell her that you two are definitely over, why not tell your fiancée? If that was the case, April would surely back you up."

Alec grimaced. If I was a betting girl, I'd wager that Alec hadn't told my sister that they were well and truly done. Maybe his vanity couldn't let go of some girl pining over him.

"And you? What's your part in all this?"

Wouldn't you like to know, asshole.

"I'm just unlucky to know you, and the one they tasked with delivering the message. Just do what they ask. This photo would be a hell of an engagement gift for her."

"I can't believe you, Ember. This is my future *wife*. You'd really ruin everything for me because of some promise I made to a stupid high school club?"

We were more than a club and he knew it. I continued to aim my practiced stare at him, silent.

"I thought I was done with this crap," he muttered.

In his dreams. I bit my lip to keep from smirking. This jerk made a deal and thought he was in the clear. It was time he learned the Red Court motto.

"Don't you know? You never stop owing them."

I was nearly back to my car a few blocks down from Alec's house when a twig snapped behind me. I whirled around, searching the darkness, and groped desperately in my hoodie pocket for the key-chain pepper spray my mom had given me. *Safety first.*

"Hi," a quiet voice from the shadows murmured.

"Umm…hi," I said back. My numb fingers finally grasped the pepper spray bottle. Carefully, I pulled the tiny canister out, trying to keep it concealed in my palm.

A petite dark-haired girl stepped into the light. Gretchen Goldberg.

Uh-oh.

"So, you're Ember Williams." Her voice, so shaky when she was talking to Shauna, now sounded sure.

"Yeah. You're Gretchen, right?"

She smiled and gave an encouraging nod like I answered a question correctly. "I was wondering who they were going to give my job to. The Red Court always finishes its jobs."

There was something almost childlike in her lilting words, like wonder, or like she was one of a set of demonic twins in a horror movie. I checked behind me to be sure there weren't two of her. We were alone, but the back of my neck still prickled, alerting me to the dangerous situation I was in. If they weren't frozen, my palms would be itching.

"Lucky me." I unsuccessfully tried to choke out a laugh.

"I wanted to see it through, even though I'm on probation. But you knew that."

I shook my head fervently. "I don't know what you're talking about."

"You overheard my conversation with Shauna. I saw you and Gideon when you went up the stairs."

Shit, shit, shit.

I couldn't pepper spray her, could I? No, I needed to find a way out of this.

"Don't worry. I won't say anything. It's just a little secret between us. I was worried until I saw you here tonight and figured out that you're one of us, too." Gretchen leaned in, a conspiratorial smile on her lips. "What you said to Alec was genius, by the way."

I faltered, completely off-kilter. "Thank you. But why are you talking to me? You had the upper hand knowing who and what I am. I would have never said anything to you about what I heard."

"I was curious. I know that's a dangerous thing to be in our line of work, but I couldn't help myself. I want to know everything about the Red Court. That's why I called her. I just had to meet her."

Her? *Shauna.* She didn't pull her fire alarm because of her boyfriend's suspicions; she was playing Shauna that day in the hall.

Well done, Gretchen. She sure fooled me. "But you only get one and you wasted it. I don't understand."

Weirdness notwithstanding, her stunt seemed like a poor use of a valuable resource. Maybe I only felt that way because when I pulled my alarm, I really needed it.

"It wasn't a waste. It was the price of knowledge. Aren't you curious about everyone else, too? We were chosen to be part of the Red Court, and there's so much we don't know about it."

Of course I was curious, but I had a feeling that my curiosity and Gretchen's were not the same. Still, maybe I could use this to my advantage.

"Gretchen, why did you join the Red Court?"

"I wanted to be part of something great."

The Red Court may have been great, but in the worst sense of the word. It was powerful and bigger than any of us, but it was also terrible.

She continued, "I even got a position as a TA in the main office because I heard a rumor they were always looking for ways in there. You have a lot of access."

I tried to remember if she was the girl who'd dropped off my note, excusing me from class the day I received my invitation, but my mind was spinning like a top and I couldn't recall. I shook my head to bring myself back to the conversation.

"What about you? What brought you to the Red Court?"

"The favor," I lied. It was too cold outside for a more elaborate story.

She nodded her approval in return.

There wasn't a way I could accurately describe the girl from the carnival, but I wanted to know if Gretchen had found out who the Queen of Hearts was and if there was a chance I was right. "Have you found any other members besides me and Shauna?"

"Like the most important member?"

Busted.

She gave me an impish grin. "Not yet, but I have my suspicions."

I swallowed my disappointment. "Well, I better get going." I pulled my keys out of my pocket and gave them a nervous jingle as I backed away. "I'll see you around, Gretchen."

"Not if I see you first," she said, the eerie smile back on her face.

I flicked my eyes to the rearview mirror as I pulled away. Gretchen was washed in red from my taillights and I had a terrible premonition. If my plan didn't work out, I could see Gretchen as the next Queen of Hearts. The fanatical gleam shining in her eyes was unsettling. For the first time, I was really scared—not for myself—for everyone else. Someone like Gretchen, who loved being in the Red Court with a fervor I couldn't fathom, could wreck the entire school without blinking an eye. I couldn't let that happen.

If the Red Court always finished its jobs, so could I.

CHAPTER 24

ONLY ONE CROSSFIRE stood between me and a place on the stage. After a long day, the Public Forum final was the last event of the debate tournament. I looked over at Gigi and gave her an encouraging nod. Her confident smile was a far cry from the despair of that morning.

I'd arrived at school bright and early to catch the bus with the rest of the debate team to our in-district rival's tournament. I stood at the door of the motor coach checking everyone in as they climbed onto the bus. Our car wash turned out to be a roaring success, probably thanks to Chase's on-stage stunt, and the team could afford to ride in style instead of in the standard banana-yellow bus. When everyone else was on board, I noticed Gigi lingering in the parking lot, throwing anxious glances back to the road in front of the school. I checked my list and noticed her partner hadn't checked in yet. If she didn't show up soon, we'd have to leave without her.

"I don't think I'm coming," Gigi murmured when she finally walked over, eyes downcast and voice defeated. "I can't do a two-person event by myself."

It took me only a millisecond to decide I was ditching the original oratory I was scheduled for. "Yes, you are. I'll do it with you."

Her head snapped up. "Really?"

The hope and awe in her tone made my chest swell. Gigi had worked so hard to improve over the last few weeks. She deserved a chance to compete. "We went over your argument so many times, I think I know it by heart."

She bit her lip, obviously wanting to say yes and being too decent to accept my offer right away. "But what about your event? You've been killing it all season. I can't take away a chance for you to place."

I shook my head and grinned. "You won't. We're going to win."

And round after round, she rallied with killer rebuttals and more composure than I'd ever seen from her. I was glad I didn't have to compete against her. Gigi was a force.

Gigi organized the notes she'd been taking that highlighted the other team's last rebuttal points. I handed her my counter-arguments for review and she scanned through them quickly, starring the ones she felt were the strongest. This was our last chance to make an impression on the judges.

As we'd planned, she opened with a systematic dismantling of the argument our opponents had just made.

"The decriminalization of marijuana at a federal level

should be a national priority, despite what our esteemed opponents have stated. The numbers don't lie. The majority of those incarcerated on drug offenses are persons of color from a lower socioeconomic background. Keeping laws in place that are known to adversely affect specific minorities at a higher ratio is wrong.

"According to a study cited in an article from *HuffPost* last July, the number of persons detained pretrial for small drug offenses at any given time in the United States is in the tens of thousands. Pretrial means that these people do not have the means to post bail, compounding the economic imbalance and putting additional strain on the households who rely on the financial support of these family members."

Gigi turned to me, eyes wide with surprise at her own performance. She'd just handed the two guys across the stage their asses, and from their shocked expressions, they knew it. I couldn't help the smile that stretched the limits of my face. I recovered quickly, glanced at my notes, and picked up where Gigi left off.

"In Colorado, we've seen the marijuana industry flourish under decriminalization. The funds raised from taxes on recreational marijuana have gone to support substance-abuse programs and to provide more affordable housing. Other countries have also decriminalized low-level possession of illegal drugs, such as Portugal, which made the move in 2001. Together with learnings at the local level from states like Colorado, and opportunities to leverage practices from the international community, we feel that the US could successfully decriminalize within three years and instead focus on providing more accessible treatment options for those struggling with addiction."

I sat back, taking a deep breath as our opponents fumbled through their stack of notes. I slyly held my hand out to Gigi under the table and she slapped her palm into mine. The adrenaline firing through me was a different sort of thrill from my Red Court work, but seeing Gigi's confidence grow with every round was a reward itself.

It occurred to me that Gigi would make one hell of a Red Court member. The thought put a knot in my stomach, and not just because I hoped Gigi would never get involved in the kind of work we did. She could easily be the next Queen of Hearts, too. I needed to stop thinking in terms of who the next leader of the Red Court would be. If all went as planned, there'd never be another Queen of Hearts again.

I fought my way through the main hall the following Monday in an attempt to make it to the third floor for Lit on time. Unless the crowd magically disappeared, I was going to be late.

"Hey, Ember!"

I turned to see Chase lope toward me, long legs striding easily. It was stunning to watch the sea of students part before him like he was freaking Moses. Popularity probably had other perks, but what I wouldn't give to be able to move so effortlessly between classes. Being a petite underclassman made getting swept away like a twig caught in the current all too easy.

"Hi!" I worked to keep the wary edge from my voice. I'd already been busted with Chase twice before. There were a lot of eyes trailing him, making another scolding from Haley almost inevitable. Plus, my put-up-with-Chase's-nonsense meter hadn't climbed back down from nuclear threat levels after he struck with his origami heart.

Chase arrived at my side with a wide, easy grin. "How are you?"

"Good. How are you?"

See? I could be normal and polite, unaffected even.

But when Chase looked at me, it was like his whole self was attuned to my every move. His gaze wove invisible threads binding us together, if only for the moment. My theoretical pacemaker was probably firing up in preparation for cardiac arrest. Being with Chase was a sharp, exquisite exercise in being alive.

"I bet you're better than good. I heard that you took first at your last debate meet. Congrats!"

Despite my best effort to quell it, a blush crept up my neck and flushed my cheeks. Gigi and I took first; our impromptu duo shredded the competition in the finals. I'd never been more proud to share the stage with anyone.

"Thank you. People think debate is all BS, but there is a lot of work that goes into it."

Chase smiled. "I don't think you're even capable of BS. When would you find the time?"

A barking laugh escaped my mouth, something between a laugh and a cough. In other words, not cute. My blush deepened, and I thought I might as well go ahead and die here. No time like the present.

"How about you? Do anything interesting this weekend?" I surprised myself with genuine curiosity. What did Chase fill his hours with when he wasn't plotting against me as my nemesis?

My shoulder collided with his as we bobbed along the corridor. The brief contact sent a jolting thrill through me. I quickly dismissed it as the temptation of forbidden fruit. Chase was off-limits; therefore, it was only natural to be curious about what I couldn't have. Could I have him? He'd asked me out, but who knew what might have come from that. Probably nothing. For sure nothing.

"I've been really busy. My mom's been traveling for work, so I've been on babysitter duty with my sisters."

Chase grinned self-consciously. Any boy who went through the trouble to win six teddy bears for his sisters had to be the best manny. My own bear held a spot of honor on my nightstand. I could just picture him at high tea with a flower hat. Chase's sweet sincerity was a departure from our normal games, and it knocked me off my axis. No one was who I expected them to be anymore.

The warning bell rang, reminding me that we had to hustle up to the third floor for class.

"We better get moving. Can't risk my perfect attendance record."

Chase stopped me at the base of the stairs, kids parting around us like we were boulders in a stream, and looked at me. "Can I ask you something?"

I looked up the staircase, knowing we were going to have to sprint to make it in time. "Umm, yeah?"

When I turned back to him, I noticed the soft look in his eyes. No one had ever looked at me like that. Nerves struck me like the caffeine aftershocks of a double espresso, leaving me jittery.

Why did this handsome, funny guy make me feel like this? Oh, right. He was handsome and funny. *Duh, Ember.*

"I know you said you were busy, and I get it. You have more going on than pretty much anyone else I know. But I was hoping we could grab a coffee. I know you like going for coffee after Lit, so maybe we could make a run together sometime."

Chase nibbled at the corner of his lip. There was no reason for me to spend more time with him. I had been expressly told not to see him. I'd have to come up with an explanation to satisfy Haley, which was about as likely as me becoming besties with Gretchen. But, as the final bell rang, I said, "Yes."

CHAPTER 25

A PHANTOM BUZZ from my burner phone drew my attention to the special zipped pouch in my bag where I now kept it hidden but still readily accessible. Gideon and I were in the library, at my suggestion. I may have agreed to go for coffee with Chase, but I was in no hurry to sign my own death warrant.

Gideon slammed his pen down on the desk in front of me. "I swear to Gosling, Ember, if you check that damn phone one more time when I'm trying to have a conversation with you, I will take it to the chem lab and dissolve it in hydrochloric acid."

"No, you won't."

Gideon could threaten all he liked. The chem lab was the off-hour hangout of his ex, Matthew. He wouldn't step foot in there if it was the only source of hair products in a fifty-mile radius.

This was the third time today I'd thought I felt the phone vibrate only to be disappointed by continued radio silence from Haley. No jobs meant no progress in learning more. After my close call with Shauna and bizarre run-in with Gretchen the week before, I was back to square one. I felt like I was perpetually stuck in the second phase of my takedown plan.

In the last hour, the grass in front of Heller had been covered in copies of an unfortunate senior's diary entry that named half of StuCo in a binge-drinking excursion. That it happened at all was a bad look, but the implication that it was bankrolled by the activities department's petty cash landed the student body president in the principal's office. A voice in my head whispered that if I'd managed to work faster maybe it wouldn't have happened. That voice was a jerk. And maybe those kids had it coming.

Every day that passed without any word from the best link I had to the Red Court added to my anxiety. The Red Court's reach was breathtaking. With so many members' identities still a mystery, everything I learned still only felt like I was scratching the surface. I had to go deeper, not wider.

"You're right, I wouldn't, but it's no use having you over tonight if you won't be paying attention to me."

"What on earth would you do without me to worship at your feet?"

My attention was back on the novel in front of me. I was painfully slogging through *The Scarlet Letter*. Class reading was typically not a challenge for me. I was a fast reader, and a faster skimmer. Boiling all the words on the page down to a few salient points was a talent of mine. But the thread of *The Scarlet Letter* continued to elude me; I couldn't find a corner of the story to hold on to. The notes I'd scribbled were worthless, and I'd taken up most of the page trying to sketch the girl from the carnival. With no other progress in finding the Queen of Hearts, I'd returned to obsessing over the mystery girl from the carnival, but already my memory of her had faded. My brief glimpse of her was already too hazy to do me any good. The only thing I knew for certain was that I did not have a future as a forensic sketch artist. Haley would be infinitely better at this.

"I'd find someone else looking to get a tan from my radiant light."

I dropped my book and the pretense of reading. "Sometimes, you're—"

"Utterly charming? Thank you, Ember. You're forgiven."

My head fell forward to rest on the library desk. We were tucked away in the far corner, behind the stacks, out of view from most of the kids hanging out in the main section of the library.

"I love you. I really do, but right now I can't handle all of this." I emphasized my point with a wave of my hand, sweeping over his entire face.

"What's eating at you?"

I peeked up at Gideon and was relieved to see he was giving me his concerned face. It was the one he wore when he was really willing to listen and not throw every word back at me with a snarky response.

I looked around, but no other students were nearby. Most of the school was still too occupied with the latest takedown gossip. "This whole thing with the Red Court. I haven't heard from Haley in a week. I'm not making any progress and I feel like April is pulling away from me."

I debated for days whether or not to confront April over her secret meeting with Alec. Ultimately, I decided against it. April was saving toward an adapted van with hand controls, so one of my parents would have driven her. If she chose to confide in either of them instead of me, I should respect her decision, even if I really didn't want to.

Gideon slumped back into his seat, his weariness at the shift in conversation apparent. "You can't keep doing this." He paused to gauge my reaction. "Do you think everything you're doing is what April really wants?"

I shook my head. "She's made it clear that it isn't. It's hard to explain, but she was the one who always looked out for me. After she got her license, she insisted on taking me out with her for her first official ride in the Jetta. Everything she's gone through—" Tears stung the backs of my eyes, but I pushed them down with every ounce of dignity I had. There would be no crying in the library. "I can't fix everything, but I *can* get rid of the Red Court for good," I choked out when I was sure I could speak without sobbing.

"Maybe that's true, but do you think it's worth everything you're sacrificing? Your soul?"

"I hardly think rigging Homecoming Court and making Alec freaking Hardy pay up on a favor are jeopardizing my place in the afterlife."

"Really? Homecoming Court was a gateway to bigger, better things for you in the Red Court. Maybe Alec had it coming, dickface that he is, but you were prepared to ruin his life. What's next?"

I winced. True, I'd made the jump from little league to the majors overnight, but this was how the Red Court worked. Alec made a promise of payment and refused to cooperate when his name was called.

"Sometimes the Favored asks us for things and then don't like the consequences. What goes around, comes around."

"Favored? Since when do you talk like them?"

"You're the one who called me out on not owning this whole messed-up situation!"

A librarian passing by hissed at me to lower my voice. Chagrined, I said quietly, "What am I supposed to do now? Walk away? I can't. I haven't come this far not to push for the finish line. And Alec deserved what he got. You didn't hear the way he talked about April."

Gideon ignored me and went back to his trigonometry homework. As soon as I reached for my book, he captured my hand and gave it a long squeeze. This small measure of affection and solidarity from him was as comforting as a dozen hugs from anyone else. Thank God for Gideon. I would be lost without him.

I was scared to admit it out loud, but I couldn't see the line in the sand anymore. If there was a boundary I wouldn't cross to get what I wanted, I wasn't sure what it was. And that, more than anything else, terrified me.

I finally received a text message from Haley just before French at the end of the day.

Haley: ur excused from class

Haley: come meet me

I was tapping out a reply when a third message came through.

Haley: now

My spidey-sense told me Haley knew about Chase. I took my time making my way to the theater room, a dead woman walking. The lights in the performing arts wing were already shut off for the day, shadowing the stairs down to the basement in horror film darkness. For what I thought was about to go down, the whole tableau fit.

The door to the theater room swung open before I lifted a finger to open it. Haley's sneer welcomed me into the dim room, the emergency light near the exit casting us in shades of blue.

"What are you doing?" she snapped.

After a week of silence, I was in no mood to justify my actions to her. The things she'd done, that I'd done with her, left zero space for moral superiority between us.

"What do you care?"

"I care because what you do reflects on me. We're a team. We're supposed to trust each other if no one else."

How could Haley expect me to trust her when I knew she was lying about the girl from the carnival? She must be important if Haley valued that secret over our partnership. I'd already asked once; I didn't think I could again without revealing how much I suspected this girl was the Queen of Hearts.

"I don't want Chase's attention. He's seeking me out. Probably because I shot him down."

Haley looked shocked. "He asked you out before?"

"Before Homecoming. I blew him off. It doesn't matter." I scrambled for purchase in my mind. A safe place where I could tell her something true. "He just asked me to grab coffee with him during my off-hour. It's not exactly a candlelit dinner. I know you don't want me drawing attention to myself, but wouldn't it be more conspicuous if I keep shooting down one of the most high-profile guys at school?"

This hard logic set the gears turning in Haley's head. I watched as she processed my words, looking for fault, and—with a resigned expression—finding none. Triumph.

I couldn't resist throwing in another layer of rationale for good measure. "He'll hang out with me a few times at most before he realizes I'm boring and safe. A guy like Chase wants someone dynamic and exciting. We both know that's not me, not the good girl everyone knows."

Finally, Haley nodded. "You're probably right. He might talk more about you if you turned him down. You go out, he decides you're not right for him, he moves on. It's a lot cleaner and far more plausible."

That she felt so confident about my impending dumping stung just enough for me to stick my tongue out at her. "I'm glad Chase ditching me brings you comfort."

She cracked a cheeky grin. "I didn't say that. Only that it was the likely outcome, like you said."

Like I said. Why did the thought bother me so much? I hardly knew Chase outside his drive to be the best. And his humor. And the unexpected streak of goodness that underscored everything he did. Maybe that was it. I wanted someone like Chase—not popular or cute or smart, but good—to see something of value in me. I'd devoted so much time to my grand revenge plan, it didn't leave a lot of room for other admirable traits.

Her expression sobered. "While I agree with you, you need to be careful."

"I wouldn't give anything away, if that's what you're concerned about. As far as anyone knows, I'm a dedicated student and nothing more." How could she think I would blab to the first handsome boy to catch my eye?

"That's not what I mean. Don't forget that Chase has an admirer who likes him enough that she contracted us to dismantle his last relationship."

I did forget. I was so worried about the Red Court's eyes watching me that I failed to remember there might be someone else, someone desperate, who kept a close eye on Chase.

The warning felt different from the last one Haley gave me about Chase. It was more immediate, which raised the hair on my arms. Warning bells rang in my head, sounding eerily similar to Gideon's words telling me to be careful. There was no time to heed any warnings when I was hurtling down this path at the speed of vengeance.

"Is that all?" I asked.

"We got a hit request today from the same girl who had us set up your little meet-cute with Chase. It was for you."

A cold sweat broke out across my forehead. Someone wanted to take me down for talking to Chase. All we did was talk. What if they knew I agreed to go on an almost date with him? Would they have taken me out themselves?

"What did you say?"

Haley rolled her eyes at me. "That I'd be the one to do it."

Her snarky attitude served the words with a side of sarcasm. "You're safe, remember? Rule number one. I take our rules seriously, but in this case we broke rank to tell her that she'd be getting no more favors until we get a return from our initial investment. I'd be careful, though. From the sound of it, she might take matters into her own hands."

"That is both reassuring and terrifying all at once."

Haley continued, "It should buy you enough time to ensure that Chase loses interest in you. He will lose interest, right?"

"Maybe?"

Haley produced her most threatening glare. It worked.

"Yes, I'll make sure he thinks I'm a waste of his precious free time. Why would he take even a minute away from his vapid fangirls to spend time with a nobody like me?"

"Thank you. Was that so hard? Now, let's talk business."

The mention of a project brightened my mood. It meant the opportunity to make my next move in the chess game between me and the Queen of Hearts.

"We have an assignment," Haley said.

If I was working for the Red Court, I could at least have fun with a few harmless jobs.

At night, when I couldn't sleep, I would indulge myself by thinking about the possibilities for Haley and me to get our hands dirty. The winter formal was coming up, and there were probably tons of options for us.

"What is it?" Apprehension quickened my pulse as anticipation caused delicious licks of excitement to flare in my veins. I wanted another job.

"It's going to be a tough one. A takedown."

Disappointment quieted the tumult inside me. Not my first

choice, but I had enjoyed twisting the screws on Alec. There was always something to savor.

"I thought you only did election rigging and things like that."

"Not always, and this one is specifically for you. The person we have to take down is Gideon."

CHAPTER 26

I FLASHED HOT and cold and hot again. "Haley." I couldn't control the quaver in my voice. "I can't. It's Gideon. You know what he means to me."

Haley's face was a mask of indifference, but her eyes were bright with what looked like pity. "This is the job. You knew that coming in. There's a price for us to pay, too. Protection and favors don't come for free, Ember."

Emotion would get me nowhere with Haley. Regardless of whether she agreed with me or not, she was too pragmatic about our roles in the Red Court to be moved by tears. I cleared my throat and adjusted my approach. "But he's my best friend. How could I pull this off without him noticing? I know things about his life no one else does. I can be careful, but I'm not sure I can be that careful."

I was wrong. There was a line for me, and we'd just reached it.

"It's because you know him like no one else that you can do it. You said he was entering a photo in the Winter Showcase, right? That could be your platform."

No, I can't.

Panic was choking me, stealing the air from my lungs. I was fighting the frantic need to escape the claustrophobia setting in. I had to get out of here before I lost it. I needed more time to think, to think and find a way out of this. Given a few days, I could plan my way out of anything. I had to buy some time.

"Give me the dossier." I extended my hand to Haley.

Her head tilted ever so slightly to the left, her disbelief at my quick change of heart evident.

"I'm not going to do anything right now, but I'll look through what you have."

She gave an approving nod and dug out the folder from her bag. This, at least, she could believe. "I'll text you the email account details so you can access the list of people who owe us favors."

I turned without a goodbye and left the room. For once, I was glad for the lack of pleasantries. No goodbyes or unnecessary chatter, just the sound of the door clicking shut behind me.

I was on autopilot driving home, my mind tangled up in a mess of half-baked solutions. What could I do to get out of this and maintain my place in the Red Court?

Who could possibly want to take Gideon down? He was sarcastic, sure, but he meant well and mostly orbited the drama instead of being the gravitational force at the center of it all.

There was no one on my radar who might want to hurt Gideon.

Gideon was my sounding board on any normal problem; a caustic sounding board, but still someone I could air my thoughts to. Just telling him when I was struggling to make a decision helped. Who could I go to now? Certainly not Gideon. I'd have to tell him eventually, but this was not the kind of problem you presented without a ready solution.

April's window winked in the afternoon sun as I pulled into the driveway. My sister had been instrumental in helping me get into the Red Court, telling me what she remembered about its members from the ever-present rumors that cast a specter-like shadow over Hell High.

She might have some insight into my situation or another angle to consider that I couldn't see. Some perspective would do me good right now. I wasn't sure who would win if I had to pick between saving my best friend and settling the score for my sister. The mere thought of choosing between the two made my stomach seize and threatened to bring my lunch back for a curtain call.

I dropped my bags in the hall and raced to April's room, clutching the dossier. April was at her desk listening to music and looking through Instagram on her computer. I paused at her door and watched as she scrolled through Alec's feed. Why was she so intent on torturing herself with his new life? Why would she even want to get back together with him?

I cleared my throat and April startled in surprise, quickly closing the window and wiping away the happy couple in front of the azure sea and sugar-white sand, revealing a spreadsheet. I didn't miss the classic put-a-ring-on-it pose of Alec's new fiancée, holding her left hand up to the camera and a megawatt smile plastered on her face.

"Hey," I said.

April sat silent, refusing to meet my eyes.

"How's the retreat planning going?"

The physical therapy center's annual retreat was coming up soon, and from the bits April had shared over dinner, it was going to be great. She'd managed to come in under budget, with more activities and participants than ever.

A smile lit her face. She was proud of her work. I knew it was important to her to be a part of something, doing real good for others. "It's going. I'm getting tired of the last-minute changes from the director. But there's something you need, right? It's all over your face," she said with wry amusement.

Stupid face.

"Right. I have a problem, and I'm hoping you can help."

Her stare gained an interested glint.

"I got a Red Court assignment that I can't complete. I'm hoping you can help me find a way out of it. It's a hit," I continued, "and I just...can't."

April turned in her chair to face me fully. "How is this different from the things you've already done?"

April's role as devil's advocate was not unfamiliar. It's what made her a good person to talk to when you couldn't find your way. She'd force you to widen your lens—like switching your camera settings from square to pano, there was more to every situation if only you'd open your eyes.

"The things I've done, I can live with the cost. I made peace with being in the gray area between right and wrong, but I think this might push me farther than I'm willing to go." I paused, considering my words, and how even though they were technically true, I still felt that something inside me had changed. The girl who emerged from deep inside when I needed to be a heartless follower of the Queen of Hearts was making more frequent appearances, and I enjoyed being her more and more with each task, relished the fact that I could enjoy the work. Would any good parts of me remain when this was all over? I couldn't admit that to April. If I did, she would tell me to stop immediately.

"So far, nothing has changed the person I see in the mirror." My heart felt heavy with the lie. The last person I could be totally truthful with was slipping away.

She nodded slowly. "And this would?"

I swallowed thickly to clear the lump rising in my throat. The sisterly note in her voice—a comforting mix of affection and reassurance—dissolved my defenses.

April's eyes caught on the folder in my hands and I moved across the room to lay it on her desk. "Go ahead."

I settled myself on the familiar pink bedspread, smoothing my fingers against the stitching.

She picked the folder up and opened it. Her eyes darted over the page, and I saw the moment when she registered why I was here asking for help.

"It's Gideon." The sympathy in her voice cut right to the quick, exposing the soft parts of me I shielded from the world.

"April, I can't do it. Even if I could somehow engineer it to not be that bad, I'd still never be able to live with myself." Without meaning to, my mind cast ahead to the Winter Showcase, framing the outline of Gideon's takedown. If the

Red Court was going to crush him, that would be the place to do it. Last year, he'd worked for months on a collection of poems, only to be told he was "trying too hard" by his Honors Lit teacher. I knew he'd held on to those pages and the hand-written feedback. If anyone else ever saw them, he'd be beyond humiliated. Gideon was a private person and displaying some-thing so personal would gut him. Haley was right. The people who knew you best knew how best to hurt you.

I may have had a whitecapped ocean of anger and sad-ness inside me when I thought of what the Red Court did to April. But with Gideon, it was protectiveness awakening within me. Our relationship was a thread woven through my past that continued beyond the horizon toward my future. He was my friend, a true friend, and I knew enough of the world to know how valuable that was.

I let the steel shine in my voice. "I would never hurt him. Period."

April smiled. "I'd like to say that you should walk away from all this, but I know you feel like you can't. So, I have an idea for you."

April riffled through the rest of the papers in the dossier.

"Aha." She produced a note from the stack and handed it over to me. "This is what you do next."

I accepted the page with a quaking hand. Relief hit me as I inspected the page and saw what she meant. A name I rec-ognized leapt out at me. The person who made the request was Matthew, Gideon's ex.

"So? What do you think?"

"I think Matthew is about to find himself rescinding his request." My moral compass spun again, finding a new north.

If there was one thing I'd learned about myself over the last month, it was that vigilante justice was kind of my thing. Exacting revenge against those who deserved it lent a righteous angle to my position. All I needed was a cape and mask.

That night, as I lay awake in bed, I waited for an idea to form. Brainstorming was like gathering a pool of water from condensation, each drop adding a new dimension to the whole.

First, I had to figure out why Matthew wanted to take Gideon down. They broke up last summer, but it wasn't ugly or anything, and it was fairly drama-free. Granted, I had only Gideon's take on things. Matthew might feel differently. It was worth looking into.

Matthew and I had been on good terms when he was dating Gideon. Not close, but friendly. If his car had been broken down on the side of the road, I'd have been the first to offer him a ride. Blackmailing Matthew, uncovering something big enough to make him balk, pricked at my conscience. I tossed in my bed, grumpy that my conscience couldn't see the bigger picture. I was doing this for Gideon. Just like I was doing this for April.

What I needed, if my goal was to get Matthew to withdraw his request on his own, was leverage. The right amount of pressure on just the right pain point would bring him to his knees. A small voice in the corner of my mind wondered what happened for Matthew to go this far. And though I'd never acknowledge it, the small voice also wondered if Gideon deserved it.

"Gideon," I whispered aloud, "what did you do?"

When I finally drifted off to a fitful sleep, dark dreams plagued me. In them, I swam against an endless avalanche of playing cards—each one the Queen of Hearts. A girl's voice cried out for me to save her. I couldn't see where she was, but it sounded unnervingly like Gigi. Waves pounded my hands as I tried to protect myself, and a thousand tiny paper cuts nicked my palms. I was sticky with blood, and everywhere I looked, there were red hearts and red queens. Red, red, red. The color of my revenge.

CHAPTER 27

BUZZ.

Buzz, buzz.

I reached into my bag and silenced the burner phone. My fuse was short this morning and I didn't want to risk reading another of Haley's snarky texts. I might explode at the next person to look at me sideways. Days had passed since we met in the theater room, and my momentum on The Gideon Problem stalled out. With all my attention on Matthew, I couldn't spare a moment to continue my search for the Queen of Hearts. Dodging Haley's texts was only getting more difficult. She made her expectations clear, and each day I didn't deliver a design for Gideon's destruction, her suspicions grew.

Much to my disappointment, Matthew was a creature of routine—a boring routine. His route to and from school never deviated. He religiously spent his off-hour in the chem lab, studying or reading. So far, there were no telltale signs that he had a bone to pick with Gideon or any secrets I could exploit. After spending a worthless week shadowing Shauna, too, I was earning an advanced degree in stalking.

I was also getting to school earlier each day and returning home well past the normal hour. It was eating away at my precious free time and peeling myself out of bed before dawn was becoming more difficult by the day.

I was waiting for Gideon at the bottom of the stairs to the third floor, planning my campaign speech for coffee, when my regular phone dinged with a text.

Gideon: I have to stay and talk to Mr. Hall about issues with my physics project. I'll see you later.

Me: Ok. Good luck!

Tucking my phone away, I took a deep breath. Even worse than all the extra sneaking around was keeping something else from my best friend. Logical Ember knew telling Gideon about Matthew's request before I fixed it would end in disaster. Emotional Ember keenly felt the weight of the lie by omission. I was grateful for a few minutes to myself, to be myself.

As I wove between cars in the parking lot, I saw a figure lingering near the hood of my Jetta. My pace slowed as I squinted against the bright sunlight to see who it was.

"You came," Chase said with a tentative grin.

"What?"

"Our coffee run."

I had a brief moment where I thought I was going insane because I definitely did not have plans to grab coffee with Chase today. It was one of those things I'd remember. Probably forever.

He was sporting his letter jacket, buttoned up to the neck against the crisp November air. The whole system of letters and jackets seemed like old relics from the days of putting a pin on your best girl, but on Chase, it worked. His wholesome smile made his jacket charming instead of cheesy.

"I don't think we specifically said today. Did we?" I was doing my best to hide how charmed I was.

"No, but we did talk about getting coffee together at this time."

"You've been waiting out here every third period for the last few days?"

He shyly ducked his head and my Grinch heart grew three sizes. If I was truly selfless, I'd end all of this right now. I'd push him away and unequivocally state that he needed to find someone else.

I was not selfless.

"Well, your chariot awaits." I hit unlock on my key fob to punctuate my invitation with an anemic honk of my car alarm.

Chase only shook his head in amusement and folded his tall frame into the passenger side. I noticed a small piece of paper tucked under my windshield wiper and pulled it free. Maybe Chase was leaving a note when I found him?

Unlike the heart note, though, this one didn't have any flourishes.

STAY AWAY FROM CHASE

A chill swept through me. I crushed the note in my hand and glanced at the boy in question, sitting in my passenger seat. I managed a brief smile and got in the car. Whoever asked the Red Court to take me out wasn't content to wait. Just what I needed.

"What's your poison?" Chase asked while we waited in line to order.

My typical large Americano didn't sound as alluring as it normally did. Standing in such close proximity to Chase and the menace of the note stuffed into my pocket had my stomach in knots. My palms itched almost to the point where I couldn't think of anything else, and I didn't think it could handle the jolt of so much espresso.

"I might get a café au lait."

"Mmm." He glanced at me sideways. "That's a pretty serious drink."

I willed myself to forget everything else and enjoy the banter. "I'm a pretty serious girl. Didn't you know? I'm quite intimidating." My voice was a sultry slither.

He threw his head back and guffawed loudly. I had a feeling that everything he did required his whole self. All in, all the time. The idea of living like that, not reserving part of yourself from the world, was terrifying and a bit exhilarating. Maybe I could try it once my stint in the Red Court was over. It would be nice to go all in on something that wasn't revenge.

When our turn to order came up, Chase motioned for me

to go first. Damien, gorgeous barista and object of Gideon's admiration, was manning the register. I had to hand it to Gideon, Damien was a catch worth admiring. He'd graduated from another high school a year early and was currently taking classes at the community college at only seventeen.

"Where's your sidekick?" Damien asked.

And he was funny.

"He got stuck at school. I suggest you think about comping my coffee if you don't want him to find out you called him my sidekick."

We chatted for a few more moments before I ordered a café au lait and grabbed my wallet out from my bag.

"I got it," Chase said to Damien.

Damien raised his brows at me and shot Chase an appreciative look. "What can we get you?"

"Can I get a medium mocha with two extra pumps of vanilla?"

Chase paid for our drinks, I gave Damien a wave before the next customers stepped up, and we went to stand near the end of the counter, where our drinks would be delivered. After a minute, I couldn't stand it anymore.

"Two extra pumps of vanilla?"

Chase hung his head in mock shame. "Mochas are my weakness. I eat pretty clean. Food is fuel and all, but I can't pass up a good mocha."

He caught his lip between his teeth, genuinely abashed. My hand lifted toward his mouth but stopped short of touching him. A now-familiar tingle hummed through my fingertips.

Chase caught sight of the motion and grabbed my hand as I pulled it back, holding it in a light grasp. He was holding my hand. This boy, who I was not supposed to even be talking to, was holding my hand. To distract myself from the sound of my pulse pounding in my ears, I focused on the intricate dance of the baristas buzzing behind the counter.

Whatever gene I had that made me an avid planner and chronic overanalyzer kicked into high gear. What did this mean for me and Chase? What did this mean for me and the Red Court? Of the two thoughts, my mind was most drawn to the former. I wasn't sure if Chase was the kind of guy to hold someone's hand casually.

I risked a glance at his face. His eyes were asking if this was ok and telling me that this meant something. Despite the teasing and competition between us, Chase was the kind of guy who worried about his ex-girlfriend and her family. The kind of guy who didn't like the drama that was part and parcel with me. I didn't want the Red Court to take Chase from me, but how could I get any closer to him with all of my secrets between us? I pushed that thought aside, wanting something just for myself. Just this once.

Our moment lasted a little while longer until the barista called out our drink order from the bar. We moved in sync, getting in each other's way, and laughing as we collided. I'm sure we looked silly, but inside the bubble of us, it was perfect. I didn't have much levity in my life, and I drank in every moment like it could be my last.

As we walked out of the coffee shop, I noticed a familiar car a few spots down from mine. It was Matthew's. I'd all but memorized his schedule by now. He should be in Mrs. Perez's AP Chemistry class. Of every class, this would be the one I'd least expect him to skip. I looked at my watch. We had five minutes before we had to leave to make it back for next hour.

"Hey," I said to Chase. "I see a friend over there. I think I should go say hi."

He peeked around me to where Matthew was sitting in his car. "Do you want me to wait here?"

"I'll just be a minute." I handed him the keys. "You can get in if you want."

Chase shook his head. "It's fine."

It was cold, but I wasn't going to argue.

Cautiously, I made my way over to Matthew. There was no time for a proper plan. I couldn't even think of what approach I should take. If he was angry at Gideon, he might be angry at me, too.

Matthew was sitting in his car, staring down. He looked... lost. There was something vulnerable about his body language. If there was ever a time to press my advantage, it would be now. I knocked gently on his window and he startled.

"Hi," I said over the whir of the window rolling down. He looked like he needed a friend. Unfortunately, he was getting me. "I don't normally see you here. Do you have this hour off, too?"

"No." His normally velvet timbre sounded fractured. "I decided coffee was more important than learning today." There was a rueful set to his green eyes and his short brown hair was tucked under a wool cap.

I made a show of peering past him to see if there was coffee in his cup holder, but it was empty. "Well, I better let you get to it if you're going to make it back for your next class."

He didn't reply but dipped his eyes away from me and

back to his lap. There was something in his hands. A woven bracelet I recognized. It was a gift from Gideon. A small fissure cracked open in my heart. Pretty soon, these weak spots were going to cost me. But not today.

I dropped down to be eye level with Matthew. "You're not ok, are you?"

He took a shuddering breath and shook his head. There was hurt and sadness in his expression. If the tables were turned and Matthew had broken up with Gideon, what would I say to him? I wasn't sure, but it would be something.

"Stay right here. I'll be back in just a minute."

I popped up, not giving him a chance to say no, and jogged back to my car and Chase. He lifted his brows in question.

"So, I think I need to stay here. My friend might be in trouble." This was a wholly accurate statement. Gideon was in trouble. "Do you think you can drive my car back to school? I'm sorry to do this to you. I wouldn't unless it was important."

He smiled at me and something—my feelings for Chase maybe—burrowed deeper into my heart. "No worries. You help your friend. I can tell it means something to you, so it's the right thing to do."

How wrong you are.

"Thanks. Let me give you my number and we can meet up after school."

I slipped my journal out of my bag and tore a sheet out of the back. I quickly scrawled my number and handed it over.

"See you later." He leaned down to give me a quick kiss on the cheek.

My skin prickled pleasantly at the contact and I lifted my hand to the spot still warm from his lips. "Bye," I whispered.

After Chase left the parking lot, I turned to walk back to Matthew. I had to help Gideon, no matter the cost. To me or anyone else.

CHAPTER 28

UNINVITED, I CROSSED to the passenger side of Matthew's car and let myself in. Once settled, I turned to him. "I'm concerned about you. You don't seem ok."

Matthew could not have looked more surprised if I'd confessed my undying love. Not my most subtle move ever. With the clock ticking, I didn't have time for subtlety. If I had any chance of using my position to help my friend, I had to do it quickly.

"I'm fine." His speech was stilted, forced.

"That's the least convincing thing you have ever said." My aim was to appear sympathetic, but even I could see I was falling short. My nerves were frayed like the hem of an old sweater, slowly coming undone, and I didn't want him to see how shaken I was.

Matthew laughed, but it wasn't the sound I remembered.

It was angry and bitter and joyless. "I'm not fine, but why should you care? We aren't friends."

I shook my head. "That doesn't matter. You're still someone I know and someone who is clearly in a bad place. I want to help."

"How could you possibly help me?" he all but sneered, his lip curling slightly.

"I can help anyone. I'm very capable, if you didn't know." This at least got a small laugh from him. "Sometimes just telling someone about the thing you're holding on to can help. Maybe not always, but you'd be no worse off. You haven't killed anyone, right?"

He looked up sharply, and for a panicked second, I thought he might know why I was there. Then the moment passed, and his face cleared. He may not have murdered anyone, but killing someone's reputation was still pretty bad.

"You can start with how you've been. I haven't run into you since you and Gideon broke up." I could do this, have a conversation with someone I used to hang out with.

"I've been avoiding you."

"Me? Why?"

"Seeing you usually means seeing...Gideon."

Was Matthew's request born from a broken heart? No matter how I looked at things, with what I knew of their history, I didn't think so. It was like relationship algebra; I had to solve for X. There had to be a factor I was missing.

"I thought your breakup with Gideon was pretty amicable. Or as amicable as any breakup could be." How would I know? I'd never even had a boyfriend.

Matthew shrugged. "It was, I guess. We kept in touch for

a little while after. We'd text or message, but then I couldn't see a point to it and stopped."

"Is that why you're so sad? Because you fell out of touch? That's easy to fix."

"No. Other things have been...hard." His voice trailed off and he looked out the window.

I could take a cue from Matthew on how to be vague. My mind flipped through ideas to get Matthew to open up. Casting my eyes around his car for anything else we could talk about, they fell back on the bracelet he had clutched tightly in his fist.

"I remember the day Gideon got that bracelet for you."

We had spent a day at the reservoir the summer before, the bright sun broiling the gravelly beach until it was coal hot. Despite the temperature, the water was still deliciously cool, and we spent hours lingering along the shore bemoaning the lack of a real beach with sugar-fine sand and an ocean breeze.

"Me, too." Matthew was quiet. Perhaps he was joining me in the warm swathe of that memory.

A girl had walked by our trio, selling handmade friendship bracelets. I rolled my eyes dramatically at Gideon when he asked if we should get a set, but Matthew caught his eye and smiled hopefully. Gideon leapt up and produced a five to purchase a matching pair. At the time, I thought he was doing it to spite me, not realizing that the token had meant something to Matthew.

"Gideon still has his, too," I said, remembering it sitting on his dresser the last time I was at his house. "Just because things end, doesn't mean they weren't important. Both then and now."

A tear escaped down Matthew's cheek. "It's not that. I just... Things have not been the best at home. My dad left me and my mom."

"Oh my... I'm so... That has to be hard." Words were failing me, and I kicked myself for thinking this could be easy. That anything could be so straightforward that I could fix it with a simple conversation. *Stupid, stupid, stupid, Ember.*

"He said he found someone else, someone he couldn't live without. He just up and left us one day like we were nothing."

This was more than petty revenge. It was the act of a broken heart.

The floodgates opened, and Matthew's words tumbled out in a torrent. "A couple weeks ago, I saw you and Gideon walking around. I don't know what you said to him, but he laughed so hard he had to stop and catch his breath."

What did it say about me that I didn't even remember that happening? There were dozens of moments just like that one in recent memory.

"Afterward, I was upset and I wasn't thinking clearly, so I did something—"

He cut himself off abruptly, but I knew how that sentence ended. He was so angry that he put in a hit request on Gideon. Because Gideon's life wasn't crashing down around him and his was.

"Hey." I reached out and grabbed his hands, encircling them as much as I could with the bracelet still tucked between his fingers, like a weird Russian nesting doll. "It's never too late to make things right. It doesn't matter what you've done. Or what you almost had someone else do. You. Can. Fix. It."

As he looked into my eyes, I could see he knew. He knew what I was and how much I understood what he wouldn't say. But suddenly, it didn't matter. Not to me. This was for Gideon, and I would go to any lengths to help him.

"Do you hear me? You can still fix it, but time is running out."

Matthew pulled his hands from mine and blinked rapidly for several seconds. That must be what you had to do when the world tilted on its axis—adjust your eyes to the new view.

"I can?" he whispered in disbelief. I doubted he was conscious of it, but his fingers fidgeted with the bracelet as he spoke, petting it like it was a lucky rabbit's foot. "I've been sick over it for days, trying to find a way to undo what I'd done. I regretted it immediately. I even tried to force the locker open to get my note back."

"You can walk away from this, but you need to do the same thing as before and ask to stop it. Like today."

He nodded. "I will."

I waited with my hand resting on the door until he looked back to me. When he finally did, I let my gaze harden so he would see nothing but determination and know I was not one to mess with. "I'm trusting you. Don't make me regret it or I won't be the only one who does."

The warmth of Matthew's car faded from me quickly when I stepped out into the cold air. Ending our conversation with a threat felt wrong. Kindness wasn't something I could give him, but there was someone else who could. I turned and leaned back in the car. "Talk to him. He's a better person than either of us. If he knew, he'd want to be there for you."

"I know he would, but I don't want his or anyone else's pity."

The way Matthew said *pity* sounded synonymous with *poison*.

"It's not pity." I nodded toward the bracelet. "It's friendship."

CHAPTER 29

THE WALK BACK to Heller was long and cold, but I cocooned myself in the warmth of my triumph. I grabbed my journal from my bag to record my success.

November 16
Even work done in the shadows can be good.

Haley'd said she was doing me a favor by assigning this job to me. Hopefully, she'd never know how right she was. No one else could have protected Gideon. And I'd done it without compromising my position in the Red Court. Well, not entirely compromising it, anyway. Haley would have an aneurysm if she knew how it had gone down. Good thing she never needed to know.

My real phone buzzed in my pocket with a text message.

Unknown number: Do you want to meet up after school?

Unknown number: It's Chase by the way.

Unknown number: You probably figured that out though. You're smart like that.

Chase was cute when he was being self-conscious. I saved his number in my phone and tapped out a reply.

Me: Prove it's really you and not an impostor.

Chase: My Lit midterm score is going to kick your score's ass

He was insufferable.

Me: Fine. It's you.

Chase: ☺

Me: Yeah, let's meet by my locker. 1120.

My off-hour had long since ended, and my parents were likely to get a call about my unexcused absence soon. So much for my perfect attendance record. I texted my dad that I wasn't feeling well and needed to be excused from classes. He was more likely than my mom to buy the lame excuse without further explanation.

With the weight of Gideon's takedown lifted, I remembered the note in my pocket. I pulled the crumpled piece of paper out and examined it more closely. The note was slashed onto the page in hasty, garbled words. What was more alarming was that the pen looked to have punctured the paper in several places. So, the person was writing quickly but with a lot of force. And a lot of anger.

The handwriting wasn't familiar and the paper itself was

from a generic college-ruled notebook. I couldn't detect any traces of perfume or any other identifying marks. My mind strayed to Gretchen, but it didn't fit. She was after the Queen of Hearts, too, but for entirely different reasons. That only left the person who asked the Red Court to break up Chase and his ex-girlfriend and then take me out as well.

If I was looking for an admirer of Chase, the entire school was in the suspect pool. There wasn't anything to be done without more information. I tried to push the worry to the side, but a lingering unease twisted my stomach. There was only one way I could think to draw out whoever this was. I had to keep seeing Chase. Poor me.

Even being excused from the rest of my classes, I fell back into the rhythm of my schedule. When the final bell sounded, I joined the flash flood of students that tumbled into the halls after French class. The hallway with my locker was abandoned by the time I made it across the school to gather my things and head home. Opening the locker with a clang, I wished I could say I was surprised to see a playing card sitting on the shelf, but I wasn't.

The card was a Joker. On the back were only two words in distinctive block lettering:

CALL ME

The threat of the Joker was evident enough. If I didn't call Haley, I would become the next target. So far, I'd managed to hold everything together with dental floss and a prayer, but it seemed like my house of cards might collapse at any moment.

"Hey!"

Chase's voice jolted me out of my stupor. I quickly added the playing card to my pocket along with the other threat I received today. I was on a roll.

"Hi." My voice was a rasp that barely scraped by the lump in my throat.

Chase's brows furrowed in concern. "What's going on?"

I have more enemies than friends right now.

"You take my breath away," I punctuated my joke with an eye roll.

He laughed. Charming Chase led a charmed life. "I was wondering if you wanted to hang out. We could do our homework."

He made "homework" sound like something else. What an intriguing idea. Sadly, I had to plan a way to save my sorry self from the Red Court's wrath before tomorrow. "I can't tonight, but I'm grabbing breakfast tomorrow morning with Gideon if you want to join us. We're meeting up with Damien, the guy from the coffee shop, around ten."

"It's a date. Text me the address." He gave me one of his signature casual grins. "Oh, here are your keys."

He grabbed the keys from his bag and dropped them in my hand. I weighed them in my palm, noticing some extra bulk.

"What's this?"

A tiny ceramic mug key chain was hanging next to my house key. I'd seen them at the coffee shop before. He must have picked it up earlier when I wasn't looking.

"A reminder, from our first official coffee run."

"Thank you."

The hurricane of my thoughts stilled. Nothing was resolved, and this was only a temporary reprieve, but here with Chase everything was quiet. I didn't want to forget his smile and how it hovered between bashful and proud. Or the warm touch of his fingers when he reached out to grasp my free hand for a quick squeeze. Or how I couldn't hear anything above the rush of blood in my ears.

Chase closed the distance between us and tilted my face up with gentle fingers. I drew in a breath as he pressed his lips to mine. Drinking in his spicy scent, I parted my mouth to taste him. His tongue met mine in an excruciatingly slow slide. I lost the ability to think, to breathe, to exist outside of this kiss. Our bodies molded together, heat building between us.

Finally, I broke the kiss and drew in a shuddering breath. I remembered where we were and remembered the threat burning in my pocket. My scalp prickled at the phantom eyes that could be watching right now. Chase took a small step back but kept his arms around me. I couldn't remember when they'd come up to encircle my shoulders.

"I'll see you tomorrow?" he asked.

I don't want to lose you.

The thought startled me. Somewhere along the way, I'd decided that Chase was mine to lose.

I swallowed the lump in my throat and rallied with a smile. "Bright and early."

On my way out to the parking lot, I pulled out my Red Court phone. I couldn't call Haley yet. I needed to think of what to say first.

Me: Can you meet tomorrow?

Haley: noon. theater room.

If I thought about it, my interfering with Matthew's request was the most Red Court thing to do. Pressure to just the right spot would get anyone to bend, and I used Matthew's own guilt against him. Haley should be thrilled that her work as a mentor was really paying off. Now I only had to make her see it that way.

CHAPTER 30

GIDEON'S AND MY favorite breakfast spot was a small café that served the best chocolate croissants in town. It was a mostly carb-based menu, and Gideon had declared that anyone who didn't like it, or so much as uttered a word against the café, could not be our friend. He must have been pretty confident bringing Damien here. It was his litmus test for compatibility.

I arrived first, fifteen minutes before ten o'clock, to claim the best table near the fireplace. A couple was finishing up and I waited like a vulture to swoop in as soon as they showed the first signs of departure. I was still chilled after my early morning run, so I took the chair nearest the fire. The café was a bustle of movement and muttered "excuse me's" since the space was only large enough to hold half a dozen tables. Most customers took their orders to go, but Gideon insisted the croissants tasted better if you ate them right away. He arrived next and spotted me immediately.

"Nice work, Em," he said, complimenting me on my table-snagging.

"Grab two more chairs." I motioned to the tables around us with a spare chair each. I didn't dare leave the table unguarded for a moment.

"So, what's going on with Chase?" Gideon asked once he'd settled.

His hair was tousled again, like he'd given it a stern talking-to and nothing else after rolling out of bed. I'd actually attempted to do something with my hair by twisting the normal ponytail into a low bun that I'm sure screamed "trying too hard."

"He kissed me yesterday," I confessed, unable to hide a wide smile.

Gideon smirked back. "And?"

"And it was pretty spectacular." And it was. Despite the threat to stay away from Chase that had been looming at the edge of my thoughts, the memory of the kiss still brought a delicious warmth to my chest.

He nodded once, giving his approval. Gideon trusted my taste when it came to anything except movies. His seal of approval was dependent upon mine. If I thought Chase was good enough, Gideon would back me.

"I can't believe you're putting Damien up to the croissant test so soon."

He looked away before speaking. "I like him, but there's no use investing in the possibility of more if he doesn't like the croissants."

"You can't continue seeing a monster like that."

He flicked his eyes back to me and grinned. There was something shy about my friend today, like a cautious optimism. I hoped things would work out with Damien. Gideon deserved this happiness.

It occurred to me that had anyone else been assigned his takedown job, we probably wouldn't be sitting here right now. That thought left me feeling oddly grateful. I used my power in the Red Court to do something good. But it wasn't the power that made me feel alive. It was the control, just like I told Haley when I joined. I had a say in how and when things went down. If this was even a fraction of what the QoH felt, perhaps I understood her better than I thought. Maybe the destruction of the Red Court wasn't the answer. Maybe it just needed a better leader.

Before I could follow that thought down the dark path it was leading, Chase and Damien walked in at the same time. They were chatting amiably. Damien laughed, his smile bringing out the tiniest dimple in one cheek. I peeked back at Gideon, who looked like that dimple might kill him.

Damien wore a cream V-neck sweater that looked striking against his dark brown complexion. "Shut your mouth. You're drooling," I whispered at Gideon.

"Chase better like croissants," he muttered back.

I hadn't even thought of that. I bit my lip and made a show of crossing my fingers.

"Hi," Gideon and I both said in unison.

Chase and Damien sat down with us. We were on an official double date.

"It smells amazing in here," Chase murmured when he leaned over to give me a quick kiss.

Were we casually kissing in public now?

"You're in for a treat." I casually shifted back to put a little more distance between us.

A humorous light flickered in his eyes.

Play with me, it seemed to say.

My traitorous body heated, like Chase was the fire keeping me warm all the way down to my toes. His usual spicy scent curled around me and my eyes fluttered shut as I inhaled. Why couldn't he make it easier for me and not smell so good?

I rose from my seat to order our food.

"Pain au chocolat?" I asked. Gideon squinted at me in confusion. "Ugh. It's French for chocolate croissant."

"I take Spanish," he said.

Chase lifted his hand. "German."

"Merci, Ember. Je voudrais un pain au chocolat," Damien said in flawless French.

I smiled at Gideon. "I'm keeping him. You heathens can wait outside."

I spun on my heel to find the end of the line snaking its way through the tables and leading toward the door. It was like waiting in line at a theme park. A guy twice my size stepped back to let another customer pass and knocked into me.

"Ow!" I yelped as his boot came down on my toes.

A warm hand settled on the small of my back and another shot out to stop the guy from encroaching any farther. "I leave you alone for ten seconds and you're nearly run over," Chase said.

My cropped sweater left the smallest patch of skin exposed just above my jeans and I couldn't think past the point where his thumb touched my bare skin. "I believe I left you alone,"

I said with as much dignity as I could muster, wiggling my toes to make sure nothing was broken.

His thumb moved a centimeter in the tiniest caress before he pulled it away. I wanted to reach out and grab it back, then tie his arm around me so we'd never stop touching.

Calm down, creeper.

"Do you have any tips on what I need to say to win Gideon over?" Chase asked as he studied the menu. He squinted just the tiniest bit and pulled out a pair of glasses from his pocket. They were black plastic frames that, when paired with his letter jacket, guaranteed his casting in *Grease* as Popular Hot Guy #1.

"Since when do you wear glasses?" I completely ignored his question. Proof positive that he was less than perfect in some way was the kind of thing I would have noticed.

"Umm. Always? I don't usually wear them at school, but my eyes get tired by the end of the week. Why? Do you like them?"

"I do. They look good on you."

I felt like I'd taken a step closer to him without moving, like some part of me was being drawn out. Chase searched my face and I could see he recognized that something was happening to me. Maybe he knew what it was and could explain it.

"So, no tips for me with Gideon?" he asked again.

I looked back at Gideon, who was chatting with Damien. He looked more relaxed, happy even. Gideon caught my eye and smiled like he could read my mind and totally agreed with my assessment.

I turned back to Chase. "No. You don't need any. Whatever side I'm on, he's there with me."

"Are you on my side?"

"More and more every day."

When our turn came, I ordered four coffees and four pains au chocolat. Chase helped me carry everything back to the table and I passed out plates like a carb fairy. Gideon and Damien watched in horror as Chase dumped an unconscionable amount of cream and sugar into his coffee.

Chase took his first bite of croissant and groaned in pleasure. "This is the best thing I have ever had."

Gideon met my eyes and we waited for Damien to try his. He took a generous bite. "Incroyable!"

I gave Gideon a wink. All clear here.

We ate and talked and laughed. Damien told us stories of his favorite quirky regular and what surprised him most about college. All the while, I kept sneaking glances at Gideon, who looked more enamored by the second. It was perfect. Not even the looming specter of my meeting with Haley could darken the morning.

"What are you up to the rest of the day?" I asked Chase.

"I'm just watching my sisters. My mom's working today."

Ahh, yes. Chase the Manny. I would pay good money to see how much his little sisters had him wrapped around their fingers.

"You?"

"Just some errands," I said.

He shook his head. "Nothing as ordinary as errands for you. You're probably working ahead in all your classes or running a marathon or something."

I shifted uncomfortably. "Or something."

While we'd been eating, an idea was starting to fully take

root. Gretchen's claim that she wanted to be part of something great made more sense now. The Red Court was great— powerful and influential—but if someone else was leading it, could it be good, too?

If I could figure out who the Queen of Hearts was, could I replace her?

CHAPTER 31

HALEY WAS WAITING in the theater room for me, lounging on the slouchy couch as always.

"You're late." She shifted so she was staring up at the yellowing ceiling tiles, obviously not in the mood to reward me with eye contact.

My temper flared, but I kept it in check. Now was not the time.

"I'm sorry." I cast my eyes down. *Good. Now keep laying it on.* "I know what I did wasn't ok."

"Which part?" she asked.

"The part where I went behind your back and took care of Matthew myself."

A deep breath steadied my resolve, and I continued, "But I'm not sorry for making the hit on Gideon go away."

"That's not how it works, Ember. You can't interfere like that."

"Seriously? All we do is interfere. We manufacture feelings, grades, Homecoming crowns."

Haley stalked toward me, a predatory edge to her gait, but I didn't dare budge. This was another hand in our game, and I was bluffing this round.

"What am I supposed to say when the Queen of Hearts asks about Matthew pulling his request? We could need his help in the future. The Red Court isn't powerful because of the twelve of us running jobs. We're powerful because we have eyes, ears, and hands all over the school. Everyone is part of our game whether they know it or not."

"You don't have to say anything. I'll do my own explaining, thanks. Put me in touch with the Queen of Hearts. I can answer for myself." The image of the girl from the carnival came to mind.

Haley collapsed back onto the couch with a great groan. "You know that's not going to happen."

"All I need is her number. I'll text her from my burner and that will be the end of it. Unless you think she'd prefer a handwritten apology. I do have an engraved stationery set that I got for my birthday that I have been dying to use."

"You're so funny," Haley deadpanned. "Just tell me what happened. No more messing around. If you've done any damage, we need to get it under control."

I filled Haley in on Matthew. How I followed him around for days, and that something just wasn't adding up. It didn't make sense that Matthew would want to hurt Gideon, and I needed to figure out why before I could take any steps to undo his request.

"When I saw him at the coffee shop, I didn't think about

the ramifications. I just wanted to talk to him. I wasn't going in there to blow the lid off anything."

Haley cut through my argument and went right for the kill. "But you did. You told him who you are. You did the one thing that could endanger everyone."

I looked away. "I never told Matthew that I was part of the Red Court. Not exactly. If he was questioned, all he could say was that I advised him against making big decisions when he was emotionally distressed."

Haley sat with her arms folded across her chest and her legs crossed. The only way her body language could have been more closed off was if she shut her eyes.

"It's not like we still don't have Matthew." It was time to woo Haley with cold logic. "He made a request, which we will have forever. He still asked us for something, and we could use that if we had to." If they ever called on Matthew, I'd find a way to help him, too.

The whoosh of the HVAC was the only sound for a few long moments. "You're on probation."

"That's it? You don't need to discuss this with anyone else first?" It was too much to hope for that Haley would lead me to the Queen of Hearts herself.

"No one else needs to know. You're right, we have Matthew on the hook if we ever need him. This stays between us."

"Wow, I'm surprised. I thought there'd be some big tribunal with torches and cloaks where you'd get me to confess all my deepest secrets."

"Is there something else you should tell me?" A glimmer of suspicion flashed in Haley's narrowed eyes.

I met it with a sweet, repentant smile cutting across my face. "No, ma'am. Cross my heart."

And hope to die.

"Fine. We have another job to do. It's complicated."

Another job meant the possibility of earning Haley's trust back and perhaps another favor from the Queen of Hearts. I could devise something to get her personally involved this time.

"As long as it's not Gideon, you have my full attention. Let me prove how committed I am."

"This isn't something you'll be doing by yourself. Every step of this, we do together. Clear? Probation means that you don't so much as blink without asking me first."

"Sir, yes, sir." I gave her a mock salute.

She rubbed her temples like she had a headache that pounded in time with the rhythm of my name. Em-ber, Em-ber, Em-ber.

"We have to take out a faculty member—get them fired—which is never very clean."

"Faculty? I've never heard of the Red Court taking on something that big."

"We've never done it in all the years I've been a member. We don't often take requests for hits on faculty or staff. If we catered to the whim of every angry student with a chip on their shoulder, there'd be no one left to teach. But we have to."

"Why?" This seemed like a question someone should have asked by now. Why did we have to do anything we didn't want to? Why not focus on accepting jobs for people who really deserved what they got, like Alec?

"It's a big enough ask that I wanted to know why we're

taking it on, too," Haley said. "One of the Red Court requested this as her favor."

I didn't have a response for that. Haley had told me that no one had ever been denied their one big ask before.

"Here." She handed me the folder and I flipped it open.

My stomach bottomed out. It was Gigi's mom, Mrs. Martin. This couldn't be happening. My fingers seemed to stop working and the folder fell from my loose grip.

Gigi's mom. I was going to get Gigi's mom fired. My brain was overloading.

"Mrs. Martin. This is major, Haley. This is her career, her life."

Haley regarded me coolly. "You didn't seem to have any problem going after Alec and threatening to ruin his relationship with his *fiancée*. How is this any different?" She bent down and compiled all the pages neatly back into the folder.

Because Alec was a jerk and Mrs. Martin wasn't. Who would want to hurt Mrs. Martin, anyway? She was voted "Best Teacher" by last year's seniors and she wasn't even a teacher. I felt ill.

"I know Gigi Martin. She's my...my friend. Alec, Gideon, and now Gigi's mom. Doesn't it seem weird to you that I know all of these people? These feel personal, Haley, like they were created to make me suffer."

"Don't be ridiculous." Haley was looking pointedly at me. "We've all had to do things we didn't like."

"That is not my problem, I promise."

Haley placed the folder back in her bag, pulled a tablet out, and started tapping on the screen, just like this was any other job. "One good thing about this job is that we don't have to do any of the planning. Everything has been laid out for us."

I dropped onto the couch next to Haley and caught my head between my hands.

"We got a tip on the Whisper Wire that Mrs. Martin was having an affair with that physics teacher, Mr. Hall. All we need to do is get proof and send it out."

Gigi's parents were married. Maybe Mrs. Martin wasn't that innocent. I remembered the takedown in the hallway and the broken girl caught up in the mix of her ex-boyfriend's drama. My mind replaced her with Gigi and I cringed.

Haley continued, "Apparently, they have a usual spot at school." Her upper lip curled in disgust. "That's gross. We need to be in place on Monday afternoon for photos."

Two days. That wasn't enough time for me to stop this or dethrone the Queen of Hearts. It had taken me almost a week to untangle Gideon's takedown. How could I even begin to undermine the work with Haley breathing down my neck because of my "probation"?

Haley must have read the emotions broadcasting across my face. I had to think of something or Gigi's life and her mom's career were over.

"I didn't get this close to my favor to back out now. This is the job. This is what we are. I thought you understood that." Haley looked stricken, like the admission was costing her.

So did I.

CHAPTER 32

THE KITCHEN WAS quiet and dark around me as I worked on a history assignment. My paper on the fall of the Berlin Wall was going exactly nowhere. I'd been working on the same paragraph for the last thirty minutes. Out of frustration, I banged out the thought stuck in my head with furious keystrokes.

> Though she began with good intentions, Ember Williams has discovered that the Red Court isn't as black-and-white as she once hoped. It also wasn't all that red, either. They should rename it the Gray Court. In this essay, I will discuss how Ember is living a lie.

I laughed at my own ridiculous words, but reading them made me feel a fraction better. Now it wasn't a secret I carried alone. *Thank you, laptop.*

"Ember?" my dad's voice called out as he crossed through the front door. April was at the retreat with her rehab center and Mom was at an event for work, so it would be the two of us for the night.

"In here." I deleted the paragraph, sad to see it disappear.

"Still feeling better?" He set his briefcase and coat down and examined me from across the counter.

"I'm ok. I think I just need to lie low this weekend."

"Are you sure?"

His concerned eyes scanned me from head to toe, looking for anything visible to refute my claim. Anytime I brought something negative to my dad's attention, he would drop whatever he was doing to try to fix it.

"Really, Dad. I'm fine. I think it's just that time of the year when things start stacking up. I made some pasta if you're hungry."

He looked relieved, if a bit disappointed, and ruffled my hair.

"You're a trouper. I don't know where we'd be without you."

His words poked a tender spot in my heart. "Thanks, but you're the one we can't live without. You're our main man."

He stepped toward me and wrapped me up in a life-affirming hug. "But without you there'd be no point to living." Dad let go and ambled over to the stove to scoop out some ravioli I'd made from the pot.

The empty screen I couldn't fill was freaking me out. I shut my laptop with a snap. Despite my best efforts to wall off thoughts of taking over the Red Court, my mind was fixated on what it would mean for April. Could I bring her over to my way of seeing things? That it wasn't the Red Court that was bad, but the girls who ran it? I could keep innocent kids from getting hurt. Wouldn't that be better?

And then there was Gigi. The ante kept going up, and I was running low on chips. Every move came with a cost I didn't think I could pay. I didn't think there was a way for me to save Mrs. Martin. I was already on probation for my interference with Gideon's takedown. I couldn't risk my position any further. If I had any hope of reaching my goal, whatever that goal turned out to be, I couldn't draw more attention to myself. The first page of my journal flashed in my mind. What I'd committed to doing didn't feel like the right choice anymore.

I cared about Gigi, had let myself get invested in her future. She was great, but what really got me was how much more she could be. What would a public firing of her mom by her own high school's administration do to her? To her family? The most I could do was delay until I could find a real solution. I'd bought myself a little time with Gideon's takedown, but going MIA again wasn't going to fly. I'd figure it out, wouldn't I?

A text message chimed on my regular phone as I was brushing my teeth that night.

Chase: I had fun earlier

My breath caught at the sight of his name on my phone. How could he affect my pulse when he wasn't even near me?

Me: I did too. How was watching your sisters?

Chase: Still going. My mom's shift doesn't end for another hour and I am out of ideas to keep them entertained.

What did little girls like to do? An idea popped into my head. Happy for the distraction, I texted him back.

Me: How about a makeover?

Chase: I'm not good at that stuff. I tried to braid their hair once and it ended in tears.

Chase: Mostly mine.

Chase: ☹

Me: No, they get to give you a makeover.

Me: It will be so relaxing. Like a day at the spa.

Fifteen minutes passed with no response. Chase must have not liked my idea. I was just crawling under my comforter when another text chimed.

Chase: this is all your fault

Attached was a picture of him with what legitimately looked like clown makeup on. His sisters had been heavy-handed with the purple eye shadow and red lipstick. It was the best worst thing I'd seen probably ever. I saved the image to cherish forever. I was going to frame it for posterity. The world needed to revel in the glory of this photo.

Me: This is my phone's wallpaper now.

Chase: NO

Me: Too late.

I took a screenshot of my phone's lock screen and sent it over.

Me: Best. Ever.

Chase: OH GOD NO

Me: See you Monday

Chase: I have a family thing, but I'll be back Tuesday

Chase: I'll miss seeing you scowl at me in lit

Me: I'll miss scowling at you

I lay back on my bed, heart fluttering at the rush that came from flirting with Chase. Anything that felt this good had to be bad for my health.

A text from my other phone was enough to bring me crashing down to reality.

Haley: meet me by mr halls mobile after school Monday

That could only mean that we'd be catching Mrs. Martin in the act. A sick swirl of my stomach had me swallowing hard. I was out of time.

CHAPTER 33

THE NOVEMBER WIND gave no quarter as it whipped through my hair. Fall in Colorado insisted on reminding us of its presence. I pulled the hood of my jacket up and tucked my ponytail away, shivering in the long shadow of Heller. The mobiles were located on the east side of the school and the shorter autumn days left it shaded for most of the afternoon. I'd positioned myself in an alcove that had a direct line of sight to Mr. Hall's mobile. Haley was nowhere to be seen.

"Goddammit, Haley," I muttered.

"So dramatic."

I turned to find Haley leaning against the brick wall in the alcove behind me, a dark smudge in the shadows wearing all black as usual. Like me, the hood of her jacket was tugged up in an attempt to contain her mass of curls.

"Have you just been standing there watching me freeze my butt off?"

"Relax. I just got here."

She came up next to me to peer in the direction of Mr. Hall's mobile. "Anything yet?"

"No. What did the notes say about the timing of the… tryst?"

She pulled a face. Whether she was repulsed by the idea of Mrs. Martin and Mr. Hall together or the very precise way I described it, I didn't know. "Just that it would be Monday afternoon between three o'clock and three thirty."

I checked the time on my phone. It was just after three o'clock now.

"Do you have any ideas on how you want to do this?" I asked.

"Pictures of Martin going in and doing something incriminating."

Whatever that meant, it wasn't good.

Since Haley's text Saturday night, I'd devoted every waking moment to thinking of ways to get out of this. The best I could come up with was inventing an emergency for Gigi that required her mom to help. If Mrs. Martin was called away, I could buy her another week. A week was an eternity. I could do anything in a week.

I'd waited outside the only class I knew Gigi was in, but she was off-site with the majority of the other freshmen for a civics project. Without Gigi physically nearby, I couldn't craft an emergency that wouldn't trace back to me. Untraceable was the number one requirement. I'd been sloppy with Matthew and I wouldn't make the same mistake twice.

Gathering my resolve, I made one last plea to Haley. "Do we have to do this? It doesn't feel right."

For a moment I thought Haley might agree with me. There was real conflict evident on her features. This was too far, even for us.

"It doesn't matter what we think. We do our job." She paused. "It's just a job, Ember."

"Not to me, it isn't." The unsteadiness in my voice betrayed how much this meant to me. "This is bigger than us. It's her life."

"And is she innocent?" Haley moved to press against the edge of the alcove, positioning herself for a clear view of the mobiles.

"What?"

She turned slightly so her face was in profile, harsh and unforgiving. Pity wasn't Haley's strong suit. "How is what we're doing right now any different than someone else finding out and telling another person who tells another person and so on? We didn't force her to have an affair. She did that all by herself."

She had a point. She always had a point. Anyone could bust them, but there was a difference between someone else stumbling upon something like this and us lying in wait for it to happen. Maybe Mrs. Martin would do herself a massive favor and stay away.

Twenty minutes later, she came out of the school, walking briskly toward the mobiles.

Haley drew her phone out of her pocket like an assassin readying her weapon. Character assassinations required different tools.

"Haley, I'm asking you not to do this."

"I know this is hard, but you'll understand someday.

Everyone has secrets. Just hope you're lucky enough to keep yours hidden."

If only you knew the secrets I kept.

The door to Mr. Hall's mobile opened and he ushered Mrs. Martin in. I held my breath waiting for the door to shut, willing it to slam behind her without revealing anything to us.

As the door was closing, out of view of everyone but us, Mrs. Martin wrapped her arms around Mr. Hall and kissed him. The click of the camera on Haley's phone echoed in my ears like a shot.

My shoulders slumped. It was done. I wanted to kick down the door to Mr. Hall's classroom and rage at them both. They were the reason I had to be a party to this disaster, the reason that someone I cared about was going to be devastated. How could Mrs. Martin do this to Gigi?

I wouldn't pretend to know why either of them had decided that an illicit affair between colleagues on school property was a good idea. People made stupid decisions all the time, but they had made this easy and had left themselves so exposed. They couldn't sneak around off school property where no one would have ever seen them?

Haley was tapping on her phone, doubtless sending our proof off to wherever it needed to go. I reached out and grasped her wrist. She froze and stared at the point of contact and then looked up at me with her brows raised. I'd crossed a line in touching her.

"Sorry," I said and let go.

She continued to stare. "Don't give me your puppy eyes. We've been over this. I'm only glad I didn't try to have you take care of this on your own. You're clearly not ready for this level of shit."

Ouch.

"No, it's not that. I told you that I know Gigi, Mrs. Martin's daughter. She's on the debate team with me and beyond talented and driven. It wouldn't surprise me if she went on to be the freaking president of the United States."

How could Haley not see how this was going to wreck Gigi? She was fourteen years old. A major disaster at home could change everything for her, the whole course of her future. My stomach was turning over at the implications. How would the echoes of what was about to happen haunt her?

"Then she'll get over this." Haley was steady and calm, and it made my emotions feel hysterical. I hated feeling hysterical.

"The school isn't so big that I haven't had to pull jobs on people I know, too. The first one is hard—seeing people you know from your regular life suffering isn't pleasant. But neither is life. No one I've seen has ever been too far gone to recover."

If I was in control of the Red Court, this wouldn't be happening. I could protect the people I cared about. But I wasn't. Not yet, anyway. The whole school was about to find out about Mrs. Martin's affair, but maybe I could find a way to soften the blow for Gigi. There had to be something I could do to help at least in a small way.

I cleared my throat, trying to conquer the frustration and sadness warring within me. "I know there's no stopping this train. But could you give me tonight to think of something to say to Gigi that might help her? Just tonight. Then tomorrow, after school starts, you can do what you have to. Please."

Haley regarded me, tilting her head and narrowing her eyes like she was trying to find the loophole that must be hiding somewhere. I'd all but destroyed her trust in me with my stunt with Matthew.

"No tricks up my sleeves." I held my hands up and gave her a tight smile. "I'm asking you for *a favor.*"

Favor was not a word you used lightly in the Red Court. Favors were debts to be paid, but I would do it for this.

Haley nodded. "You have until first period."

When I got to my car, another sheet of white notebook paper was tucked under the windshield wiper. My admirer must have stopped by.

LAST WARNING. STAY AWAY FROM CHASE.
IT WOULD BE A SHAME IF YOU FELL FROM THE
CATWALKS...

Oh, God.

CHAPTER 34

A SHIVER SNAKED its way up my spine, cold and creeping. I'd grown too accustomed to being the one wielding threats, and I couldn't seem to draw enough breath. My lungs were screaming for air like I'd just sprinted for ten minutes straight. Paranoia pulsed through me, whispering with its insidious voice that I was being watched. Whoever had left this note probably wanted to see my reaction, my fear. I spun in a circle looking in cars and through the windows of Heller.

Empty, empty, empty.

There was no one else nearby, and the emptiness seemed ominous, like it was waiting for something. Or someone.

I ducked into my car and fumbled with the radio, needing the reassurance that everything was normal—even if it was only an illusion to make myself feel better. With music blasting through the speakers, I was able to catch my breath.

In.

Someone knows that April's accident wasn't an accident.

Out.

Or at least suspects that it wasn't an accident.

In.

Worst case, they know that I know the Red Court was behind it.

Out.

Worse worst case, it's someone in the Red Court and they know what I'm doing.

Fear seized my heart, wringing it dry of every ounce of determination I possessed. I needed to collect myself away from Heller's watchful gaze. I pulled out of the parking lot and headed home.

My house was dark when I arrived, quiet in a familiar, peaceful way. As I put the car in Park, my regular phone chimed with a text message from Gideon. Then another. And another.

I unlocked my phone and could barely read his messages before more streamed in.

Gideon: Mrs. Martin and Mr. Hall?!?

Gideon: WTF is happening???

Gideon: At the school

Gideon: Grosssssssss

Gideon: I sit in that classroom every day

Gideon: I don't even know what to think

And then a break in the barrage of texts before one final message came through.

Gideon: Wait. Isn't that Gigi's mom? Was it you?

I checked my email and found a message from "A Friend" that must have gone to the entire school. The subject was blank and the only thing in the body of the email was the photo Haley just took.

"Dammit, Haley!" I threw my phone down in disgust.

There was no way to explain over text to Gideon that this was and wasn't me. I'd have to call him later.

My Red Court phone vibrated in my bag with a message. Only one person would be texting me and her excuses didn't deserve my attention. She promised me she'd wait until tomorrow. After the latest threat, my body was on high alert and the flash of anger only added fuel to fire that began as fear but had morphed into something uglier. I grabbed the phone to let her have it.

Haley: i'm sorry

Haley had never apologized for anything before. I didn't think she had the word in her vocabulary. A simple apology could right a number of wrongs, but not this. I'd never forgive her.

Haley: it wasn't me

Haley: i sent the pic as proof that the job was done but said the email to the school would go tomorrow

Me: Who sent it out then?

Haley: you know who

The Queen of Hearts.

Me: Why couldn't it wait?

Haley: it's not like i get explanations for everything

Haley: i wouldn't have made that promise unless i thought i could keep it

Haley: i'm sorry about your friend

Me: Don't pretend that you care about her or me. Leave me alone.

I turned the phone off and threw it on the floor to join the other one.

I looked up at the rearview mirror, catching a glimpse of my eyes. The furious, burning glint was startling. They were the eyes of the Red Court girl. She'd come out without me even noticing. I grabbed my journal, feeling reckless. There was one way to make sure the fear and anger left for good.

November 19
I've had enough of being a pawn. I'm ready to be the Queen.

CHAPTER 35

THE NEXT MORNING was cold and gray, just like my mood. I'd spent the night stewing, wavering between fury and fear. The Red Court had eyes, but I needed to be more careful than ever. My plan to draw out my admirer was working, but I couldn't risk everything I'd worked for over it. I had to find out who was writing those notes. If they knew that April's accident wasn't accidental, perhaps they knew something about the Red Court or the Queen of Hearts.

The only small mercy from yesterday was that April was still at her retreat. So much had happened in the last few days, and I didn't have it in me to gracefully dodge any questions. She was due back this evening, so I had better find a way forward.

I was the first car in the student parking lot, hoping to catch Gigi, if she was coming today at all. Other kids steadily poured into the school, jostling one another and laughing. Good-natured insults were volleyed and returned, gossip was passed in whispers, and I sat apart from all of it. I had never felt less like one of them. I finally understood why Haley had separated herself from everyone else. It was self-preservation. If you didn't care about anyone, it didn't matter if they were collateral damage in the Red Court's schemes.

When the first bell rang, I finally gave up and made my way inside.

"Ember."

I jumped at the sound of my name and spun around.

"Hi." Gideon was stationed next to the main doors. "What are you doing lurking over there?"

"I could ask you the same thing. Why were you sitting in your car by yourself?" The hunched set of his shoulders and fierce expression did not bode well for me.

I kept my voice light and said, "I was just waiting for someone."

"Was that person your friend Gigi? You probably had to make sure your hard work hit the mark."

I never responded to Gideon's messages and I couldn't steady myself enough to call, either. He must have read my silence for what it was: guilt.

"Don't say it like that. I tried to stop it. I asked them—"

"You asked? Is that what you do in the Red Court? Politely request that lives not be destroyed?"

This wasn't fair. He didn't even know Gigi that well. Not like I did.

"No, we don't ask anything. I was risking a lot trying to stop the pictures from leaking. It's suspicious that I even asked.

No one else does that. If they knew what I really wanted, I'd be in serious trouble. I'm trying to help."

"And what about Matthew? Did you help him?"

He knows about Matthew. That's why he's angry.

"He just told me about your little 'chat,' and I thought he must have been mistaken. I thought, 'No, Ember wouldn't threaten him.'"

"I didn't threaten him! Not really. You don't understand. It's complicated."

Now was not the time to explain to Gideon that I saved his ass from social ruin. That if it wasn't for me, he would be the one with grainy photos pasted all over the hallways or emailed to the entire school. The mercury of my temper was rising fast. If I didn't defuse the situation, things were going to escalate quickly.

"Then explain it to me." His words were angry but pleading, too. He wanted me to give him a tidy explanation. I was fresh out.

"I was stopping him from making a mistake. He almost did something that couldn't be taken back. And when I talked to him about what he'd done, he realized he could undo it. Did he tell you that, too?"

Perhaps my approach with Matthew hadn't used a surgeon's precision, but blunt-force honesty was my only option at the time. I hadn't been as careful as I'd meant to be, and I didn't bother to talk to Matthew about the source of his anger or the result of it. I was focused on protecting Gideon, not helping Matthew. That was my real mistake.

"He mentioned something like that but seemed more terrified of you and what you would do to him if he didn't do what you asked. What did you ask him to do?"

The accusation in Gideon's eyes eviscerated the last of my control. "Save you!"

Gideon stumbled back. "Me?"

"Yes, you. I followed him around for days last week, trying to find a way to get him to cancel the request he made to have us take you down."

I could practically see each piece of the puzzle snapping together in his mind.

"He asked you to hurt me?"

I nodded, meeting his eye so he could see every wretched, wretched thing I felt in that moment, how he'd turned my pride for helping him into shame at hurting Matthew. The inadequacy of everything I did to try to protect the people I cared about was overwhelming.

"Why didn't you say anything? And don't say you were going to tell me."

Gideon's voice dropped to a quiet murmur. That meant he didn't trust himself to speak with any control. This was going in the wrong direction. There had to be a way to salvage this.

"I *was* going to tell you. I wanted to have the problem solved before I said anything."

"And this was your way of solving it? Bullying someone who has enough to deal with?"

I flinched at his words. "You know why I'm doing this—"

"Do I? Because I think it's more than that. This isn't even about stopping the Red Court. This is about you wanting to pull the strings."

"No. Yes. I did like some of what I did—"

"Like breaking up Chase and his girlfriend?" Gideon may not have realized it, but he was dragging out the very parts of me I wanted to hide—just like the Red Court did.

I dropped my bag to the floor and spread my hands in mock surrender.

"Yes, I did. I liked it. Is that what you want to hear? I joined to take the Red Court down and discovered something ugly about myself. I liked the work I did. It was easy to manipulate others." I thought of Alec. "Sometimes it was fun for me."

The confession seared my throat as the words left my mouth, as if I'd set the worst of myself loose.

"But this thing with Matthew was different. I wanted to find a way to force his hand. And I was willing to use any means possible. But when I spoke with him, I found out that he wanted to take his request back. At the time, it was the best thing to do—tell him it wasn't too late to stop this. All he had to do was ask, and then it would go away."

Gideon considered me with a critical eye. "What if you couldn't find a way to make Matthew stop it?"

I shook my head. "If he wouldn't do it, I would have figured it out myself."

"And blown apart your grand plan?"

"Yes, unequivocally, yes. I would have done it for you."

For some reason, this did not seem to make him happy. If anything, he seemed more disappointed.

"I think I would have rather had you next to me when whatever they planned went down than on the other side trying to stop it."

I let out a frustrated cry. "That's not fair. I can't control everything. I made the best of the hand they dealt me, but it doesn't have to be this way." I paused. Maybe it was time to tell Gideon everything. "I can take over the Red Court and make it better. We won't hurt innocent people."

He gaped at me, not having anything to say for once.

I pushed on. "What if the Red Court could only do jobs for good reasons? It wouldn't be so bad."

"And who makes the call as to what a good reason is to crush someone?" He'd regained his footing and was meeting my determination measure for measure. "You? It seems like you're having a tough time finding the right side of things. For God's sake, Em, you went after Matthew and then Gigi. You're messing with the lives of actual people, people you know and claim to care about."

Gideon reached down into my bag and pulled out my journal. I fought the instinct that screamed at me to snatch it back. I didn't think I could handle having any more of myself exposed.

He opened it to the first page, the one where my four-step plan was written out in my neatest handwriting, and held it out to face me. "Have you forgotten why you began in the first place? I was worried when you started that this revenge plot would consume you. I never thought that it would go this way."

"You're thinking about it all wrong. You could help me."

Why couldn't Gideon see that things would be different, better?

"Leave me out of it. As long as you're part of the Red Court, you don't know me."

My eyes nearly bugged out of my head. "You can't mean that. We're in this together."

His sorrow cascaded off him in waves that slammed against me, an unending barrage on my heart.

He handed my journal back to me, the words on the page mocking me, reminding me of just how far I had fallen. He turned to go and said over his shoulder, "Not anymore. You're on your own."

CHAPTER **36**

WHEN THE BELL rang at the end of Lit class, I automatically stood to meet Gideon. His parting words came barreling at me like a punch to the gut and I sat back down. There was no one waiting for me.

Chase came over from the other side of the room, ready with a smile. "Hey."

That smile disarmed me completely. "Hi."

My capacity to feel so many conflicting emotions at once was maddening. How could I be angry at the Red Court for Gigi, heartbroken over Gideon, and ridiculous about Chase all at once? I struggled to gain control over myself, but my body was fighting against me, flashing hot and cold.

"Are you headed to meet Gideon? Maybe we could all grab coffee."

"No, not today." I busied myself with my bag to hide how upset I was.

Honestly, I had no clue what Gideon would be doing. Maybe he was running to Damien to tell him all about our argument. I didn't even know if it qualified as an argument. It felt more like the breakup he'd joked about so long ago.

"Ok, do you want to come hang out on the double *H*'s with me? I normally have some friends over there."

There was a lounge at one end of the school with benches shaped like two capital *H*'s for Heller High. It was notoriously frequented by the upper echelon of popular kids, not a place I ever dreamed I'd be invited to. Or one I really desired to go to, either.

"Maybe the library?" I suggested. "I have a ton of work to do."

He smiled even wider. "Of course you do. No rest for the wicked, right?"

If you only knew.

As I made my way to the track after school, I finally found Gigi leaving the main office. I pushed my way past a group of boys, murmuring apologies as I went.

"Gigi!" I called.

She turned, and her mouth lifted in a thin copy of her normal smile. "Hi."

I was not what people would call a "hugger," but Gigi's swollen eyes broke something in me and I pulled her into a hug. "I'm so, so sorry."

"It's ok." She pulled back, looking down as she blinked away tears. "Well, no, it's not. I don't know why I said that."

"Because you're tough and being ok is probably a reflex."

I put force into the words, trying to get Gigi to believe them. She would get through this. She had to.

"I'm just glad the school is letting me take some time away until everything calms down. Not that I'm allowed to take time off classes. I'll just be completing assignments from home for a little while."

"How generous of our Hell High overlords."

Gigi snorted and wiped away a tear. She looked back up at me, resolve flashing in her eyes. "I wasn't surprised, you know? I feel like I should tell someone that. About my mom, I mean. I wasn't surprised."

"What?"

Granted, I wasn't her child, but the revelation that Mrs. Martin was having an affair shocked the hell out of me.

"Things between my parents aren't that great. Really haven't been for a while. I've kind of gotten used to it, I guess. That's why I was so happy to be on the debate team." Her burst of emotion faded and she was left hollow-eyed, devoid of the spark that made her Gigi.

I understood what she meant. I hadn't been able to help April, and I had felt helpless until I harnessed my anger and shaped it into a plan for revenge. "Having something to focus on can help. What will you do now if you're taking some time off?"

Gigi shrugged. "My aunt and uncle live close by. I'll probably stay with them and lie low."

"And your mom?" I couldn't help but ask. Did the Red Court succeed in getting her fired? If not, would Haley and I have to do something worse?

"She's resigning right now. I'm going to wait in the car until she's done packing up. Some friend, huh?"

I blanched. Was she talking about me? "Excuse me?"

"*A Friend.* That's who sent the email out."

I weighed my question, examining it from all sides, before asking, "Do you know who did it?"

"It could have been anyone. There are a lot of kids who would like to stick it to a teacher or counselor. But who did it doesn't matter. Not to me."

"How could it not? Aren't you angry with the people— or person—who did this?"

I was part of the group that did it and I was livid.

"I'm mad at my mom. I'm so mad." Her voice broke, and she swallowed hard. "I don't think I can be anything else on top of that."

My heart shattered watching Gigi shake with the force of her anger. The Red Court destroyed Mrs. Martin's career, her family, and Gigi's relationship with her mom.

Gigi shifted her bag on her back, pulling herself together. "I better get going. Bye, Ember."

I lifted a hand in a weak wave. "Bye."

I didn't move as Gigi, head down and dark hair shielding her face, marched out to the parking lot. Haley had questioned if Mrs. Martin was innocent and she wasn't. But Gigi was. So was Alec's fiancée and that girl from the hallway whose boyfriend was cheating on her. It didn't matter if we only took down people who deserved it. Everyone had someone who loved them who would suffer because of the pain the Red Court caused.

It was—*we* were—toxic. I could almost hear Haley's argument. The Red Court was only an instrument in the orchestra of lies and misery. The kids were the ones conducting the symphony, but how many of them lashed out in a moment of despair and used the tools we provided to turn their pain into action? Probably a lot of them. Just like Matthew.

It was true that some of our requests, like Reece's for Maura, were born out of something other than anger. But they shared a commonality with the calls for hits or grade fixing—desperation. Everyone was desperate for something, and we were the ones enabling them, feeding that need.

When you gave people a shortcut, they'd take it. I was that shortcut. And everyone else in the Red Court was using it for their own ends—whether it was the favor Haley needed or the chance to be part of something that Gretchen was desperate for. Until this moment, I hadn't thought of the work that way. The kids at school were using and being used in a vicious cycle that would only stop if I stopped it.

I didn't have all the answers, but stopping the Red Court was about more than just my sister or anyone else they'd ever broken in one way or another. It was about stopping the cycle of hurt. It was about crushing the wheel to keep it from turning another person into Matthew—a mess of anguish.

I was so stupid for thinking I could be the Queen of Hearts and make the Red Court into something better. The ends didn't justify the means when it meant hurting people. It was time for it all to stop.

CHAPTER 37

THE TRACK BENEATH my shoes was cold and damp, giving it about as much spring as a concrete block. On any other day, this might have bothered me. But right now, I could have been running on lava rocks and it wouldn't have mattered.

Chase was supposed to join me after he met with his lab partner to go over their last assignment. There was so much to mentally unpack; I needed space to sort through my thoughts in private. As my legs found their rhythm, I let my mind wander through the day's hellscape.

Flashes of Gideon dominated my vision, and I pushed my pace. Thoughts of Chase's smile came next, and guilt followed knowing I wasn't who he thought I was. I pushed harder. The hunch of Gigi's shoulders came at me next, and shame chased me like my own personal demon.

Though I was all-out sprinting at an unsustainable pace, my

breath coming in ragged gasps, I didn't stop. I kept pushing for more, digging down deeper for the drive to go harder. I was determined to push through it all until there was nothing left to purge.

My stomach gave out before my legs and I dropped to my knees, vomiting what was left of my lunch into the grass next to the track. Shaking, I stood and stumbled to my water bottle on the bleachers. The freezing aluminum greeted me with a clang when I collapsed onto the metal bench.

A few tentative sips of water left me cringing as the cold liquid hit my stomach. Out of habit, I reached for my journal in my bag, wanting to get my feelings off my chest and onto a page, but threw it back down. There wasn't anything to say. My breathing was nearly back to normal when I saw Chase's familiar silhouette making its way down the hill from the parking lot to the track.

"Hi," he said when he got close enough to speak instead of shout.

"Hey."

His easy smile made my own flimsy one feel false. Chase set his water and keys next to me and shook out his arms, then lifted them overhead, revealing a sliver of his sculpted stomach.

"Looks like you've been at it pretty hard." His eyes skimmed my flushed cheeks and the sweat clinging to my hairline.

"I have a lot on my mind and running helps me think."

"Now I know your secret to being the best. Better watch out."

Chase's laid-back manner coupled with the word *secret* cut through my haze to the parts of myself I was trying to hide.

"Good luck. No one else seems to be able to keep up."

Confusion crossed Chase's face. "Did I say something wrong? I didn't mean anything by it. I admire your work ethic." He'd elevated me onto some pedestal I was bound to topple from. "I've never met anyone as focused as you are. I know I could learn a thing or two."

I scrubbed my hands over my eyes. "I'm sorry. I'm terrible company right now."

He continued loosening his muscles. "Well, let's get to work and fix that. I'm here to learn from the master. Show me what you got."

It was impossible for me not to smile. Chase was like a walking ray of sunshine to my permanently cloudy day.

"Actually, would it be ok if you led the way today?"

Chase's surprised expression highlighted a thin scar running through his right eyebrow. It was a small imperfection of his otherwise flawless features. My hand itched to reach out and smooth my fingertips across the raised skin.

"We can do that. Why don't you take a lap with me to warm up and then we might do some sprints I've been working on."

I pushed myself up from the bench, my wobbly muscles feeling like Jell-O left to warm in the sun too long. Chase set an easy pace as we made our way around the track in companionable silence. If only everything were as easy as jogging next to the boy who made my heart stutter.

"Hey, aren't you friends with Gigi Martin? Have you talked to her?"

"I saw her after school. She's not coming back until things cool down."

"God, I can't imagine what that's like. If you talk to her again, and there's anything I could do to help, let me know. I feel so bad for her."

"Yeah, I will."

Chase didn't know Gigi at all. But he was the sort of person who could feel empathy for someone he didn't know. He was the kind of person to help a girl he previously hated when she was having a fake crisis in front of him. How could he have more room to care for anyone else? Caring for another person seemed to take up physical space inside me; there was only so much I could take on, only so many people I could truly care about.

"I overheard some people saying that it was the Red Court that did it."

This conversation could not be headed in a more dangerous direction. The truth of who I was pressed down on me, fracturing my foundation.

"Could you imagine what kind of messed-up monster you'd have to be to destroy people like that? To enjoy it?"

My arms and legs felt leaden with the weight of my secret. Living so much of my life in secret was exhausting. I wanted nothing more than to be transparent with Chase. He deserved that, and I didn't want to lie anymore. Not after what happened with Gideon and Gigi.

I looked at him, committing his face, and the way he looked at me, to memory. "I'm part of the Red Court."

"You're what?" Chase's expression hadn't changed at all, like he was positive he'd misheard me.

The only thing worse than admitting something terrible about yourself was having to repeat it. I stopped, pooling my courage for a second shot at the truth. "I am part of the Red Court. I have been since the moment we ran into each other in the hall and I told you about my sister."

"That's not possible. How could *you* be one of *them*?" Incredulity was working its way into his words.

"Because I chose to join." The simplicity of the explanation belied the twisted reason behind it, but it was the easiest truth. No one forced me to do any of this. I chose it and continued to choose it.

I could almost see his faith in me slowly unraveling; I expected to find the remains of it—the tattered scraps of what Chase felt for me—spooled around my running shoes.

"But you're not like *them*."

There was something there. Something in the way he said it knocked an idea loose in my head, an idea that had been lingering in the back of my mind since we saw the hallway takedown. Chase seemed so certain in his assessment of the Red Court and the girls who ran it. Almost like he knew us, was involved with us.

"What favor did you ask for?" I was taking a shot in the dark. When Chase winced, I knew my words hit their mark.

"Wouldn't you know?" He refused to meet my gaze, fidgeting with the cuff of his hoodie.

His quiet words and the accusation they held tore a hole in the life raft I was desperately clinging to; without it, without him, I wasn't sure if I could stay afloat. I was no longer me, the girl he kissed in the hallway and texted with at night. I was the monster.

"Actually, I wouldn't. I'm a nobody underling."

"Does that make you any less guilty?"

Shame washed over me, leaving me vulnerable. I pushed back at it the only way I knew how. "You made a choice, too. No one forced you to ask for anything."

I took a step away from Chase and was overcome with the horrible feeling that I would never be that close to him again.

"And I've never stopped paying for it. You don't know what it's like to live every day wondering if today is the day when they ask too much, want something I can't give."

I did know that feeling; I'd already faced that fear and come out the other side without my best friend. "What did you ask for?" I repeated my question without avarice or assumptions.

"At the end of last year, I was struggling in Honors Biology. I took on too much, too many advanced-level classes. There just wasn't enough time to maintain my GPA and my sanity with how much I have to help out at home. My grades are everything to me. A scholarship is the only way I'm going to college." His shoulders, normally strong and steady, were hunched and his head hung low in defeat. I wasn't alone in my shame, but if I was misery, I wasn't in the mood for company.

"So, you asked for help and got it."

"No, not really."

That couldn't be true. The Red Court always finished its jobs. "What do you mean?"

"Turns out I didn't need the help. I studied my ass off and did all the extra credit I could. Just before summer, I got some anonymous note that said they looked into it for me and confirmed my A, but because they had to check at all, I still owed them. Owed you."

"Not me. I wasn't even involved until last month."

A small amount of softness returned to his gaze. Maybe

knowing I wasn't a part of one of his darkest moments bettered me in his estimation. It shouldn't.

"I don't get it, Ember. You already have the grades, and a place on the track and debate teams. Why would you even need to be a part of something like this? Do you get your kicks from controlling other people's lives?"

I wanted to tell him about April. And how I thought I could make the Red Court better. But I realized that there was nothing that could justify the pain it inflicted. But he owed the Red Court and would do what he had to. If it ever came down to it, would he use me as a bargaining chip the day they asked too much of him? I couldn't be sure.

"I can't—" My voice came out in a choked whisper. I was about to tell him that I couldn't trust him, but the words wouldn't come out. I wanted to trust him, craved his trust in return even if I didn't deserve it.

It didn't matter that I couldn't say it. His hurt expression told me he understood. "What? You don't trust me? I guess I don't blame you. You're part of some screwed-up group that likes to mess with people. You probably can't trust anyone. Not even yourself."

My story, the real story of my life, was burning in my throat. I ached to let it out. It wouldn't budge, wouldn't let me say the words that might win Chase back to my side.

The time had come to do the thing I should have done weeks ago. I had to push him away for good. "That day in the hall, when you helped me, I was only there because the Red Court told me to be." My words hit Chase like bullets, each killing a part of him that cared for me. "My job was to be helpless so you'd get close to me and I could get a picture of us together. They sent it to your girlfriend. She was jealous, but she had every reason to be."

"Why would you do that?" He stared at me in disbelief, but I had to drive my point home.

"Because someone else was willing to pay us for it. It's how this whole thing works. We give you whatever it is you want most and then use that against you when we come to collect again and again."

"Who asked you to break up me and Madison?"

I threw my hands up in the air, unwilling to tell him I didn't know. It was ridiculous that I could be on the inside of the Red Court and barely know more than one of my marks.

"That's the worst part in all of this. I don't get to know why I'm doing something or who is handing out orders."

"Then why do you do it?"

The impulse to spill my guts to Chase hit me again, harder than expected, but I held off. Behind his warmth and goodness was a person who wanted something bad enough to pay an unknown price for it. Behind his soft brown eyes was a liability I couldn't afford. Not now that I'd given up so much.

He read the lack of a response in my reaction. "Fine, don't tell me." For an aching moment, it seemed like those would be the last words he would ever say to me. Then he said, "I'll tell you why I did it. I was scared of what would happen if I didn't have my GPA. When it looked like I might lose that, I panicked."

My sensitive stomach gave an angry twist at the tears pooling in the corners of his eyes. How the Red Court affected Chase wouldn't be erased the moment he received his diploma. He'd carry the weight of his mistake long after high school ended.

I reached for words, and found the truth waiting for me. "I wish things could be different. For both of us. But it would be better for everyone if we weren't friends anymore." At least my admirer would get their way. I would be staying away from Chase just like they wanted.

"Friends?" Chase scoffed. "How could we be friends when you were lying to me the whole time? This—" he pointed between us "—was never anything, because it all came out of your part in your club. I really can't believe you, Ember. I thought you were better than that."

I cleared my throat against the emotional asphyxiation strangling my vocal cords. "You're right. I guess there's nothing left to say."

Chase leveled a blank glare at me, not a trace of his usual warmth or even the anger of the last few minutes. It seemed he was already past grieving the loss of whatever we were to each other.

"I guess so. See you around, Ember."

CHAPTER 38

IT WAS SEVERAL minutes after Chase disappeared over the top of the hill leading back to the school's main building that I noticed the snow falling lightly around me. The first snow of the season was always my favorite. The cold without snow seemed pointless, but the gathering flakes coating everything in an even white blanket was beautiful.

My legs were heavy, weighed down by the rubble that once was my life, as I bounced from foot to foot trying to loosen my frozen muscles. I didn't have anywhere to be. No use going home to my too-quiet house. Only a week ago, with a rare free moment to burn, I would have already texted Gideon and had a plan to spend some quality time doing absolutely nothing with my best friend. I felt his absence like a phantom limb, remembering what it was like to be whole when he was in my life.

After two miles at an easy pace, I couldn't ignore the stitch in my side any longer. It wasn't the workout leaving me short of breath. No matter how much I tried to focus on my breathing and the sound of my shoes slapping the track, my thoughts strayed back to Chase. I longed to talk to someone and release the pressure of my thoughts like a steam valve, but who was left? The flurries ebbed, leaving only the overcast gray sky as my companion.

The walk up the hill back to the school left my fatigued legs shaking and I stumbled to a secluded bench next to the theater wing's entrance. Large bushes shrouded the cluster of cement blocks from view. During school hours it was usually occupied in a do-not-disturb kind of way. My stomach was still unsteady, and in case it turned inside out again, I'd rather not let anyone see me vomit.

Over the sound of my deep breaths, I heard the door to the theater wing open. Harsh, hushed voices were arguing, but the words were unintelligible from my spot. Curious, I crept to the edge of the bushes and peered out. Haley stormed past my hiding spot and halted, turning back to the girl she was with in a tornado of blond curls.

"I said don't worry about it," she snapped.

The girl behind her pulled up short, looking hurt at the sharp tone in Haley's words. It was only then that I looked closely at her face, shaded by a baseball cap. It was Shauna, the Fire Alarm. She recovered her composure quickly. "Your pick doesn't seem to be working out."

"She'll get there. It's hard for a lot of newbies at the beginning, but she could be great. Let's give her more time."

The Fire Alarm did not look impressed by Haley's reasoning. "It wasn't hard for us."

Haley rolled her eyes. "That's hardly a ringing endorsement for us as decent human beings."

"Since when do you care about being decent? This is supposed to be about stacking the deck in our favor. I've earned my place, and next year this is all supposed to be mine. You need to start thinking about your legacy as our leader."

Leader? That would mean...

I mentally revised my tally of Red Court members to thirteen. It seemed Haley was pulling double duty.

"I told you not to worry. I'm handling it."

The Fire Alarm huffed, seemingly resigned. "It's my job to worry."

"And it's *my* job to make it work."

So much for the girl from the carnival. Haley marched away from the school without a look back at her partner. Her *real* partner in all of this. The Fire Alarm stood silently for a few moments, her poker face firmly in place. Whatever she was feeling, I couldn't read it. She left silently, but I could hear the echo of Haley's words reverberating around us. It was her job to make the Red Court work. And what the Queen of Hearts says, goes.

"I thought I would know what to do once I found out who the Queen of Hearts was," I said to April.

I'd ambushed my sister the moment she got home from her retreat, still glowing from the success of her event. Now, after I'd unloaded everything that had happened over the past few days, she was sitting on her bed with a notebook in hand to record the so far terrible ideas I'd brainstormed on how to destroy the Red Court.

It had been hard to talk about what happened to Mrs. Martin and Gigi, my fallout with Gideon, and everything with Chase. But the hardest thing was admitting how far I'd fallen into the Red Court, and how I'd foolishly thought by taking control I could change the nature of it. Layer by layer, I stripped all of it away, leaving me raw and ashamed.

April set the notebook aside. "You know I love you."

"Oh no." I put my hands up. My sister was notorious for delivering hard truths after those five words.

"Hear me out, please. I've supported your revenge plan even though I don't agree with it. I never want to take your choices from you. I'll never force your hand because *I* think it's the right decision. It's a lesson I learned the hard way. But I think you've been doing this for too long, pouring too much of yourself into it. I'm worried about you."

I crawled onto the bed next to her and put my head on her shoulder. "Thank you for being here for me."

"I'll always be here for you. I just want you to know that you can walk away, even with everything that's happened. I don't want you to have to live with more regret than you have to."

I almost laughed. My sister, in all her sincerity, couldn't know how much I already regretted what I'd done. But if I could get rid of the Red Court, I could move on. Things would be better. For me. For everyone at Heller. I could do this.

I knew the players, and now I had to stack the odds in *my* favor. I needed to refocus all my energy into dismantling the

Red Court like I should have from the very beginning. Instead, I'd let myself get swept away by the current of power that the Red Court ran on. The regret would fade if I succeeded. I knew it would.

When I didn't respond, April moved on. She was giving me the space to make my own choices, no matter that she'd chose something different for me. "Are you upset that it's Haley?" April's tone was careful, questioning, and it felt like her keen eyes asked me the same question a thousand different ways.

"Yes." There was no point in lying about what I so obviously couldn't conceal, but I couldn't admit the whole truth to April. "I'm upset that she was there, right in front of me, and I was too caught up in...other distractions to see it."

April seemed to accept my answer, but the lie cost me. My sister was probably the last person who saw me, the whole truth of who I was, and had yet to turn away. Choosing to lie to her again was choosing to further the distance between us. But the truth was that I was angry with myself for not seeing Haley for what she was, and a small, naive part of my brain stung at her betrayal. She was my partner, and she'd kept her part in the Red Court a secret.

The Queen of Hearts was always the goal, but perhaps my narrow focus on her alone was what held me back. My plan was to cut the head off the snake. That no longer seemed like enough. "My original plan was never going to work. I need to get all of them, not just Haley. The Red Court's foundation isn't built on her." I considered how dangerous someone like Gretchen could be if she moved into Haley's vacant role. "It's designed to withstand the defection of any one member, even the Queen of Hearts. She may be the most power-ful player on the board, but any pawn could take the game."

"You're mixing metaphors. What are you talking about?"

"I'm saying that it isn't enough to remove Haley. I need to find every other member, too. All of them have to be taken out all at once, or they could just rebuild the Red Court without her."

April nodded in understanding. "So, what's next?"

"I have four of the thirteen members if you count Haley, Shauna, Gretchen, and me. Haley is the key to unlocking the rest, but I don't know where the door is."

When Haley granted me access to the Red Court's ledger of favors owed for Gideon's takedown, I'd saved a copy for myself and pored over every entry but didn't find anything that indicated who the rest of the Red Court was. The Red Court relied on playing cards for communication from the Queen of Hearts, but the rest was done via text. I grabbed my phone from my bag and stared at it.

"What are you thinking?" April shifted my way and I held the phone closer for her to see the contacts list.

There was only a single number with no label for Haley and the Fire Alarm. Haley had the same phone and no other. Not even a personal one.

"I wonder if everyone else's phone numbers are in Haley's phone. If I could get ahold of it, I might be able to check."

April chewed on her lip, thinking of holes in my thought process. "Would she have names and numbers stored in her phone or just numbers? Seems like a liability to keep names—even first names—on a phone like that."

"Burners and their numbers have to change every so often

or they could be lost or stolen. I don't think she could reliably remember every new number. My gut says the bigger risk is in leaving only the numbers listed. She could accidentally message the wrong person. If it were me, I'd label them."

I felt a flare of excitement as my mind raced ahead of our conversation and began to forge new paths, chasing ideas like they were the White Rabbit. Haley wouldn't be so careless as to leave her phone unattended, even for a few minutes. That would be the hardest part.

"So, how do you get the phone?"

"I need her to willingly leave her bag with me. That's the key. She has to trust me so implicitly that she doesn't think twice about walking away. That might be hard. She's been keeping a careful eye on me, and I don't think she does trust me anymore."

The best way to get Haley to do something she wouldn't ordinarily do was to put her in an unfamiliar situation away from her routine.

"What's something you have in common, something you could build on?" April asked.

"The only thing I know she loves is art." I couldn't think of a foothold for me to grasp onto when it came to art. The closest thing I had to any art knowledge was the handful of trips I'd made to the art museum. "The museum."

"The art museum?"

"What if I could get us into Final Friday?"

Final Friday was a popular series of events at the art museum. The best local restaurants provided appetizers and drinks, and they always had great live music. It was a hell of a way to spend a Friday night, eating and drinking your way through a mostly empty museum. It was also twenty-one and over.

"How are you going to get in? I can't even buy tickets."

"April? Are you ready to go?" our mom called from down the hall.

My thoughts churned ahead, already planning this new angle. There was one person who could most definitely get tickets, but I couldn't be the one to ask. "I was hoping you might ask Mom."

"Ember," April said. "Come on."

As kids in the Williams household, we learned quickly that asking for something for yourself was the quickest route to a hard no. If we asked for something for someone else, we stood a puncher's chance. It was a risk.

"This could work. This could be the thing that ends the Red Court for good, April. Please."

Our mom appeared in the doorway of April's room to take her to a doctor's appointment.

"Are you ready, darling?" Our mom's delicate features were tired, but she rallied with a warm smile.

April's eyes held the hint of annoyance as she said, "Mom, Ember and I have been thinking of something nice to do for a friend of hers. She's really into art but hasn't been having an easy time lately. Do you think you might be able to get them tickets to Final Friday? It was my suggestion, but I completely understand if you don't think it's a good idea."

Mom's job as an event director at the nonprofit she worked for meant she had connections at venues all over the city, including the art museum.

"Well, I'm not sure if it would be allowed. Although,

Henry will be there to keep an eye on you, and he does owe me a favor. I'll give him a call and see."

The following day, I breezed through the doors of Hell High in possession of a plan. My mom had sweet-talked her friend Henry into reserving two tickets for me. Now all I needed was a plus-one for Friday night.

I shot a quick text to Haley before first period.

Me: Can u meet?

A moment later brought her terse reply.

Haley: is it important?

Me: Yes.

Haley: whatever

I took that response as implied agreement and bolted to the theater room to wait.

I'd barely sat on Haley's usual slouchy couch before the door banged open and I leapt back onto my feet.

"What?" Haley was in torn black jeans splattered with white paint, looking like she was wearing her art.

"I'm sorry."

Haley turned to leave, but I reached out and tugged on her bag before she could duck out.

"Wait! I didn't ask you to come here so I could apologize." She turned back to glare at me. "Then why?"

"My mom got tickets to Final Friday this week at the art

museum, and I wanted to see if you wanted to go. If we're going to keep working together, we need to be a team." I kept my tone light and widened my eyes hopefully.

"You want me to go...with you?"

"Yeah, as a peace offering. I know you said you weren't interested in being my friend, but I don't know anyone else who would appreciate it more than you. And..." I paused and pretended to struggle with my apology. "I'm sorry for what I said about you not caring. That wasn't fair. If you don't want to, I can let my mom know. She can release the tickets back to the museum. I'm sure they'd have no problem selling them—"

"No, I want to go. But I don't have a fake ID. How are we going to get in?"

"Don't worry about that. My mom's contact said it was fine. They just won't give us ID-check bracelets for the bar."

Haley looked skeptical, but I knew I couldn't push. If this was going to work, Haley had to come on her own.

"I have always wanted to go." She spoke like it was an admission of guilt, and I laughed.

"Like I said, it's up to you." I held my hands up and let them casually fall to my sides. "You don't even have to go with me if you don't want to. I can have them leave the tickets at will-call for you."

I left my baited trap wide-open and waited. This was the make-or-break moment in the plan. There was no further cajoling. I had something I knew Haley wanted; I just didn't know how badly she wanted it and what she was willing to risk to get it. If there was one thing I learned through the Red Court, it was that wanting was a powerful thing.

"No, I would feel bad if you didn't get to go, too. Thanks for the offer. I would like the extra ticket."

Her gratitude seemed genuine, but we didn't live in a world where I took anything she said at face value. Not anymore.

"Ok, let's meet there. Doors open at 7:00 p.m." The first bell rang, and I gathered my things. "See you later." Saying goodbye, when I'd been explicitly told not to, was my final test. Her response would tell me where I stood.

"Bye, Ember." She gave me the smallest of smiles.

A flare of triumph rose up inside me and I gave her my brightest smile in return. It was my turn to deal the cards, and I was working with a stacked deck.

CHAPTER 39

I STOOD AWKWARDLY outside the art museum that Friday night, trying to look like I belonged. Among the glittering crowd in designer jeans and stilettos, my standard jeans and T-shirt would have stood out too much, and not in a good way. April served as my stylist for the night, vetoing almost every outfit I tried on. We'd finally dug out a teal sequin tank and black jeans that I paired with an old pair of her heeled boots. My mom contributed the black satin blazer to complete the look.

I felt ridiculous. And cold. Ridiculously cold. Even with all my ploys as part of the Red Court, I'd never felt more like a fraud than I did amid a crush of adults like a kid playing dress-up. Plus, the kohl eyeliner April had insisted on was irritating my eyes. My hands itched with anxiety, and it took all of my practice not to rub them along the rough denim fabric of my jeans.

"What are you doing?" I heard Haley's voice from behind me. She emerged from the throng pushing their way into the warmth of the museum and looked me up and down. Her critical expression confirmed I looked like as big of a fraud as I feared. Haley was in her standard black-on-black ensemble, wild blond curls fluttering around her face in the icy wind.

"Blending in." I gave her a slight sneer.

She slowed her steps and eyed the security stationed at the door checking IDs. "Are you sure we're going to get in? If I paid twenty dollars to park for nothing..."

"Relax. It's going to be fine. We're not even going in this entrance."

We skirted the side of the building and I located the service door for employees in an alley. A guy a few years older than us stood outside in shiny black shoes and a black wool coat. He was cute in a I-probably-like-to-sail-and-have-a-ski-chalet-in-Vail kind of way.

"Are you Ember?" he asked as we approached him.

"I am." I flashed him a confident, toothy smile. "Is Henry coming to meet us?"

"Unfortunately, he had to deal with a catering issue and asked me to wait for you." He eyed us critically and had probably surmised we were not twenty-one. "I'm Ethan. I intern for Henry."

"Well, thanks for waiting for us. I'll be sure to let my mom know that you guys took such great care of us." I reached out and gave his arm a squeeze to punctuate my words, lest he get cold feet about letting us in. Haley glanced sidelong at me. It was amazing how much desperation could motivate a person to step out of their comfort zone.

After another moment of hesitation, he stood to the side and passed an ID badge over the door's keypad. "This way." He swung the heavy door open and a blast of hot air blew my hair up around my face in an honest-to-goodness Marilyn Monroe moment.

Ethan led us through the busy kitchen. Servers in black vests swooped in and out of the melee while white-coated cooks bellowed that more duck confit appetizers were ready. My stomach rumbled in response to the intoxicating scents of citrus and spice.

Shutting down the urge to reach out and swipe some of the hors d'oeuvres from the silver trays moving swiftly past me, I risked a glance at Haley. The grin plastered on her face told me I made the right choice in bringing her here. Already her hard exterior had cracked, revealing a girl giddy with the thrill of stealing into a VIP event.

"Think I can get us a couple of wristbands for the bar?" I whispered to Haley. My mom trusted Henry enough to keep us out of any real trouble, but she didn't know Ethan.

Haley seemed to remember herself and tucked away her smile, giving me an indifferent shrug. "If you think you can without getting us escorted out."

I quirked my brow at her. "Challenge accepted."

We followed Ethan out of the kitchen and into the atrium at the museum's entrance. The airy space was lit with strands of lights overhead and an electric guitar could be heard crashing down from somewhere on the second floor.

"Thank you again." I turned to head up the escalators before pulling up short. Making a good show of looking around, I turned back to Ethan. "Is it going to be weird that we don't have bracelets like everyone else? I just don't want to look too obvious."

My performance lacked delicacy, and Ethan took the bait, shooting me a skeptical look. "Oh, so you promise if I get you two wristbands that you won't touch a drop of alcohol?"

I raised my palms to him in coy admission. "Ok, so I wouldn't go that far. But I won't tell if you won't."

He shook his head at my exaggerated wink and ducked behind the docent's counter. There were a few small boxes stored out of sight and I watched with a smile as he produced two red wristbands from a packet.

I held my hand out for him to fasten it around my wrist. There was no use in hiding the sparkle of triumph I felt. Ethan gave me one more indulgent smile before doing the same to Haley and excusing himself.

"Alright, I'm impressed." Haley flicked her finger against her wristband. "That was pretty great."

My heart was still pounding, and I took a deep breath to calm myself. "I don't know what you're talking about."

"Please. You played that guy hard. And the best part is that he knew he was getting played and did it, anyway. He was happy about it."

I let out a laugh and we joined the crowd at the bottom of the stairs. "Yeah, he did. Couldn't you see how much he wanted to do it?"

My smile faded as Gideon came to mind. I wished he was with me to witness that. Maybe he would understand why being in the Red Court was so easy. How grifting Ethan the intern was second nature to me. It was hard to dislike something you were so good at, but I was trying to keep my head above water this time, keeping my goal in mind. The Red Court wouldn't pull me under again.

Gideon's memory was a palate cleanser for my mind. I remembered that the friend standing next to me wasn't Gideon. She was a lie.

"Where should we go first?" I asked when we stepped onto the second floor.

Haley was reaching for her phone and I watched as she typed in her password. Her lack of care at my seeing it told me all I needed to know about the likelihood of her leaving the phone with me. She didn't look up until I cleared my throat loudly at her.

"What?"

"I asked where you wanted to go. Is something going on…" I left room for the unspoken words in my question: *With the Red Court?*

"It's nothing." Haley tossed her phone carelessly back into her bag. "I want to see the Warhol pieces they have on loan."

She marched in the direction of the Modern & Contemporary Art wing, her gait easy but her shoulders tight. How did I not see before how hard she worked at not caring? Her demeanor was more curated than the art on display.

I gave Haley a bit of distance and stopped the first harassed-looking server with a tray of drinks that came my way. Someone already put out with other patrons was less likely to look at me twice. My hesitation nearly gave me away as she asked if I wanted red or white.

"Can't we mix them together and make a rosé?" I asked as a joke.

Nothing.

"I'll take one of each, thanks."

Following in Haley's direction, I reviewed my plan. Haley needed to either give me her phone or leave it unattended for long enough that I could check it. The bathroom seemed the most logical way to separate her from her bag, but that was a long shot.

One of the special collections rooms was set up with a black curtain draped in front of the door and a couple of museum staff and security guards stationed at the entrance. I wedged myself in with the crowd slowly trickling their way into the room.

"What's this?" I asked the man in front of me. He wore a patterned shirt buttoned all the way up to the neck and thick black glasses that he pushed back up his nose.

"The museum has some of Picasso's sketchbooks on loan from Paris. They aren't open to the public to view yet, but they're giving us a sneak preview for the next half hour. This alone is worth the price of the ticket."

I made a noise of agreement, but my eyes caught on the museum staff at the front of the line. They were collecting bags and phones and offering claim tickets in return.

"They're not letting us bring in our stuff?"

"No, and I really wanted to get something for my Instagram story about tonight." His disappointment was almost laughable, but I gave him an enthusiastic nod.

I stepped out of line and went to find Haley. If I had only thirty minutes to get her into the exhibit sans bag, I had to hustle.

"There you are!" I practically shouted when I located her

on a bench across from what were presumably the Warhol pieces she'd mentioned.

Haley was a charcoal smudge against the bright canvas of white walls and warm-honey wood floors, and yet she fit in the space so naturally. Perhaps it was how at ease she seemed from just a few minutes ago, like she belonged there. I still knew so little about her—apart from her biggest secret—and I'd never seen her expression so open. It was easy to forget art was her passion when plotting her downfall.

"I've been waiting right here. Must have lost each other in the crowd."

I held out the two glasses of wine for her to pick her poison. She regarded them carefully and took the red. "I don't actually drink, but I'm guessing having something in my hand will help me blend in better, right?"

"You don't drink at all?" I wasn't much of a drinker, either, but she was correct. The whole goal of my clothes and the wristband was to look just like everyone else.

"No, not since..." she trailed off, looking uncomfortable.

The reference had to be to her stepdad. My instinct to exploit this weak spot for information was difficult to ignore. I wanted to peel her words back and look deeper, but I couldn't risk pushing her away, so I let it go.

"Are you picturing your own work on the walls? Visualization really works for me when I'm preparing for a track meet." I pointed to a bare patch of wall. "That really pretty blue-and-green piece that you have in your room would look amazing right there."

Haley looked down, still not comfortable with open praise. "Thanks for bringing me. You'd be a good friend."

It was my turn to look away. I was no one's friend and it had to stay that way.

"Oh!" I said as if a thought had just occurred to me. "I was held up because there's a big crowd waiting to get into an exhibit that's not open to the public yet. I guess they have some Picasso sketchbooks on display for the next twenty minutes or so? Did you know that?" I let my words hang in the air and hoped they'd be enough to lure Haley to the exhibit.

Haley stood abruptly. "We should go check it out."

I waved a disinterested hand. "I'll walk over there with you, but there's a ton of people cramming into a tiny room. I don't want to see them that badly."

She gave me a look, but it was more tolerant than suspicious. Careful to seem caught up in all the splendor of the night, I gathered a few appetizers from the trays floating around and shadowed Haley's progress toward the Picasso exhibit.

The mezzanine that overlooked the atrium was packed with a crowd jostling into the small space, salivating at the chance to see the sketchbooks before anyone else. I found a small slice of unoccupied balcony and planted my back firmly against the railing to wait. Haley anxiously surveyed the crowd and tried to time her entrance into the fray, but I caught her eye and waved her over.

"I bet you could slip right in if you left all your stuff with me. They're stopping people at the door to check their bags and drinks." My tone was even, and slightly conspiratorial.

I'm being helpful. I'm being helpful. I'm being helpful.

The mantra played in my head and hopefully translated

into my smile. Haley might be able to read people, but she was playing my game now, even if she didn't know it.

"Yeah, that would be great. I just heard someone say that they're about to rope it off for the night."

"Hmm." I stuffed a bacon-wrapped scallop into my mouth and gestured to the floor where my purse was thrown at my feet.

Haley's bag and coat joined mine and she marched into the crowd without looking back. Bingo.

CHAPTER **40**

MY HEARTBEAT QUICKENED as time seemed to slow. I measured my breaths and watched Haley slip behind the black curtain into the exhibit. There wasn't a way for me to tell how long she'd be in there, but I doubted it would be more than a few minutes; people were being cycled through quickly to accommodate as many guests as possible.

Casually setting my drink and appetizers on the ground, I located my real phone and pulled out Haley's from the bottom of her bag. I unlocked it and tapped her contacts. The screen lit up with a short list.

AB
BC
ES
EW
Fire Alarm

GG
JL
KQ
OV
SA
SH
TK

They weren't first names, but initials. I could tell because my own—EW—were listed as were Gretchen's. I drew a stuttering breath. Every member of the Red Court was here in my hand. A small, irrational voice inside screamed at me to run, to grab the phone and make a break for it. If I worked fast enough, I might be able to find out who they all were before Haley could clean up after me. Or take me out entirely.

No, that was too risky. This was the kind of job that required the finesse of a scalpel, not a wrecking ball like with Matthew. I didn't need to be taught the same lesson twice. With another quick look at the exhibit's curtain and the stream of people filing out, I took pictures of every contact name and number with my phone. When I had them all, I opened Haley's text messages and captured photos of those as well. By far the most texts she had were with the Fire Alarm. They messaged each other daily with updates on other Red Court members, requests for jobs, and miscellaneous comments on everything from the principal's bad tie choices to whatever the weird smell was coming from the boys' locker room. My first thought was: they're friends. The second was: How could I use this? I was surprised by how much the former hurt and how much the latter bothered me.

My internal alarm clock reminded me that now wasn't the time to examine my conscience. Before I could put the phone away, I caught my own name in the text message chain between Haley and the Fire Alarm. Without time to read it, I blindly snapped more photos. A swish of bright blond hair flashed in the corner of my eye. I was out of time.

Scrambling to toss everything back into our bags, I knocked over Haley's wine. The liquid spilled from the shattered glass in a ruby-red pool. *Shit. Shit. Shit.*

"Party foul!" A teasing voice rang out from a woman in front of me. All I could see from my position on the ground were her purple combat boots. She had better be gone by the time I sorted this out or she'd find herself with her shoelaces tied together.

My breath came in a hitch. I had two seconds at best to put away our phones and get the mess under control before anyone looked too closely at the teenage girl who made it.

"Ember?" Haley's voice came from behind the woman with the boots. Bless Purple Combat Boots for being too stubborn to get out of the way.

If I couldn't hide the evidence of my spying, I had to destroy it. Standing abruptly, I purposefully slipped in the wine and kicked our stuff to the side in my efforts not to fall—which I did anyway, landing hard on my butt. My hand roared in pain as a shard of glass sliced across my palm.

In a moment, Haley was by my side picking me up and gathering our stuff.

"Oh my God! Do you need help?" Purple Combat Boots asked. "I've never seen anyone actually slip in wine before."

Her eyes were wide, but she stood there smirking at me like I was an amusing anecdote she could tell all her friends.

"There's a first time for everything," I muttered and turned toward the bathroom.

I was already washing my hand when Haley eventually followed me into the ladies' room.

She set our bags and coats down on the counter with a thud. "What was that?"

"Sorry. I accidentally spilled your drink and kind of panicked. The whole point of tonight was to play it cool. Nothing like falling on your ass to get people to notice you."

I hissed as the soap stung the cut. It didn't seem very deep, but it still hurt like hell.

"Do you need stitches or a hospital or…"

Haley was pointedly not looking in my direction as she rambled.

"I'm fine. I just need to get this cleaned up. If I keep pressure on it for a bit, it will probably stop bleeding."

Haley fiddled with a chip in the tile wall, still not looking my way.

"Are you… You're not afraid of a little blood, are you?"

She scoffed. "That was not a little blood. It looked like a crime scene out there."

I waved her away and grabbed a few more paper towels to wrap my hand. "That's nothing. I once sliced my arm open a good six inches when I fell off a trampoline."

Haley's head fell forward to rest against the cool tile. "Don't talk about it," she moaned.

"Wow. I didn't know you were such a baby."

Blood didn't scare me. What scared me were the scars you

couldn't see. The hurt people kept hidden under smiling faces. Cuts could be stitched, and bones could be mended, but healing a mangled heart was another thing entirely.

"Lots of people are squeamish about blood," she whispered between deep breaths.

"And lots of people are babies."

She gave me a rude gesture and I laughed softly to myself. Why couldn't Haley and I have met under different circumstances? We might have been friends.

Once I'd cleaned myself up, I collected my bag from Haley and we headed back out into the museum. Someone, probably Ethan, had already cleaned up the mess and a CAUTION WET FLOOR sign was all that was left of my brawl with the wineglass. *Sorry, Ethan.*

"Where to next?" I asked Haley with a cheer I didn't feel.

"We can leave if you want to," Haley said, though she was edging slowly toward the Asian Art collection.

"I'm not wasting tonight because I fell. In front of the whole museum. And left a huge mess behind me for Ethan the intern to clean up. Why would you think that?"

Haley let out one of her rare laughs. "Fair enough."

I let myself be led through the vast halls, eating appetizers off nearly every tray that passed my way and sipping a club soda with lime the whole time. I'd barely escaped dousing my mom's blazer with red wine, so I wasn't taking any more chances.

Haley read from every placard and pointed out what she liked and what she loved. She never mentioned the things that didn't resonate with her, like she didn't want to tear any piece or artist down with her criticism.

The crowds began to thin around ten o'clock, and polite caterers and museum staff informed us the doors would be closing soon. Haley and I made our way back to the entrance, some of the last to leave. We were about to head our separate ways for the night when Haley stopped.

"Thanks for tonight."

"I take it you had fun?"

"Anything where you fall on your ass and I get free food is guaranteed to be a good time."

"Ha ha. You're welcome."

"Good night," she called out as she turned to go.

I spent the walk back to my car shaking, but it had nothing to do with the frigid air. My close call was a little too close for me to be entirely pleased with the way the evening turned out, but it worked.

I pulled my phone out of my pocket and dialed April.

"I did it."

The following day, my mom roped me into holiday shopping. When we returned home weighed down with bags of presents for aunts and uncles and cousins we never saw, I ran up to my room to store my haul under my bed like I did each year, even though April hadn't attempted to search for gifts in years. Just an old habit I didn't bother to break. It was nice that some things remained the same, even when the rest of the world couldn't bother to stay consistent.

When I got home from Final Friday, my tired eyes had refused to focus on the pictures I had taken. The plan was to take a look first thing this morning, but my mom woke me up extra early to tag along with her to the mall; it wasn't wise to look through photos of a phone I'd broken into without permission in front of her.

Finally alone, I brought them up on my phone and flicked through the first few images of initials and phone numbers. I wrote them down on individual sticky notes that I pinned to my corkboard.

While I had done laps around the mall vetoing many terrible gift ideas for my dad, I had outlined the next phase in my plan. Part of me wanted to line up the members of the Red Court like dominoes, knocking over each girl one by one, my casualty list creeping up as the days passed in agonizing slowness. It would take effort to research each one and find what would get them to bend. That angle had its benefits, like letting the Queen of Hearts sweat it out as her protection was stripped away until no one stood between her and what she deserved.

Haley. The Queen of Hearts was Haley. It was hard to make the mental switch from plotting the downfall of some nameless, faceless tyrant to the girl I'd spent countless hours with. The chances of getting through everyone before Haley figured out it was me were too low to bet the house on.

With the members of the Red Court's initials pinned to the board, I went back to the photos of the texts between Haley and the Fire Alarm, where my name came up. It was dated from the day we got Matthew's cancellation request.

Fire Alarm: what did ember do to make matthew take his request back???

Haley: what makes you think it was ember

Fire Alarm: please i told you she couldn't hack it she was never going to take gideon down

Haley: now we know her limits

Haley: everyone has them even you

Fire Alarm: are you going to keep throwing him in my face?!?

Haley: no I'm reminding you that everyone reaches this point...we just pushed ember to hers sooner than most

I clicked away from the exchange. Without more context, I wasn't sure what the Fire Alarm's breaking point was, but it was good to know she had one, too. But what stood out to me the most was that Haley seemed to be defending me when she knew it was me who interfered with Matthew. A flash of doubt flooded my body, but I pushed it right back down. She was the Queen of Hearts, a master manipulator. And I was going to end her reign.

I dragged out my old yearbooks to find likely candidates for the rest of the Red Court. Under each set of initials, I wrote the names of possible matches. It was surprising how easy it was to find some of them. There wasn't a way for me to be completely sure, but there weren't that many people with the same initials, even in a school of two thousand five hundred students.

After a few hours, I had a list of members with mini dossiers on every girl. I stood back to admire my handiwork. The colorful patchwork of sticky notes was strung together like a spiderweb with our Queen of Hearts at the center. Each pair of initials held branches of names that matched up with a piece of yarn linking it to the most probable candidate. Below the names were as many details I could think of on my own and what could be gleaned from public Instagram and Twitter profiles.

> AB (aka Addison Betz)
> BC (aka Brianna Cho)
> ES (aka Emma Song)
> Fire Alarm (aka Shauna Lopez)
> GG (aka Gretchen Goldberg)
> JL (aka Jenna Lowell)
> KQ (aka Kayla Quiroz)
> OV (aka Olivia Vaughn)
> SA (aka Samantha Allen)
> SH (aka Sasha Harrison)
> TK (aka Taylor Kent)

I rolled my neck out and stretched my back, considering whether I had time for a run before dinner. A text notification from Haley lit up the screen of my burner.

Haley: thanks again for asking me to come with you last night

Haley's gratitude sat uneasily with me. How was I supposed to destroy someone who kept thanking me?

Me: Of course! Is it lame that I loved it even more because no one else our age got to go?

Haley: extremely lame

Haley: and also true

Haley: see you Monday

The most important thing was to act as normal as possible until I could figure out my next move. I'd reached the end of what I had planned, but the journey was far from over. I was a roller coaster out of tracks, unsure of how the ride would end.

I carefully flipped my corkboard around, keeping my spiderweb facing the wall and feeling like a boy hiding porn under the mattress from his parents. It wasn't only my parents I was worried about. Truthfully, I didn't want April to see it, either.

When I called her last night and gave her the entire story in an excited rush, she was reserved. I'd made her a reluctant part of my plan, a plan she didn't approve of, but it felt like something more. She stonewalled me when I pressed her this morning. She wouldn't even meet my eyes and I didn't know why. April had made her position on my plan clear, sure, but she'd never shut me out like that.

She'd been hurt so badly and seeing me in danger as part of the Red Court had to be hard for her. No matter that she wanted the Red Court to fall, I was taking risks that I knew she didn't agree with.

You're almost there. Just hang on.

My fingers itched to scribble a quick journal entry, to purge some of the more difficult thoughts. Only enough to take the edge off. The worn leather and cracked spine of my journal felt like butter beneath my fingertips. I had to look insane stroking the binding, but I'd become so attached to its familiar pages. The weight of it alone soothed my nerves, though I'd torn out my last entry. I couldn't bear to have proof of what I'd wanted staring at me.

November 24
I've lost so much with very little chance to gain any of it back. Will it be worth it?

It has to be.

CHAPTER 41

WALKING THE HALLS at school was an exercise in avoidance. I couldn't find a route to any class that minimized the risk of running into Gideon or Chase enough to ease my nerves. When the inevitable happened and I stumbled across one of their paths, I did my best to keep my chin lifted and pretend that seeing them didn't matter.

With Gideon, the urge to talk to him pulled at every fiber of my being. I wanted to ask how his day was going or if his dad missed me or if he had plans to see his mom for Christmas and did he need me to come. Instead, all I could do was keep my face neutral when his eyes slid right past me like I wasn't there, like I was another unfamiliar face in the crowd. Maybe I was.

When I saw Chase, remorse coated with regret twisted my stomach and a ridiculous longing squeezed my heart to the point of breathlessness. How was it possible to have two very different reactions to seeing someone? My feelings for him were so tangled up with my involvement in the Red Court. I didn't think it was possible anymore for me to see or think of him without experiencing a sensation like I was endlessly falling backward. I could prepare for class; knowing where he would be made it easy to pretend he wasn't there.

The Friday after the art museum was cursed. Mr. Carson gave us a pop quiz in American Lit that I was not prepared for, which was the first time I'd ever turned in a test knowing I failed. When Carson handed the graded quizzes back at the end of the class, mine included a long note that he was both disappointed and concerned.

After the bell rang, I literally bumped into Chase on my way out of the classroom. His friends all stopped to look at me, their faces acknowledging that he and I had a something that was currently a nothing.

"I'm sorry," I mumbled into my armful of notebooks, avoiding their knowing glances.

Chase stared at me, and for a moment I thought he might talk to me and smooth things over like he would have only a few weeks ago. Then he gave me his easy smile and said, "No worries." With a courteous nod, he kept walking with his friends and resumed conversation. Like *I* was a someone who was now a no one. Maybe I was.

Tears stung at the corners of my eyes and I hauled into the bathroom before the whole school saw me cry over Chase Merriman. With a great sniffle, I slammed the door to the first open stall in the corner shut behind me and leaned against it for good measure, not that I thought anyone would follow me or attempt to talk to me. The closest thing I had to a real friend was the girl I was plotting to destroy. Everything was so screwed up.

The warning bell rang, and I thanked whoever was in charge of scheduling that I had my free hour. There was no chance I could pull it together in time to be Ember Williams: Model Student in the next sixty seconds.

A group of girls giggled their way into the bathroom and took up residence at the sinks in front of the mirrors. I thumped my head hard against the door to dislodge the cackling echo and sighed. There was also no chance of my leaving the bathroom and facing whoever was out there with puffy crying-over-a-boy eyes.

"So, wait," one of the girls whispered. "You're telling me that you asked him to do it?"

"Shh!" another girl scolded. "I didn't *ask* him to do anything."

"But you dropped a major hint like a boss," a third accused. "I was there."

I risked a glance through the crack of the door. It was Maura Wright and two of her friends.

"Well, I guess I did mention to him that it would be the best thing to ever happen to me if I won," Maura admitted.

"He asked the Red Court to do it?" The first girl was clearly in awe.

Maura gave a shrug and a devious smile. "He won't say so exactly...but yeah. He totally did."

The other girls giggled again. "I swear that boy would lie across train tracks if you asked him to." The third girl was checking her lip gloss and eyeing Maura appreciatively.

"Maybe I will. Our one-year anniversary is coming up." Maura laughed her high girlish laugh, one that was nothing like the laugh I remembered from when we were kids. It was 100 percent fake, and I was kicking myself for not seeing through her before. "When will you be at my party tonight? You're coming early to help me set up, right?"

"We'll be there by five."

After another few minutes, the girls made their way out of the bathroom, still laughing about Reece and planning for the party Maura was throwing while her parents were out of town for the weekend. Sliding to the ground, not caring about how gross it had to be, I cried in earnest. My one good act with the Red Court—getting a nice, deserving girl like Maura elected Homecoming Queen—was a lie just like the rest of it. It seemed no one was innocent.

It took nearly the entire period for my tears to dry, but once they did, I pulled myself up and revisited my plan, or lack thereof. How could I stop the madness, this cycle of hurt that the Red Court fed? As long as we existed, girls like Maura were going to manipulate their stupid boyfriends into signing a deal that never expired.

With a splash of cold water on my face, I stalked out of the bathroom and headed for the closest exit to the parking lot. My mind was on the corkboard at home. I had to get back to it. I had to put the last pieces together and figure out a way to take them all down in one move. It was checkmate time.

"Ember," a familiar voice called. A familiar voice that hadn't spoken two words to me in over a week. A familiar voice that wouldn't return my calls or texts. I didn't have anything left for a fight with Gideon.

I stopped near the door but didn't turn. Turning meant looking at Gideon and seeing whatever disgusted expression was on his face. Why would he be coming to talk to me?

"Hi," he said when he stepped in front of me. The corners of his eyes tightened when he took in my tearstained face.

I wet my dry lips. "Hey. What's up?"

"Are you ok?"

A frustrated noise escaped my throat. There wasn't an answer to that question. I was so far from ok. If "Ok" was a star, the light could go out and I wouldn't know for ten thousand years.

"So, no, not ok?" Gideon's concerned expression made me want to throw my arms around him and sob or shove him hard. Probably both.

"Why are you here?"

"Because I saw you bump into Chase and then basically run into the bathroom. I waited to see if you were alright when you came out, but you were in there a long time. Crying and hiding at school is not Ember Williams. It was…distressing."

Gideon's face shifted from concerned to skeptical, as if I was about to pull off my Ember mask and show him that I was someone else entirely.

"No, Gideon, I'm not ok. I have not been ok for years. I have been plotting to destroy the Red Court since I was in middle school, and the further I get into it, the more I realize that it is so beyond complicated I can't begin to unravel it on my own. And I am so on my own here. My sister isn't happy with me, Chase won't talk to me, and the one person who I have always had on my side left me. You. Left. Me."

I dashed around Gideon and pushed open the doors to the

parking lot. The cold wind whipped across my face and froze the tears on my cheeks. At some point I must have started crying again, but it didn't matter. Nothing mattered but getting to the finish line.

CHAPTER 42

PLEAS TO MY DAD fell on deaf ears. He refused to call the school and excuse me for the rest of the day. Worse than that, I landed myself on his "something's up" radar and would be questioned after dinner. Without him covering for me, I had no choice but to return to class.

The day dragged, and I checked out of each period. My teachers noticed, and I got more than one stern look for not paying attention. It never occurred to me that my carefully cultivated reputation would backfire so badly on the one day I was off my game.

When the day finally ended, I tried to duck out of debate practice but was caught in the hallway by several teammates who asked for my help and pulled me bodily down the hall to the debate classroom. After two hours, I excused myself to my car and collapsed into the driver's seat. My emotional exhaustion manifested into a pounding headache. The ten-minute drive home seemed almost insurmountable, but I started my car and drove out of the parking lot.

Before I blinked, I was sitting in my driveway, my car next to my mom's, wondering where the miles went. I stepped through the front door and heard my mom talking to some-one from down the hall. I knew Haley's voice. The cadence of it was imprinted in my mind.

Before I could throw my bag down on the hall bench, my mom appeared at the end of the hall.

"Hi, sweetie," she said breathlessly. "I was just talking to your friend Haley. She's hanging a gift on your wall, as a thank-you for bringing her to the Final Friday event."

"A gift?" What would Haley leave for me?

"Yes, she's very talented."

The corkboard. My stomach flipped as I raced toward my room.

"Do you think she'd be interested in an internship at the museum?" my mom shouted down the hall. "I could call Henry and see if they're looking for anyone this summer."

"I'll ask her!" I shouted back. "Haley?"

I found her with the beautiful blue-and-green piece from her room on the floor in front of her and my corkboard in her arms.

"What are you doing?" My body flashed cold with dread. It was clear what she was doing. She was looking at pictures of her and every other member of the Red Court. And I was looking at years of planning collapsing in front of me like a house of cards.

"What is this?" There was a deadly note in Haley's voice,

made all the more terrifying for how quiet it was. Her eyes were glued to the photo in the middle of my spiderweb—it was her.

"I don't know what you're—"

"Don't lie to me, Ember. Tell me what's going on."

Haley set the corkboard down on my bed and took a step back from it, like it was a grenade and she was waiting for it to detonate. Finally, she took her eyes from the mess of photos and sticky notes and looked to me.

"I'm taking down the Red Court. It has to stop."

Haley looked at me like I was an algebra problem that just wouldn't equate. "You're taking down the Red Court? What makes you think you can?"

"Because I know who everyone is, and I've been planning this for years. It's only a matter of time."

Her expression fell and rebuilt itself as a mask of incredulity. "Years? You've been planning this for years? Why?"

"Because what the Red Court does to people is wrong."

"What the Red Court does? Don't you mean what *you've* done? Don't act like you're better than any of us. Your picture is on here, too. You're just as guilty."

Haley stabbed an accusatory finger at the web as proof positive. I was just as bad, just as guilty for what I'd done, but she didn't understand that I wasn't in it for the same reasons as her and the rest of the Red Court.

"I know I'm responsible for my actions, but I didn't join the Red Court for myself like you did."

Haley threw her arms up and looked around, eyes furious. "You're some kind of vigilante superhero? Taking us down for the good of the school?"

I'd never seen her so angry, not even when her stepdad was tearing her down. She expected that kind of behavior from him, but not from me.

The front door opened, and my dad's and April's voices floated down to us, reminding me how dangerous it was to have this conversation in my house. What if my parents heard? What if April heard? I wasn't sure which was worse. April didn't know Haley, and if they came face-to-face, I wasn't sure how April would handle it.

"I started planning to end the Red Court the day I found out what it did to my sister." My voice was quiet, my anger gone. I knew what I was doing was right. The Red Court had hurt so many, and I allowed the sharp edge of my focus to be dulled by the sense of power and importance that came from belonging to something bigger than myself. Not anymore. With Haley, here in my room, in the house I shared with my sister, it was never clearer. The Red Court was done.

Comprehension surfaced on Haley's face, but I could tell she didn't understand the depth of my anger.

"This is all about your sister?"

"The Red Court hurt her, hurt countless others. It's over." I kept my voice low and prayed that everyone stayed down the hall.

To my surprise, Haley laughed. It wasn't a pleasant sound. She laughed until tears formed at the corners of her eyes. "Did she tell you that?" she asked between gasps.

"She did. She tells me everything." I didn't feel the confidence I put into my words.

A noise behind me caught my attention. April was in the doorway, staring at Haley, a look of shock covering her face.

"What is she doing here?" April asked me without taking her eyes from Haley.

"She was just leaving, actually." I ignored the frustrated noise Haley made and kept my eyes on my sister.

A look of warning crossed April's face as Haley began to speak.

"Ember," she said. "It's true. The Red Court was involved in April's accident. I would know—I was a sophomore when it happened. It was my first year as a member."

Hearing someone else talk about April's accident was surreal. Finally, I was getting somewhere.

"But we weren't the ones who hurt her."

"Haley. Stop it." April's voice cut through the thrumming in my head. It was too high maybe, or her words too fast.

Haley kept talking. "Her accident wasn't part of some plan to do anything to her. She was part of a plan to hurt someone else. April was one of us, part of the Red Court. She was my partner, the one I inherited the theater room from. What goes around, comes around. That was our saying. Right, April?"

The sound of blood rushing in my ears muffled April's response. Dizziness came over me as my eyes unfocused. As I inched backward, my knees bumped the edge of my mattress and I collapsed onto it.

"What?" I looked to my sister convinced that whatever she said would explain away Haley's story.

April's eyes shifted to me, and the truth of Haley's words was written on her face. I couldn't believe it.

April had been part of the Red Court.

CHAPTER 43

"APRIL, NO." My voice was nothing more than a whisper. Still, the words cut through the silence like a shout.

No one said anything for several beats. Had I said that aloud or were the words only spoken in my head?

"You should leave." April's words scraped out of her in a rasp.

"Happily."

Haley's eyes dropped to the painting she brought me, and an uncomfortable corset of guilt squeezed my sides. Haley was many things: a liar, the Queen of Hearts, and, somehow, a friend. "Enjoy your painting."

Haley moved past me and out the door. My dad's voice filtered through my haze, alarmingly jovial. Haley wouldn't say anything to him, would she? No, that would reveal her own part in this Greek tragedy. Mutually assured destruction was not part of Haley's game plan.

"Do you want to stay for dinner?" he asked her.

"No," she quickly replied, before adding, "Thank you."

Haley quietly excused herself and my dad's feet padded down the hall.

Coming back into myself, I scrambled across the room and moved my corkboard to the floor before he appeared behind April.

"Your friend Haley seems nice. Is that the painting she brought you? Your mom said she was very talented." His voice, so light and familiar, pricked at my skin. My whole body felt like an exposed nerve.

"Yeah, she is." I managed to keep my voice steady, though tension shimmered in the air like heat waves in the desert.

Dad looked between the two of us, about to open the lid on Pandora's box, but April rallied quickly. "Ember was telling me about Haley's home life. Her stepdad is a nightmare."

It seemed April knew Haley better than I did. It seemed I didn't know April at all.

"Oh, that's terrible." Dad's brow furrowed in concern. "I wish she'd stayed for dinner." Food, the universal cure-all in the Williams household. "You girls should head into the kitchen. Get it while it's hot."

April looked at me with a sad stare before following after Dad. I couldn't look at my corkboard or at the painting Haley left, so my eyes fell on my reflection in my mirror. I watched, detached, as tears filled my eyes and fell down my cheeks. This wasn't me. This crying girl, whose heart had been ripped out moments ago, wasn't me. It wasn't even the ruthless girl I'd grown accustomed to being, the one who could endure the horrible things I'd done.

I was Ember Williams, ace student, track star, debate team captain, and…idiot. My sister had been lying to me for years. The Red Court didn't hurt her; she was injured hurting someone else. How didn't I see it? Her reluctance to help me once she realized what my plan was looked different in this new light. April never wanted me to uncover the truth.

"Ember!" my dad called.

"Coming!"

I swiped at my face, angry at the tears that proved how naive I'd been. With a few deep breaths, I went to join my family.

By the time I reached the kitchen, I was composed. By the time I sat down at the table, I was smiling. By the time I took my first bite of chicken, I was asking my parents how their day had been. April sat in silence, cutting her chicken into tiny, precise bites.

"School was ok," I answered when my mom asked. "I'm just tired, I think. Winter break can't come fast enough for me. I'm exhausted. I think I might sleep the whole time."

Babbling was a dead giveaway that I was definitely not ok. I was a mess, and if I didn't shut up soon, I would end up talking about how broken and angry I was. My view of the Red Court was so different than when I began. I'd seen the damage it could inflict in a dozen different ways and witnessed how the hurt could ripple through a life, leaving destruction in its wake. There were more reasons besides my sister for why the Red Court had to be stopped, but it all started with the need for revenge. Revenge was the catalyst that put me on this path for the last two years. And it was a lie.

"I think I need a run," I said and pushed away from the table with only a few bites gone from my plate.

"Now?" My dad's confused face was edging toward concerned, and I had to get out of the house before he came to his senses and stopped me.

"Yeah, maybe not a run. Just a walk. I need some air."

Throwing on the first pair of shoes I saw, my rattiest sneakers, I dashed out the door into the cold night air before my coat was on. I had zero intentions of walking around my neighborhood. That would only give me time to think, and my thoughts were what I had to escape. There had to be a place where I couldn't think.

A car's horn blaring caught my attention, and several shouts from inside a packed SUV followed as it raced down the street past me. Curious, I watched as it continued a couple of blocks and stopped in front of a house. Judging by the other cars and groups of kids streaming toward the house, there must be a party going on.

Maura lived two streets down from me. Maybe it was her party. My feet moved of their own accord, heedless of the battered sneakers and hoodie I was wearing. Hardly party attire. Not that I really knew. My frame of reference was what April used to wear when she went out to parties. April. My feet moved faster. I was desperate for a distraction loud enough to drown out my thoughts.

The party was as advertised. Kids dotted the lawn and front porch, sipping from red plastic cups and speaking in hushed whispers. Once inside, I was pushed into a crush of people, and they seemed to all be part of one huge conversation. Everyone was laughing and shouting at each other.

I tried to melt into the shadows and give myself some time, unsure what to do now that I was inside. Even unsettled by the music and the crowd, I was happy to have a new set of problems to think about. Like what to say if I ran into Maura, who I hadn't spoken to in ages and whose house I had invited myself into.

With more people coming through the door, the inertia of the crowd moved me toward the back of the house and into the kitchen. A silver keg was parked in a kiddie pool full of ice. A senior I recognized from my math class was manning the tap and regarded me appraisingly.

"Wouldn't have picked you for the partying type, Williams," he drawled around a toothpick perched between his lips like he was James Dean with a cigarette.

"Me, neither. Can I get one?"

No use in lying. I did not belong here, but I'd probably look less out of place with a cup in my hand. He smirked and poured me a cup of whatever kind of beer it was. I kept a careful eye on him, remembering the sole piece of advice I'd heard about parties: watch your drink being poured.

"Thanks." I took the cup he offered with little appreciation.

He held his cup up for me to knock with mine. "Have to cheers the Kegmaster."

We clinked cups and I took a tentative sip that was more like letting the liquid below the foam touch my lips, before I pulled the cup away and gave him a nod. I turned to hide my horrified expression. The beer was bitter and tasted like I'd taken a bite out of my shoe.

With my cup in hand, I felt slightly more at ease. I was having a drink at the party. Just like everyone else. I had no idea why anyone else was here, but the noise and warmth of the room took up all my attention.

I took a drink, a real one this time, and was less shocked by the alcohol's bite. It wasn't as terrible as the first, but not improved enough that I'd be using my beer cup as anything more than a prop.

A small corner of my brain, probably one where the thumping base hadn't yet reached, scolded me for stuffing my problems under a rug and dousing the rug in alcohol. It wasn't a permanent fix, but I just needed a break.

"Ember?"

I turned and came face-to-face with Gideon.

"What on earth are you doing here?" he asked.

"Same as everyone else." I stepped away from him to find a new corner to skulk in.

Gideon snagged me by the arm and tugged me out the back door.

"Hey," I said indignantly.

He led me to a table and pulled a chair back. "Sit."

Without much choice, I took the seat, wincing at the jolt of the cold metal chair against the thin fabric of my leggings.

"Talking to me twice in one day. Must be a special occasion."

Gideon glared his disapproval at my sarcasm. "Well, we'd have only had to do this once if you bothered sticking around earlier."

My throat tightened against the dam of emotion threatening to break just because I was in my best friend's presence. My problems would not disappear with Gideon back in the picture. In my head, I understood this fact. In my heart,

I wanted to dump out the fifty pounds of emotional baggage I'd gained in the last day for us to pick through. Together.

"What are you doing here, anyway?"

"I didn't have anything else to do tonight." Gideon looked away from me, like the statement cost him something he didn't want to pay. It occurred to me that Gideon would have been as lonely as me.

He turned back to me, his normal smile playing about his lips. "Besides, something interesting always happens at parties."

"Like me showing up." I peered into my cup and set it aside. The beer lost its appeal with Gideon nearby.

"Ember," Gideon started, "you're not ok."

"No, I'm not ok!"

Gideon only half raised a brow at my snappy attitude.

"What I'm saying is that I've been watching you and every day you seem worse. More run-down."

How creepy. And endearing. And infuriating.

"You've been 'watching' me?" My voice was teetering on the edge of hysteria. "You've just been hanging around watching me drown—"

"Yes, in a shallow pool of your own drama," he added.

I laughed, giving in to the agitation that overflowed like a pot of boiling water, and tears followed. It was the most Gideon thing to say, which was to say that it was ill-timed and a little mean but totally truthful. Was I laughing so hard that I was crying or crying because I couldn't remember the last time I laughed?

"What are you doing?" Gideon reached out and smoothed

my hair, tucking a piece that had fallen from my ponytail behind my ear.

I drew in a shuddering breath, wiping at my runny nose inelegantly with my sleeve. "I'm losing everyone I ever cared about."

Gideon chewed the corner of his lip before he came to sit in the chair next to me and gathered my hands in his.

"You have me."

I shook my head. "You abandoned me."

"I couldn't stand by and watch while you lost yourself to the Red Court. I'm guessing something's happened?"

All I could manage was a nod in return. He studied me closely, his gaze flicking from the bags under my eyes to the frizzy state of my hair.

"Can you tell me?"

So I did. I told him about Gigi and Chase. I told him about the art museum, my corkboard with the likely members of the Red Court, and April. I spent the most time talking about the few moments I'd had with my sister, dissecting every word and the tiniest details. Part of me, probably the soft, mushy part, wanted there to be an explanation. But the most damning evidence were my own memories; small things that, when seen in a different light, took on entirely new meaning. April had known more than she should have about how to get into the Red Court. The sorts of things they'd find appealing in a potential member. At the end of my story, I was left with two questions. Who was my sister? Who was I?

Gideon made a small, annoyed sound. "You know who you are."

"A 4.0 student. Runner. Debate captain. First-class fool."

A few kids stumbled out back toward the hot tub across the yard. We watched them pass us, and I wondered what their problems were. If any of them were running from something, too. Maybe we were more alike than I knew.

"Those are things that describe you. I could add friend, daughter, and sister to that list."

The word *sister* sizzled like a brand against my skin.

"But," Gideon continued softly, as though he was sharing his biggest secret, "those things aren't *who* you are. I believe, beneath all the bullshit labels we put on ourselves, there's a place only you know about. A place where you can feel what you're made of."

I thought about the person who lived inside my skin, past the hurt and anger and the Red Court girl I'd let take over. Allowing my eyes to lose focus, I delved deeper inside myself, looking for the girl who wanted to be good. Who wanted to be like Chase. Who, no matter what, knew what the Red Court did was wrong, even when it felt right. That person wasn't angry at any betrayal. That person was tired of hurting people.

My fingers slipped over the fibers of that girl, grasping at them like they were wisps of smoke. The more I thought of her, the more real she felt, I felt. This was the me I was when I wasn't pretending to be anything else. The insubstantial girl materialized, and I felt the weight of her press into my chest while I wrapped my arms across my stomach to hold on to the feeling.

"I know what I have to do."

CHAPTER 44

THAT NIGHT, I grabbed my burner and started a group text.

> **Me:** Attention, ladies of the Red Court
> Mandatory meeting
> Monday
> 7am
> Theater room

I quickly shut it back down before any potential replies could come in. Then I went to my sister's room.

Without bothering to knock, I invited myself in. April was propped up in her bed, eyes rimmed in red and tissues scattered around her.

"Ember, I'm so sorry."

I let her apology fall at my feet without bothering to acknowledge it. "Were you ever going to tell me?"

April looked away and hiccupped a sob. "Every day. I wanted to tell you every day. Since you joined the Red Court, I've been sick over it. It's been killing me."

Ice like fire licked through my veins, searing everything in a cold that left me numb. "It's been killing *you*? Do you know what this has cost me? I've given everything I have to destroying the Red Court."

"I never wanted this. I never asked you to destroy them for me!" Her frustration was palpable.

It was true. Nothing I did was because April asked it of me, but this was a path I was set on over a lie.

My breath gusted out, taking the bite from my words. "You didn't have to. What kind of person would I have been if I just stood by and let the Red Court continue to hurt people?"

"There were a lot of ways to stop them that didn't revolve around revenge."

I flinched. The words only hurt because they were true. "You should have started that sentence with 'You know I love you.'"

We stood on opposite sides for what felt like the first time. "Why? Why did you lie to me?"

April gathered her composure, putting her tears away. "I didn't mean to lie to you. That first summer, I was such a mess. I'm still a mess, but everything was so fresh then. When you came into my room that day, so young and asking questions, I couldn't tell you the truth."

"You made someone else the villain in your fairy tale so you could save face with your fourteen-year-old sister?"

"Ember, you don't understand."

"No, I don't, but I want to. I have only ever wanted to understand."

April reached out to me, and because she was my sister, I went to her and wrapped my arms around her slight shoulders.

"I'd compromised who I was for the Red Court. I played games with people who didn't deserve it, took choices away from others without a second thought. The control, the power it gave me was addictive. What happened was my own fault, I know, but I couldn't lose you. If you knew the things I'd done, I would have lost my sister."

Despite everything, I did understand. After her surgeries, starting on a road to recovery with a destination she didn't yet know, I was one thing April refused to lose. Me and my adoration for my big sister. But I couldn't let it go, even knowing why.

"I take responsibility for everything I've done, but at no point in nearly two years did you tell me the truth, either."

"Would it have stopped you?"

My words escaped without a second thought. "I don't know."

The desperation in April's face was nearly my undoing. "When you tell a lie, every day it grows. It gains life and turns into something else. I never thought it would go this far. I tried so many times to come clean. After a while, I thought maybe you wouldn't end up in the Red Court. I hoped you wouldn't, and then I could tell you everything."

"The lie did gain life. In me. It became part of who I am." A sob escaped me. To my surprise, I was relieved. Letting the anger drain from my body left me lighter.

"I'm so, so sorry. I will never stop being sorry."

"You were going to tell me everything. Tell me now."

April spoke until her voice was hoarse. She explained how she slipped her name through the slot of locker 1067 on a dare during her junior year, not even knowing about the favor and never expecting the playing card that appeared in her own locker. How she enjoyed the thrill of it and was partnered with Haley the year after. April acted as her mentor, similar to how Haley had with me. The fact that the two had known each other all this time brought my worlds colliding together all over again.

"I was too scared to quit, though, even when it was hard. I didn't know who I'd be if I didn't have the Red Court." Just like me, April thrived on the thrill of the work and struggled with the guilt of what we did. "I think about it now, how stupid I was, and I'm ashamed."

"What happened the night of the accident?"

April fiddled with the loose threads of her comforter. "I was setting up another senior to be busted for our stupid prank. We knew the punishment wouldn't be too serious. The mark was a good girl, never in trouble. She would have gotten community service at the most. Still, I think about how cavalier I was about getting someone innocent in trouble for nothing. For a stupid favor."

A stupid favor. Everything we've done in the name of the Red Court was for something of no actual worth.

April continued, "The plan fell apart when the alarm was tripped early. But I stupidly tried to salvage it and ended up falling from the catwalks like I said. I think it scared everyone, because they left me there. And I haven't seen any of them since. I was so angry when none of them came to see me in the hospital. Not even Haley. I had dedicated two years to the Red Court, yet she cared more about anonymity than seeing if I was ok. So I painted them as the bad guys and somehow recruited you on my side against them. I'm not the person I was when I joined the Red Court. I'm not the person I was when I lied to you. If I could change things, I would."

"You wouldn't have joined the Red Court?"

If April had never joined, her accident would have never happened.

"No, not that. I love my job and studying psychology. I am where I am because of the choices I made, but I'm happy. I would have never lied to you. If I could change that, I would. I wish I'd had the courage to tell you the truth."

When she finished, I rose from her side. "Thank you for telling me."

"What are you going to do?" April looked truly afraid now.

"What I've planned to do all along. It stops now, April."

"Now that you know everything, can't you just leave it all behind? You don't have to do this for me anymore."

"I'm not doing it for you. I'm doing it for everyone the Red Court has ever hurt. I've gone this far, and I have to see this through. For myself as much as anyone else."

"Please be careful. I know what some of them are like, and they won't go down without a fight."

Maybe I should have been scared, but I wasn't. Maybe the smart thing would be to walk away, but I couldn't. I bent down and kissed the top of April's head. "It will be ok," I whispered.

Then I walked out of her room and into my own. Firing up my laptop, I began to write. And I didn't stop until Sunday night.

CHAPTER 45

THE SCHOOL WAS mostly abandoned when I arrived early on Monday morning. Only a few cars were scattered across the student lot. I grabbed my bag, heavy with supplies for the final step in my plan, and caught my reflection in the rear-view mirror.

"You can do this."

A sharp rap on my window startled me from my pep talk. A figure in a dark Heller hoodie stood next to the car, back to the blinding sun breaking over the horizon and face in shadow. I scrabbled for my pepper spray, convinced a Red Court member had sent someone here to murder me.

The figure leaned down.

"Chase?"

"I, uh, wanted to talk." His eyes flicked around the lot, but there wasn't anyone nearby. He looked paranoid, like I was going to reveal a Red Court ambush at any moment. I swallowed down my irritation. He had no reason to trust me. I was a liar. April wasn't the only one who had a complicated relationship with the truth.

I climbed out of the car and checked my phone. "Ok." I had to be in place in ten minutes, not exactly enough time for a heart-to-heart or whatever Chase had in mind. "Can you walk with me to the theater room?"

I didn't wait for an answer before I started walking as quickly as I could. There were several very likely scenarios to come out of my confrontation with the Red Court and most of them weren't great for me. I couldn't handle another round of hearing why I was the worst. I sucked. I thought we'd moved on from that. Next.

"I wanted to say I'm sorry."

I pulled up short and spun around to face Chase. "You're what?!" Thank goodness there was no one around to hear me roar at Chase. In my defense, an apology from Chase was about as likely as the entirety of the Red Court politely agreeing to disband over a nice cup of coffee.

He grimaced at my tone. "That day when you told me about the Red Court, I was angrier with myself and what I'd done than with you. I'm the one who made the choice to bargain with the Red Court."

I dropped my bag to the ground and then promptly joined it. I squeezed my eyes shut and pinched the inside of my arms. I was keyed up, true, but I didn't think this was a hallucination or a stress dream. Chase sat down next to me and I risked a peek at his face. He looked concerned.

I laughed, embarrassed at my reaction. "I...appreciate the apology. But you don't owe me anything."

"Why didn't you tell me you were trying to stop the Red Court?"

Chase's presence and apology shifted into focus.

Gideon, I swear to God I will wring your neck when I see you.

"Because it didn't matter. Some of what you said about me was absolutely true. I got caught up in the worst of what the Red Court stands for."

He looked at me, and it was then that I noticed his expression. He was looking at me the way he used to, like I was his favorite puzzle.

"I was tired of lying, and you deserved the truth."

"I should have seen it," he murmured.

A smile stretched my face. It felt unpracticed. I hadn't had much to smile about recently. "Seen that I was trying to destroy the Red Court from within and went a little too far down the rabbit hole? Of course. How could you not?"

"I should have seen how conflicted you were. It was tearing you apart. I should have tried to help you."

I shook my head and placed a hand on his. "It was something I had to do myself. Even Gideon couldn't bring me to my senses."

"I've been thinking that we both made mistakes with the Red Court, and that no one can understand what we went through better than each other."

He was right. This was the first time we'd talked without our biggest secrets between us. We knew who the other was, even the darker parts, and we weren't looking away.

My internal alarm clock chimed a reminder. I had somewhere to be. I stood up and heaved my bag onto my shoulder. "Well, it's not over yet."

"Right. Gideon mentioned something about that. What can I do to help?"

"Gideon might need a hand. He'll be in Carson's room in a few minutes. I need to do my part solo."

"Are you sure?"

I nodded. "Positive. I've got this."

"If anyone can do this, it's you."

Chase pulled me into a tight hug. I leaned my forehead against his chest, drinking in his spicy scent. "I missed scowling at you."

"I missed being scowled at. It's not enough to just beat you in everything anymore." He looked down at me with a smile and I couldn't help but laugh. "I want to be with you."

I stood on my toes and placed a soft kiss on his cheek. "Thanks for coming back."

I turned and faced the doors to Heller while Chase went the other direction toward Carson's classroom on the third floor. One way or another, nothing would be the same after today.

CHAPTER 46

MY HANDS SHOOK as I waited alone in the dark theater room. The damp cold of the basement seeped into me, chilling my bones. I was by myself, but I wasn't alone in this anymore. Two people I thought I'd lost were backing me up. I felt invincible and quickly checked myself. It could all go south in an instant. I had to be ready.

Unsurprisingly, Haley was the first to arrive.

"What are you doing, Ember?"

I merely motioned to the tattered couch where we first met and invited her to sit. "You'll see."

"Whatever you're planning, watch out. I might be the Queen of Hearts, but I'm not your biggest worry."

"I know."

I didn't want to underestimate Haley, but the more I considered our partnership, the more it seemed like friendship, however unlikely that might have been at the beginning. I had no reason to trust her, but I did. It was also time to trust myself again.

In the minutes leading up to seven o'clock, more girls filed in. I mentally checked them off, picturing my corkboard. The only one who surprised me was Jess Lantz. Jess was a sophomore as well, but she was quiet and unassuming. She led the coat drive for the freshmen class last year. I never considered putting her on the corkboard with other likely candidates. She went right to the list of distant maybes.

Gretchen shook her head sadly at me as she found a seat. Gretchen was clever. She must have figured out that the Red Court's reign was ending. It was hard to forget the fervor in her eyes when she'd approached me at Alec's house. I wasn't most worried about her, but she was a close second.

The last to grace us with her presence was the Fire Alarm. She swept into the room, looking balefully at me before raking her gaze over the rest of the girls, then finally Haley, who held her eye for a full five seconds before the Fire Alarm plopped onto the floor with her back against the door.

I cleared my throat. "Thank you for coming—"

"Cut the shit," Shauna said. "What do you want? Favors? How many?"

Clearly some of the other girls thought the same thing as they nodded their agreement. Half of the girls had malicious twinkles in their eyes, which seemed to say they were angry at themselves for not blackmailing the whole of the Red Court for their own gain. Others seemed unsure, disbelieving.

"No, I don't want favors. The Red Court is done. I want it all to stop."

Several dramatic gasps cut through the tension.

The Fire Alarm scoffed and stood up, dusting invisible bits of lint from her skinny jeans. "I can't believe I woke up early for this. There is no stopping the Red Court." Each terse word was thrown at me.

"Yes, there is."

I picked through the stack of manila folders in my bag, each labeled with a different name. I removed the one for Jenna Lowell and grabbed what I had collected for Jess from the collection of backups, glad I'd overprepared despite how unlikely some of the candidates seemed. I handed the edited stack to Haley. "If you wouldn't mind, Haley?"

I noted Haley's curious expression before she delivered a folder to each girl. She didn't seem angry. The mood in the room shifted slowly as each girl was faced with her own photo and the words *Red Court Member* emblazoned across the top. Under that was a list of each member's friends, boyfriends, girlfriends, exes—anyone they knew—who'd been targeted by the Red Court or owed us a favor.

"You all have been under the protection of the Red Court for long enough. Now it's time you understood what it's like for someone to hold a secret over your heads, to bend to some-one else's will because of your choices."

Olivia, a pretty blonde junior, slammed her folder shut, causing soft-spoken Jess next to her to jump. "We all stop or you rat us out? To who? Our friends? Our parents?" All the color in her face drained away, and her mouth was pulled into a tight, colorless line.

I nodded, casually checking my nails. "That's the gist of

it, but just in case a piece of paper doesn't feel immediate enough, there's this."

I picked up my phone and brought up the video Gideon had texted me. The screen filled with more than a dozen bewildered kids sitting in Carson's otherwise empty classroom. "I've called a few *friends* of the Red Court for their own little meeting this morning."

I turned my phone toward the other members. "How do you think your boyfriend Nate will feel, Brianna, when he hears you're a part of the same Red Court that broke up his last relationship? Or your best friend Cecelia, Taylor? Do you think she's still going to want anything to do with you when she learns that the Red Court sabotaged her bid for varsity soccer captain? Each one of you has someone in this room, someone I'm sure you don't want to know what you've done or what you are." I slipped my phone into my back pocket before anyone could examine the video too closely. Gideon and I had gathered as many students as possible on such short notice to cover nearly every possible Red Court member, but there were bound to be some people missing.

Haley rose from her seat and moved to stand in front of me. She looked at the burner in her hand for a long moment before turning to Shauna.

"Maybe Ember's right. What we did to Mrs. Martin wasn't right. I've regretted accepting your favor request ever since it happened. I let you bully me into it and that is something I'll have to live with forever. We ruined her life and destroyed her family."

Even the Queen of Hearts had a line in the sand, one she had to cross to realize it was there. Whispers began to rise as every person in the room recognized Haley for what she was: their leader.

Shauna sneered at Haley, like her display of conscience was deplorable. "She only got what was coming to her."

"Don't pretend like that was why you did it." Haley's eyes shifted to me.

Me?

"What do you mean?" I asked.

Haley turned to me. "When you said that everything with Alec and Gideon and Mrs. Martin felt personal, it was."

"Be quiet, Haley." Shauna was shaking with anger.

"It was Shauna's idea to use Alec even though he'd graduated. We could have done that job a hundred different ways."

"Haley!" Shauna looked around the room in a panic. "Stop it."

"The request from Matthew was real, but Shauna wanted you to take down Gideon, and when I objected, she told me I was going soft. I'm sorry, Ember. I knew it would hurt you, but I let her convince me that it would be better if you did it. It wasn't until she asked for the job on Mrs. Martin and you told me that you knew Gigi that I figured it out. All this time, Shauna was trying to hurt you."

"Don't be ridiculous," Shauna snapped. "Why would I care about her? She's nothing to me."

Haley rounded on her. "And it just so happened that *your* friend asked us to break up Chase and his girlfriend. That *your* same friend came back again when Chase showed interest in Ember. Come on, Shauna. I wasn't born yesterday. You knew I couldn't accept the request, but that I'd warn Ember off of Chase, anyway."

"This is about Chase?" I thought I was the only one with a surprise up my sleeve.

Shauna's eyes were wild with anger. "Don't you dare say his name. Do you think he'll want anything to do with you when I tell him what you are? Your little game works both ways."

"He already knows. I told him." I added a small smile to throw her off balance.

Shauna stepped back, considering me. The trump card in her hand held no power over me. When you lived honestly, it was hard for people to use your secrets as weapons against you.

"Was it you leaving those notes on my car?"

Haley narrowed her eyes at Shauna. "What notes?"

I looked back at Haley. "Someone has been threatening me to stay away from Chase. It started after you told me someone asked for a takedown on me to break us apart. The last one threatened me with an accidental fall from the theater catwalks like my sister."

Haley paled and looked to Shauna for an explanation. "That's so messed up. Even for us."

Shauna pursed her lips, refusing to meet Haley's eyes. Haley gave a frustrated shake of her head. "You don't get it, Shauna." She glanced at me before saying, "Neither did I for the longest time. But I've ruined enough reputations and cheated too many people out of the things they've earned. The Red Court doesn't make me happy. It just makes everyone else as miserable as I am. It's not worth it. I'm out."

Shauna was glaring daggers at Haley. This was a girl used to getting what she wanted, and watching her partner call it quits had to be killing her. "This isn't how it was supposed to be, Haley." Shauna jabbed an accusatory finger in my direction. "You've let her ruin everything we've worked for. This was going to be our time to make the Red Court better than ever before. You can't just walk away. I won't let you."

Haley handed me her folder. "I don't speak for anyone else, but I can't do this anymore." Haley dropped the burner in the trash can to my left.

The other members of the Red Court shifted uneasily. Olivia whispered something to Jess and she nodded back. They must have been partners.

"We're out," Olivia said. "I thought being in the Red Court meant immunity from this kind of thing. If members are turning on each other, I think we're better off on our own."

Both Olivia and Jess rose and handed me their folders. They followed Haley's lead and dropped their phones in the trash before walking out, shooting wary glances at Shauna. That gave me an idea.

I turned my eyes back to the rest of the girls. "If Shauna did this to me, who's to say she won't turn on you? You can't trust her."

Shauna stalked to the middle of the room, taking center stage. "We don't need them. We can still be the Red Court and I'll be the Queen of Hearts. It will be like it was before except better. Haley has been holding us back, denying requests she thought were too much. No one in this place is scared of us anymore. It's time to remind them all who really runs this school. I'll admit that I pulled some strings for myself recently, but haven't we earned more than one favor? I'm offering you more. We can be more together."

A few of the girls, Gretchen included, were nodding their heads. I had to hand it to Shauna. She was good.

I cut in, eager for my rebuttal. "She might have you do bigger jobs, but how will you know that they're legitimate requests and not self-serving ones to settle her petty arguments? Or even if they're against other members. She's proved that she comes first. Take the deal and save yourselves."

A handful of other girls rose and followed Olivia and Jess, giving me their folders and tossing their identical phones in the trash. Once the last of them filed out, only seven remained, including Haley and me. No matter what went down between us, I was grateful she was on my side in this.

I struck first. "We've all done things we're not proud of." Matthew's face flashed to my mind, followed by Gigi's. "Things we're going to regret for a good long while. Just like Haley said."

A few girls shifted uncomfortably in their seats. These were the ones whose consciences had already been nagging at them. All they needed was a little extra push.

I looked to each girl for a moment before starting. "How many more sleepless nights are you going to give to the Red Court? And for what? The promise of a favor? Look around at how few of you are left. What kind of favor is this group even going to be able to pull off for you?"

Silence met my words and I let it settle, let them consider if a watered-down favor was worth their souls.

"I, for one, got tired of looking in the mirror and hating the person I see." My voice cracked, but I pushed through. "And I was sick of changing my route between classes all so I could avoid seeing someone whose relationship I'd destroyed."

A few scattered nods bolstered me. "I'm not the only one. Tampering with people's lives is wrong, and decisions we make can affect people for the rest of their lives, not just high school. We can all get out of this together. Start making amends."

Two more girls stood and dropped their phones and dossiers off with me. When they'd left, the Fire Alarm came forward, tore her folder in half, and tossed the remains on the floor in the middle of the room. It felt like a challenge from medieval times, as though she was throwing a gauntlet for a duel.

But I didn't fight fair.

CHAPTER 47

SHAUNA'S SUPPORT WAS all but depleted, but that didn't stop her. "Your little sob story might have worked on the others, but you don't fool me. I know who you are, where you come from. For girls like you and your sister, being part of the Red Court is in your blood. That's why we tapped you, Ember. Your sister was one of the best. So don't act like you're all holier than thou when we both know what you're capable of."

The mention of my sister shook me. Shauna would stop at nothing to keep her position. She needed power like boys needed cheap body spray—it masked the things she didn't want the world to know.

"Maybe that was true, but not anymore. I've seen the hurt the Red Court caused people who didn't ask for it, who didn't deserve it. And seeing it, being a part of it, has changed me in every possible way. I'm done. We both are."

"So, why don't we forget all about this and go our separate ways? I'll swear to leave you and yours alone. I'll sign it in blood if I have to." She gave me a winning smile, the year-book kind that was all teeth.

There was no guarantee I'd get a better offer. It was tempting to quit while the chips were up and walk away. I could save my friends and myself. That was worth something.

But not everything.

"I can't. It's already over. You have to see that."

She slapped her hand against the wall. "It's over when *I* say it's over! You think you can get everything you want? Take us down and walk away free from any responsibility?"

I stuck my chin defiantly in the air. "I know I can."

Fire blazed in her eyes. "The Red Court has always been bigger than one person. Losing your sister was nothing more than a bump in the road. We'll survive this. As long as people are willing to bargain for what they want, the Red Court lives."

Being part of the Red Court took so much from my sister, and she'd never stop regretting what she'd done and what it cost her.

I looked to Gretchen and Emma Song, the last ones standing, and saw their wary glances. "This doesn't have to be ugly. You can walk away and that's it. I destroy all the folders, send your friends on their way, and we all go back to being strangers." My voice seemed thin, easily lost in the fog of anger that had settled in the room.

Shauna laughed, hard and ugly. "Have you thought this through at all? What's going to happen when you expose us? You think we won't take you down, too?"

All the eyes in the room landed on me like a weight pressing against my chest. If they were going down, they'd take me with them. No doubt.

I reached into my bag and pulled out another folder for her. "I'm counting on it, actually."

When the Fire Alarm remained standing in the middle of the room, I rose from my chair and handed the folder to Haley and said, "Go ahead."

She opened the folder and stared at its contents, her expression inscrutable.

"This is yours." I could see the question in Haley's eyes.

"You're not the only ones who've hurt people. I'm just as bad as you. If the Red Court is going to stand judgment, I'll face it with the rest of you."

"You wouldn't." Shauna's face now read like a construction sign flashing *warning.*

"It's already done. Copies of all of this are in the hands of someone else right now. If he doesn't hear from me by eight o'clock, he'll deliver the copies to the school office, school paper, and members of the school board. Along with a letter signed by me, explaining everything. There's no bluff to call here. I'm ready to go down with the rest of you."

For a few moments, no one moved or spoke. They barely breathed.

"Shauna," Gretchen said finally. "Come on. We have to go."

Shauna had to be led forward by Gretchen and Emma, and together they relinquished their phones. Her unfocused eyes settled on me and sharpened.

"We're not finished," she murmured. "The Red Court might be down, but I'm not out. I don't forgive and forget."

I shivered at the threat in her tone. "You should give it a try. There's no washing away hurt and anger with more hurt and anger."

She stared at me, lip curling in disgust. Her expression wasn't one of someone who'd lost everything. It was of someone who'd had everything *taken*.

I watched while the remnants of the Red Court gathered their things and went to the door.

After they'd all left, and Haley and I were alone in the theater room, I sent a quick text to Gideon to cut the room full of hostages loose. It was over.

My tension unraveled like a spool of ribbon, and I let out a sigh. I turned to Haley and said, "I can't believe those cards with the flowery handwriting were you all along."

She laughed. It sounded as exhausted as I felt. "What can I say? I'm an artist." Haley's smile crumpled and her eyes shone with tears that wouldn't dare to fall. "I don't know whether to thank you or strangle you."

I considered my options. "Maybe the first one? I'd rather not die."

"You know, I never wanted to be the Queen of Hearts. I just wanted my favor. I justified everything I did over and over again for a favor. All of it ended up being for nothing."

I nodded, remembering the night Haley talked about getting out of her house and securing an in with the financial aid department at her dream art school. She was talented enough to get into the program she wanted and maybe even earn a scholarship, but there were no guarantees.

This might be the last conversation I had with Haley, so I asked a question I never got to ask before. "Why did you pick me?"

Haley sighed and went to gather her things. "For April. I never spoke to her after her accident, but I wanted to know if she was alright. When she got hurt, I abandoned her, and I've never been able to live that down. I tried to visit her in the hospital a few days after it happened, but the nurses wouldn't let me through. They asked who I was, and I panicked. I didn't want to get in trouble, so I left. I know it was selfish of me. I was always scared she'd tell on us, but she never did. I guess I wanted to bring you in as a way of redeeming myself for leaving her alone in the theater that night. Do right by you the way the Red Court never did for her."

I nodded. The twisted logic actually made sense to me. "What about all those 'personality markers' I supposedly have?" Not supposedly. I knew I had them.

"Yeah, that, too." She bumped my shoulder with her knuckles and gave me a smile. "Don't act like you didn't enjoy part of the work. Your double-agent act required more deception than the rest of us."

She sobered, the light sparking in her eyes fading quickly. "I am really sorry about your friend. If we're laying our cards out, I want to tell you that I made the mistake of sending the picture of Mrs. Martin to Shauna."

That made sense. Haley had seemed genuine in her promise. Now that I knew it was Shauna's request all along, I would have come to the same conclusion eventually. "Thanks. I wish it didn't go down that way. That there was something

I could have done to spare Gigi from that." I'd find a way to help her somehow.

The bell rang, signaling the first day without the Red Court. Haley handed me a folded-up piece of notebook paper and turned to go.

"What is this?"

"My real number. Call me sometime. Maybe I can introduce you to Brit. I think she's the one you saw me talking to at the carnival. We've been hanging out for a while. She goes to Denver School of the Arts."

My mouth dropped open. So she did matter to Haley, if not exactly in the way I thought. Even if she wasn't the Queen of Hearts, I was glad my instincts weren't wrong.

Just before she closed the door behind her, she looked back at me. "See you around, kid."

By the start of first period, dozens of signs were posted around the school.

The Red Court is no longer in business.
We kindly suggest that you handle your own dirty work
from now on.
Anyone caught making requests will face consequences.

EPILOGUE

THE DAY BEFORE winter break came, and I was finally getting used to the quiet life. The gossip about the signs and the demise of the Red Court was starting to ebb. I heard rumors passed around that the Red Court disbanded because business had dried up, or that the school administration had posted the signs to keep students from making requests, or that there was never any Red Court to begin with and this was some elaborate prank.

I kept an eye on the locker mailbox and was surprised when not even a single request was made. With winter break looming, the chatter about the Red Court fizzled. Students were too busy planning excursions to the mountains for early season skiing or trips to the mall for holiday shopping.

"Do you want to grab dinner with me and Damien tonight? You can bring Lover Boy," Gideon said as he sidled up next to me at my locker after school.

"You have to stop calling Chase that." I kind of loved that he did.

Gideon laughed. "I'll call him what I want. He's still terrified that I don't approve of him."

"That would be great. I'll ask him. Maybe I could invite Haley, too? And Brit?"

My conversations with Haley were mostly over text, but on our own phones now. Her responses grew longer each day, from one-word answers to nearly complete sentences. And after only light pestering on my part, she did introduce me to Brit. I thought back to the dinner at her house when she said she wasn't close enough with anyone to share her relationships. I counted it as progress on the friendship front.

"Ugh. Fine, but I liked it better when you didn't have any other friends."

Gideon could grumble all he liked. Haley won him over the moment she praised the composition of his photo in the Winter Showcase, where they both received an award in their categories. Plus, Haley's piece caught the attention of Sally in the Heller postgrad office, who offered to connect her to contacts at two top art schools. It was no Red Court favor, but it was a start.

I opened my locker and froze.

"What?" he asked.

A Queen of Spades sat on the top shelf of my locker. Just the sight of it was enough to set my hands shaking as I grabbed it.

Gideon examined the card in my hand. "What does it mean?"

"I have no idea. We didn't use this one on its own."

"Do you know who sent it?"

"I have one really good guess." Shauna had been lying low the last few weeks, but I knew it wouldn't be forever. She'd bide her time and wait for the right moment. After the final meeting of the Red Court, Haley changed all the passwords for the accounts and deleted as many files as she could find. It wasn't a guarantee that she got rid of everything, but it was the best we could do. It wasn't enough.

I looked back down at the card in my hand and turned it over, knowing I'd find something written on the back. Just like the notes from the Queen of Hearts.

I read the note aloud.

> **THE RED COURT IS DEAD.**
> **LONG LIVE THE BLACK COURT.**

★ ★ ★ ★ ★

ACKNOWLEDGMENTS

I'm so grateful to all my friends and family who helped me along my journey. It's a surreal moment to be sitting here, writing the acknowledgments for a book I have worked on for YEARS. It's been a process, one that wouldn't have been possible without the help of so many people.

To my writerly friends, Julia and Bex, thanks for cheering me on along the way. Melissa, thank you for your never-ending support. Alyson, thank you for keeping me sane.

Tess Callero, thank you doesn't even begin to cover it. Thank you for taking a chance on me. Thank you for your support. Thank you for your guidance. I will never forget our first call, when you told me that even if I didn't decide to go with you as my agent that you would always be a fan. I knew then that you were the kind of person I wanted in my corner. I am so thankful we get to work together. You're the best!

Lauren Smulski, thank you for choosing my book. Your yes was the one that put this book on the path to publication. I can't thank you enough. Thank you, thank you, thank you!

Connolly Bottum, thank you for stepping in and taking me on. Your insights and guidance have been integral in getting Ember's story to the finish line. I'm so glad this book found its way into your very capable hands.

Bess Braswell, Justine Sha, and the rest of the Inkyard team, thank you for your support. I feel so lucky that this story found a home with the Inkyard family. To Cara Liebowitz, Jung Kim, Mark O'Brien, and Anna Prendella, who offered guidance on the characters I love so dearly, thank you. Kate Studer, thank you for helping me connect the threads of this story and making it into something stronger. Elita Sidiropoulou and Gigi Lau, you are both beyond talented, and the cover art you created is stunning. I will love it forever. Thank you!

My fellow Roaring '20s peeps, thank you for all the support. Writing can feel like a lonely business but having others at the same point in their journey to talk to and commiserate with is invaluable. Congrats to everyone! We did it!

Amanda and Sonya, I love you girls so much. Thank you for celebrating every milestone in my writing career (and outside of it!) with me. They say you need to write what you know, and what I know is what true friendship is like. "Always."

Mom and Dad, thank you for being proud of me, for pushing me to do better, and for teaching me how to be strong when things are hard. I know who I am and that comes from the two of you. Without that, I wouldn't have been able to accomplish anything in my life. I love you both.

Dan, John, Danielle, and Savannah, thank you for being

part of my foundation. No matter where we go or what we do, we have each other. I love you guys.

The Laurin and Pottorff Families, thank you for loving me as one of your own. I am so blessed to be able to count you as family. Love to you all!

Henry and Asher, I'm so proud to be your mom. I hope one day you'll read my work and be proud, too. You two inspire me to follow my dreams and work hard every day. I love you both more than the words can say.

Justin, I love you. I love that you support my ideas. I love that you and I are in it together. I love that you are both the anchor that keeps me grounded and the wind that lifts me higher. I can only hope to be those things to you. Our partnership through life has made all things possible. Thank you.

Thank You, God, for answered prayers, for the strength to see things through, and for the love present in my life.

Dear Reader, thank you for giving this story a chance. I am so grateful. I hope our paths cross someday.